A DARKER SHADE OF NOIR

NEW STORIES OF BODY HORROR BY WOMEN WRITERS

Laurel Hausler

EDITED BY **JOYCE CAROL OATES**

AKASHIC BOOKS
BROOKLYN, NEW YORK

T0000500

©2023 Akashic Books
Copyright to the individual stories is retained by the authors.

Paperback ISBN: 978-1-63614-134-3
Hardcover ISBN: 978-1-63614-137-4
Library of Congress Control Number: 2023933940

"Breathing Exercises" by Raven Leilani was originally published in an earlier form in the *Yale Review* (January 2020).

Cover and interior artwork by Laurel Hausler.

Akashic Books
Brooklyn, New York
Instagram, Twitter, Facebook: AkashicBooks
info@akashicbooks.com
www.akashicbooks.com

For those Harpies, Furies, Gorgons, and Fates
through the centuries who never had a chance to tell their tales

TABLE OF CONTENTS

INTRODUCTION

A buried dream could be reborn
like a curse in the wake of the dead.
—Tananarive Due, "Dancing"

Of mythological figures of antiquity, none are more monstrous than harpies, furies, gorgons—Scylla and Charybdis, Lamia, Chimera, Sphinx—nightmare creatures representing, to the affronted male gaze, the perversion of "femininity": the female who in her physical being repulses sexual desire, rather than arousing it; the female who has repudiated the traditional role of submission, subordination, maternal nurturing. Since these fantasy figures have been created by men, we can assume that the female monster is a crude projection of male fears; she is the embodiment of female power uncontrolled by the male, who has most perversely taken on some of the qualities of the male hero—physical prowess, bellicosity and cunning, an appetite for vengeance and cruelty. As in the most lurid male fantasies of sadism and masochism, the female monster threatens castration and something even more primeval: humiliation.

Consider Medusa, the quintessential emblem of female body horror. We all know who Medusa was, yes?—a demonic female figure, a gorgon, with writhing venomous serpents springing from her head, and a face of surpassing ugliness; a bestial creature so horrific to behold that anyone who gazed upon her turned to stone. Since Medusa was also a mortal woman, the "hero" Perseus succeeded in beheading her, by observing her not directly but through a shield; as a favorite of the goddess Athena, Perseus then used Medusa's severed head as a weapon of his own, turning enemies to stone.

Less generally known is that, in some variants of this legend, Medusa was originally an exceptionally beautiful young woman, with particularly beautiful hair; like many other mortal women in classical mythology, Medusa was raped by a god, in this case Neptune, king of the sea; because the rape occurred in the temple of Athena, the goddess was outraged, and with the cruel illogic of the patriarchy—Athena, born out of the head of Zeus, with no mother, was a male cohort—she punished the rape victim, not the rapist, transforming the beautiful Medusa into the horrific gorgon, with snakes springing from her head, and a very ugly face.

A cautionary tale: women should be beautiful and desirable even as they will be punished for being beautiful and desirable, at least outside the protective perimeters of marriage.

Should we know nothing of the female monsters of antiquity, still we would know that body horror in its myriad manifestations speaks most powerfully to women and girls. To be female is to inhabit a body that is by nature vulnerable to forcible invasion, susceptible to impregnation and repeated pregnancies, condemned to suffer childbirth, often in the past early deaths in childbirth and in the aftermath of childbirth. Fairy tales abound in stepmothers precisely because so many young wives died in childbirth that men naturally remarried as many times as their resources allowed. Even in civilized Western nations, to be female has been to be a kind of chattel, in lifetime thrall to the patriarchy; women could not own property, divorce, vote, take out mortgages, even acquire credit cards until relatively recently. Throughout history the female body has been condemned as the occasion for sin, for arousing sexual desire in the male. Strict dress codes for women are a characteristic of patriarchal religions in which female physicality is considered repugnant, while male physicality—virility—is revered. The punishment of Medusa is in line with age-old punishments for women and girls who have the bad luck to attract unwanted sexual attention from men; but to spurn such a role, refusing to marry, to procreate, to acquiesce to the model of meek, subservient femininity, symbolized, for instance, by the Virgin Mary, has been to risk being declared unnatural—"bitch," "witch." The ultimate punishment of the female who resists femininity was to be burned at the stake, condemned to death by religious patriarchs for the good of the commonweal.

In Mary Shelley's *Frankenstein; or, The Modern Prometheus* (1818), a fever dream of an epistolary novel, the most powerful passages spring from dreamlike, surreal sources of anxiety: the creature assembled by Dr. Frankenstein is the very embodiment of a freakish birth, oversized, with ill-matching parts taken from a graveyard and a yellowish, parchment-like skin. We know that Mary Shelley was only eighteen at the time she began composing *Frankenstein;* she was unmarried and pregnant, living with the Romantic poet Percy Shelley with whom she had eloped to Italy, in unstable circumstances; Percy Shelley had left behind a teenaged wife in England, the mother of his child, who would soon commit suicide. Amid such turmoil and uncertainty, Mary Shelley created one of the most horrific of literary monsters, as if fantasizing the worst possibilities of the impending birth; it's likely too that Mary Shelley identified with the creature, in his feelings of isolation and exile. (As it happened, the baby Mary Shelley was carrying during the composition of *Frankenstein* would die at birth; she would have three other babies who also died, and only one who survived. Until the sudden death of Percy Shelley, Mary Shelley was almost continuously pregnant or nursing for eight years.)

In recent decades, body horror has been established as a literary subgenre of horror and dark fantasy. Monsters and freaks of all kinds have always abounded in popular fiction and movies, and in such cult classics as Tod Browning's *Freaks* (1932)—a graphic film more disturbing in our time than it was decades ago when the casting of grotesquely disabled people as "freaks" was not viewed as morally repugnant. A director generally recognized as a master of high-quality body horror is David Cronenberg, whose films (*The Brood, Dead Ringers, Crash, Crimes of the Future)* contain visceral, visual shocks that function as both literal and psychological horror. (The sight of the naked body of the estranged wife and mother in *The Brood,* whose hatred of her ex-husband has hideously deformed her body, is one of the most memorable.) Nor is anyone who has read Katherine Dunn's *Geek Love* likely to forget the carnival family whose grotesque brood has been deliberately created by the parents with the aid of amphetamines, arsenic, and radioscopes—a Dickensian tale in which the surreal and the "real" collide in an exploration of a capitalist-consumer society from the perspective of self-defined "freaks" who are not ashamed but proud of their lineage.

The body horror of *A Darker Shade of Noir* is as varied and unpredictable as the writers exploring the genre, and as unclassifiable as the hauntingly sinister illustrations by Laurel Hausler that accompany them. Though the protagonists of the stories may wreak havoc upon others or are victims themselves of bodily horror, it is only in Cassandra Khaw's lyrically realized evocation of lycanthropy, "Muzzle," that a female protagonist *is* a monster—"My own wolf, the one that had slept encysted in my lizard brain." In Aimee Bender's bizarrely conversational "Frank Jones," a young female office worker creates her own miniature Frankenstein out of peculiar growths emerging from her body, which she employs to keep her coworkers at a respectful distance; she has been accused of "loneliness" and "weirdness" in the workplace, and this is her self-defense.

Megan Abbott ("Scarlet Ribbons"), whose prose fiction typically moves with the disconcerting swiftness of a suspense film, depicts the terrifying night world that lurks beneath the day world of an ordinary suburban neighborhood in which a grisly family murder has occurred, as it is experienced by a young girl mesmerized by tales she has heard of a loving father bludgeoning his family to death—a loving father not unlike her own. In Joanna Margaret's suspenseful "Malena" a female sculptor must contend with the monstrous being—a "parasitic twin"—emerging from within her own body, while in Tananarive Due's "Dancing," a selfless forty-year-old woman who has devoted half her life to caring for her infirm grandmother succumbs to a fit of dancing and demonic laughter after her grandmother's death—her body "at war with itself." The spirit of her grandmother, denied a career in ballet because of her race, becomes a curse, frenetically dancing through her.

The curse of the body at war with itself in a woman who is both a creative artist and Black amid an insidiously racist society is explored with unnerving intensity by Raven Leilani in her harrowing "Breathing Exercise," which is likely to leave the reader breathless by its end. Lisa Lim's graphic tale "Dancing with Mirrors" is a terrifying grandmother-mother-daughter parable of how a "toxic tongue" can indeed be a curse on subsequent generations of women; how body dysmorphia may be inherited, not genetically but through the tales we tell about ourselves.

Amid this gathering of highly imaginative stories, Margaret Atwood's "Metempsychosis, or The Journey of the Soul" is very possibly the strangest; but then Atwood, one of the most inventive and original prose writers of our time, is never predictable. In this fabulist tale of a most unusual metempsychosis, a creature of another species finds itself peacefully "space-sharing" with a human woman, a midlevel customer service representative at a bank, with unexpected results for both. In Lisa Tuttle's savagely satirical "Concealed Carry"—set, appropriately, in the most rabid of American gun states, Texas—a firearm acquires a malevolent life of its own, parasitically attaching itself to a human woman.

Aimee LaBrie's "Gross Anatomy" is the only story in *A Darker Shade of Noir* with a male protagonist, a medical student whose behavior, with a female corpse in the school's morgue, is indeed gross—but does not go unpunished. Yumi Dineen Shiroma's "Her Heart May Fail Her" is a bold appropriation of Bram Stoker's hapless female characters Lucy and Mina (*Dracula*), revisioning them in a sensuously evoked erotic triangle, one side of which is a female vampire; while Elizabeth Hand's "The Seventh Bride, or Female Curiosity" appropriates the centuries-old tale of Bluebeard and his victim-wives, in this case as a traveling theatrical troupe in nineteenth-century England with a most unusual cast of characters both living and deceased.

Set as well in the nineteenth century, Valerie Martin's "Nemesis" pits a vain, callow, narcissistic young man against a canny middle-aged wife and mother whose smallpox-disfigured face the young man finds repulsive, with fitting results for the vain man whose beauty is destroyed forever; while Sheila Kohler's "Sydney" depicts the marriage of a naïve young girl and a duplicitous older man in a triangular relationship with a most unusual lover. (Since much of *A Darker Shade of Noir* is, indeed, dark, it seemed appropriate to both begin and end the collection with stories of victim-women who become, in the course of confronting their situations, ingeniously empowered.)

"The Chair of Tranquility" may be read as prose fiction or prose poetry, the lone contribution in *A Darker Shade of Noir* that involves neither the surreal nor the supernatural, but is based upon historical records: the interior monologue of a woman entrapped in a diabolical but widely respected nineteenth-century medical treatment for so-called hysteria. This treatment, known as the "rest cure," advocated by the distinguished physician Silas Weir Mitchell (1829–1914), was in effect the enforced infantilization of women who may have been in (healthy) revolt against the confinement of their roles in society; any variance from the norm of obedient daughter/wife/mother was considered an aberration, indeed "hysteria," of which they had to be cured no matter how extreme the price.

Through these very different stories, something like a pulse beats in defiant opposition to the confinement of the female by the patriarchy, as by images of self-laceration and defeat internalized by tradition. Whether the rebellion is overt or indirect, successful or fatally thwarted, we are moved deeply by the varying ways in which, in Tananarive Due's words, a buried dream could be reborn like a curse.

Joyce Carol Oates
May 2023

PART I

YOU'VE CREATED A MONSTER

Laurel Hausler

FRANK JONES

BY **AIMEE BENDER**

had a tag on my skin, a little growth around my hip area the size of a flat baby tooth. I twisted it off by myself. It had no nerves. It didn't hurt! I don't mind that kind of thing, even pride myself on not being wimpy in such a way. My college roommate couldn't even put her own earring in, no joke. I had to poke the stem through the hole in the lobe because the act of feeling her own lobe bothered her that much. She also couldn't deal with shots. She also didn't like sandal straps, or bread. What happens to such a fragile little soap bubble of a person? I never bothered to keep in touch, or if I did, she never wrote back. She gave me the feeling of wanting to obliterate, and I didn't do anything to her, no, but she had to feel the rage sometimes, lying in her little twin bed across the room with her sensitive earlobes while I, in silence, twisted the tag right off my hip even though it usually grew back in a few weeks. I had a little wax paper cup of them. I did not share that cup; it was hidden behind some books. It is gross, I understand. But I felt some kind of continued draw to these parts of me unneeded.

The cup grew higher with tags, and I kept it going, traveled it with me through college, through graduate school, until it was pretty much full. It was, I would sometimes chuckle to myself, the clearest marker of my education. Was the tag supposed to grow back as often as it did? According to Google, it's not so uncommon. At one point I did examine one closely with a high-power microscope but it looked fine as far as I could tell, all the cells as neatly lined up and orderly as bricks mortared into a wall.

I, one time, went to an art exhibit of a man named Tim Hawkinson, and right before arriving my date had abruptly bailed on me with a dumb excuse about car issues, but maybe it was better after all because in walking around the galleries and circling the constructions of pipes and ships and noses, I came across a tiny dirty bird skeleton in a glass case tucked in a corner, something I might not have ever found if distracted by the talky presence of another person. The skeleton looked like it belonged to an extremely young baby bird, so small and delicate it was, and I wondered how it fit into the sculptor's oeuvre and even if he'd mercilessly killed it for art, when I stepped up to look closer and found, beneath the title, that the materials were listed as fingernails and glue. He'd built a skeletal bird baby from his fingernail clippings, and the dirty white of his fingernail tips had indeed resembled bird bones. It evoked the way our nails and hair grow after we're dead, those photos of skeletons with long streaming hair—these are creative materials, really, they have force beyond us, and it was also like he'd birthed a little bird from his body's detritus. Anyway, it was great. From that point on I looked to Hawkinson as inspiration.

So it wasn't such a stretch once I had about forty or so tags, and was settling into my new work situation, to make a little creature of my own. I had purchased a very sharp needle, and black thread to enhance the stitched quality. I was working, in those days, in a computer lab, my first job after graduating. In a basement. With three other people I found highly annoying. I went through the cup and discarded the less usefully shaped tags and placed the good ones into a rough person-like shape, with tag arms, and tag legs, tag head, about the size of my thumb. I did not need to stuff it—it had a solidity all its own. Each tag was square-shaped and created a quilt of a person, stitched with black thread, with little x's for eyes, and a small straight mouth. What did Dr. Frankenstein do to awaken his creature? I took the book out from the library to remind myself, yet it wasn't at all clear how he activated the magic. I tried to hook my little guy up to some cords but that didn't work, of course not. It was performance art at that point; I knew it wouldn't animate. It needed something to animate it, and where does one find the spirit? I'm the spirit, I told myself, pocketing it. It can just impact what I do, it can exert influence via its presence in my pocket. I spent many long hours in the lab, hunched in my chair, but to improve work conditions and mood bought a new red shirt with a buttoned front pocket in which to hold the being, the little guy. The unnamed skin tag fellow. Frank, I called him, after Frankenstein, because I especially liked how, over time, over centuries, the monster had stolen the doctor's name, transforming himself into the offspring he so wanted to be. He pretty much got himself named through the power of his presence in the book and eventual movie. Who says Frankenstein is the doctor's name? Only the sticklers. As a way to honor this, I gave the tag guy my own last name, Jones. Was I worried about decay? Not really. Skin can last just fine. Have you ever kept a scab? They just get harder and drier.

Frank Jones did get smaller, dehydrate some, but that just made the stitches look better, more official, made his eyes and smile more real. Smile, did I say? He wore an uptilt now that I had not made myself.

One morning, I tucked him in my buttoned pocket and brought him to work with me for the first time, him keeping me company while I did all my sorting and tracking. It was soothing to have him there. The day had started irritatingly; my colleague Francisco as usual did the work by himself and then said it was mine to check, even though the fun part was finished, and then he complained I hadn't done enough to help. He had pulled this routine a number of times. So while he was out, I left Frank Jones on his desk. Tied a little string around the taggy waist, so I could pull him back.

A little while later, Francisco came back from lunch, patting his belly, sighing, making some comments about the glory of what he'd eaten. Every day, he went to the pho truck or the taco truck or the boba truck and never asked if anyone else wanted anything. Did I? No. I am a bring-my-own-sandwich person. But is it nice to be asked?

He sat down to work.

After a few minutes he stretched out his hand and it touched the dry quilt that is Frank Jones. Where was I? Just at my desk. Holding the string lightly like a fisherperson united with the line and the bait. I didn't want to lose FJ; he was, at that point, a real companion. Unlike Frankenstein, who was rejected, FJ was cool to me, a pal.

"What's this?" Francisco moved his hand away. "Fuck, man, what is this?"

I laughed in my corner. I pulled the string, and within seconds had FJ back and safe in the buttoned pocket.

"You putting voodoo dolls on my desk or something?"

"It's not you," I said, offended. "That is nothing like you, no likeness at all."

"I'm calling HR," he said.

"Go ahead," I said. "No one else saw."

"I saw," said Timma, across the room.

"You can't see that far," I said, recalling a lunch conversation from months before. "You are nearsighted."

"I," said Timma, pointing, "wear glasses."

Timma is the nicest of the group but still not very nice.

Francisco was already on the phone. "Sure, I'll hold," he was saying.

"Listen," I muttered, "I was just trying to be funny. It was just a joke."

"That's what the assholes say," said Francisco. "Yes, sure," again to the phone.

Timma was back to typing. Luc was, as usual, asleep at his desk. He's on permanent jet lag because he's keeping to French time so he can Zoom with his love, even though when I listen in, the tone of her voice seems so biting and critical. Both of them stuck in a bad feedback loop, but I felt like I was breaking out. Breaking out with little FJ in my pocket, finding new frontiers.

"I would like to report an incident," said Francisco, into the phone. "My coworker put a voodoo doll on my desk. Sewn up. It was disgusting." He nodded a little. "Okay," he said. "No, first time . . . Okay."

When he hung up, he looked at me thoughtfully. And I did think then, for the first time, that I had been the subject of previous conversations among the others, something that had never occurred to me before but that I was beginning to glean from his gaze. Laughing about me, maybe. Wondering about me.

"I won't file a report this time," he told me. "They said I could come in, make it official. I could. But I won't. Just no more. Okay? We're all on guard around you a little bit. Dial it back."

"Me?" I said it aloud. "Around *me?*"

"You come across weird. You know that, right?"

Timma, across the room, nodded. "The sandwich, the loner quality. A person's gotta be careful these days."

"What's wrong with my sandwich?" It was one slice of turkey on plain white bread. Perfection.

"Nothing is wrong with it," Timma said. "It just speaks of—"

"Loneliness," finished Francisco. "Inflexibility."

I shook my head. Patted my pocket.

"And whatever that thing was," said Francisco, "it was gross."

Later that night, after some pasta and some television, I took FJ out of my pocket and placed him on my bedside table, next to the phone charger.

"Go on, little fellow," I said in a whisper. "Be free. Go make some mischief."

I slept well, better than I had in a while. The dreams light and easy, like skipping stones over my sleep self. And he was still there when I woke up, little FJ, in his same lying-down position, his smile of stitches large and almost warm over his features.

In the lab, both Francisco and Timma looked exhausted when they walked in. Luc was slumped at his desk, napping again.

"Didn't sleep well?" I said, settling into my spot.

"Horrible," said Francisco. "Dreamt I was fighting a skin army."

"What the fuck," said Timma. "I dreamt I was fighting a suffocating skin sky."

"How gross," I said.

They stared at me.

"What, now you're going to accuse me of messing with your dreams?" I laughed a little. Took out my morning snack, a bar that contained every vitamin and then was coated in chocolate. Sometimes that was also my dinner—is that a problem? I do not like to cook! I do not know how to cook! I do not feel motivated to learn! Fuck you all.

"Weird we both had skin in them," Francisco mumbled. "Taylor, what was in that doll yesterday? Was it made of skin? It looked like it. A skin doll."

"Nooooo," said Timma. "Really? That is barbaric."

"Is it?" I said. "Is it really barbaric when you wear leather shoes every single day?"

She stared at her feet. She was wearing plastic flip-flops.

"Anyway," I said, "it's not really public information."

"Isn't it when it's on my own desk?"

"It's there no longer."

"Come off it!" Francisco waved his hands in the air. "What are you, British?"

I returned to my work. I had so many lists to scour. On a break, they whispered in a corner together.

When I took out FJ later that afternoon, in a bathroom stall, he looked robust—ever smaller as he dried, but somehow strong, wiry, leathery, like he could withstand a lot. Was he more powerful than I'd realized? Had he somehow messed with their dreams? My wicked devil arm, reaching into their world? I admired my sewing; I had worked hard to get the stitches so neat. I had some skill in this way. I could've been a surgeon, my mother used to tell me, in the windows of time when she was coherent and encouraging.

HR called me up. They wanted me in for what they called a routine check, though it was clear Francisco had named me at some point. Fine, I said, pulling on my jacket. No big deal. I need a break anyway! I could use a walk! I could use fresh air!

Once there—who designed the office? Someone not in touch with a single feeling. The bland cushions, the artless walls with art on them. Even the window coverings spoke of robot-like intention. They—a man and a woman, in clothing they clearly did not enjoy wearing—asked me about guns. Guns, ha! "Oh, that's for the masses," I told them, leaning in. "Obvious, lame, sans courage. I am uninterested in brute weaponry."

"Like?"

"Like *what?*"

"Like what kind of weaponry are you interested in?" asked the man, while the woman clickety-typed away on her computer screen.

I laughed. "I don't collect weapons," I said. "I'm not that person. You can look through my apartment anytime. You can peruse my Internet searches."

"We can?"

"Sure."

"Right now?"

I handed over my phone.

The man poked around for a while, and handed it back.

"I also enjoy Thai food," he said.

"Pad see ew," I said. "Right?"

"Who's that artist?"

"Tim Hawkinson. Does these great fiberglass structures."

"Cool."

They asked about my loneliness; I lived alone, I ate alone, I cultivated no friendships. I told them it suited me, it was my best style of managing the constant chitter-chatter of the human-being din. I have a cat, I told them, which was a lie, but they seemed comforted by it. "What's the cat's name?" and I paused.

"I refused to name her," I said, after a minute. "I call her kitty."

One of the HR officers admitted her named cat was usually called kitty. "Her actual name is Aladdin," she said, "But it's just too formal most of the time."

"Is she genie-like?"

"She really is."

We smiled at each other. FJ in my pocket.

"Well," said the man, "thanks for coming in. We'll let you know if we have any follow-ups. But that's all good for now."

"I still have a job?" I said, standing.

They laughed cordially. "You do indeed."

Back at the office, Francisco and Timma had clearly received the news via email or telephone, and they waved at me. They looked disappointed; that was obvious.

"Still here," I said. "Sorry."

"Blah blah blah café!" Luc was saying, emphatically, to his girlfriend.

At night, I told FJ to keep it up. "Whatever you did," I said, "do it more. It's just dreams! Have fun."

Again, I slept so well, like I hadn't since childhood. Deep, pure, empty, long. When I woke, I did some stretches which I never, ever do, even took a walk around the neighborhood and bought myself a little espresso cup in a cute and tiny mug which I drank at a counter. I tipped the barista! This was not my usual, any of it. The effort usually stops me cold. When I arrived at work, Luc was awake, typing, and Francisco was absent.

"Where is he?"

Timma shuffled in from the bathroom. "Another shitty

sleep night," she said. "Like two hours? I dreamt I was battling bugs made of skin. It was revolting. This is fucked up. Did you curse me, Taylor?"

"I should call HR on you," I said. "That is offensive."

"It just all started—"

Luc cleared his throat. "Francisco does not feel well. He is taking a day off. We have a lot of work to do."

Luc looked sad. I wondered if he had broken up with his girlfriend. It wouldn't be the worst thing. He deserved better. He was the least asshole of the assholes, now that my opinion of Timma had changed.

We got to work, and got a lot done, actually. Turns out Francisco chats a lot, makes a lot of jokes, takes up space with his sparkling personality, whereas the rest of us are busily hunkering down thinking our own whirlpoolian thoughts.

At a pause, I returned to the bathroom stall. Took out FJ. Who was ever smaller. Almost wizened.

"Don't hurt Francisco," I whispered. "He's just a guy I work with."

FJ smiled at me.

"I don't want you out hurting people," I said. "I'm not the villain here, and neither are you. We're buddies, okay?"

I ran a finger over his bald skin tag head. He really did look like a voodoo doll at that point. Unlike the monster Frankenstein, he did not seem to want anything from me. His smile was not sinister, was only sinister because it was a smile.

"Lay off, little pal," I said. "Okay?"

We worked really well together all day. Luc gave me some kind of French compliment before his midday nap.

Francisco was out again the next day, and Timma called and he picked up and told her he still wasn't sleeping well, like barely at all, like minutes. I could piece this together from her questions and replies. Her face scrunched up, listening with concern, and after a few minutes, she held the phone out to me.

"He wants to talk to you."

We both shrugged, surprised. I held the phone close to my ear but not on my ear. I don't want a brain tumor.

"Taylor," he said, in a quiet voice, "release me. Will you? Please? I'm sorry for whatever I did. I truly am. I'm eating turkey sandwiches on white bread every day. It's like all I want to eat. I'm collecting my hair in a jar. What the fuck is going on?"

I laughed. I felt so relaxed. Had FJ switched us? I'd had a chicken taco with salsa for lunch. I made a joke about orcas that Timma laughed at.

"It's just hair," I said. "Why not collect it?"

"I love mustard!" Francisco wailed. "I practically drink hot sauce."

"I'm sure it'll pass," I said. "Don't fret."

He asked for Timma again, and she urged him to come in. "Don't just hole up at home," she said. "Be with us, here, in the basement." She was dangling a flip-flop off her toe. Were they a pair?

He did return the next day, almost lurching, with big purple bags under his eyes, all of him monstrous. I waved. I'd had another espresso. He held up his sack lunch.

"Turkey," he said, mournful.

Close to noon, when Luc was in the bathroom, maybe weeping, because he'd been doing that, I'd heard it once or twice, Francisco and Timma approached my desk. I was just busily doing my work, minding my own business, looking for mistakes, when Timma suddenly reached down and pinned my shoulders with her strong hands and Francisco dove his fingers toward my pocket. He flicked the button, fished around.

"Hey!" I shouted. "Stop that!"

"This?" he said, pulling out FJ. "Is it this?" He dropped it. "Yuck! What the fuck!"

"Give me that!"

Timma peered down. Her glasses are basically magnifying lenses.

"Looks like an old piece of bark or something."

"That is mine! Hand it over!"

"Or not," said Francisco. "Or a human organ. For a tiny human. Toss it."

"No!" I yelled.

"Definitely toss it."

Francisco was now holding me down hard, and Timma used a piece of paper to double up as a kind of rag and picked FJ up, dumped him in the trash.

By the time I'd shoved Francisco off and was kneeling at the can, searching, ready to grab and rescue FJ from its depths, I caught, out of the corner of my eye, Francisco reaching into his own pocket, his own new buttoned shirt, and from it removing a hair creature. It was small, wiry, made entirely of hair, tied at the waist by a hair string.

"Dude!" said Timma. She burst out laughing.

He dumped it into the trash.

"They can hang out," he said.

The room fell quiet, broken only by the sound of Luc washing his hands in the restroom, and Timma snorting little gasps out of her nose. The three of us stared into the trash together, and when I shoved aside the yogurt cup, I could see, against the sunset-colored backdrop of an empty cheesy chip bag, FJ's little tag hand holding the little hair hand. No kidding. What was I to do? Didn't he deserve his own life?

We returned to our desks. I pushed Francisco. I pushed Timma. Oh, I wanted to explode them both into bits, true, but I also sort of wondered if FJ had made them do it, in his own weird telekinetic way. Maybe he needed outside intervention to meet his hair love. Timma was still laughing. "What the fuck," she said, shaking her head. Luc exited the restroom, his face splotchy from crying.

"We broke up," he said. "For real."

No one was ready to work right then, so we all went over to Luc's desk and Timma told him all the things his girlfriend had said that had bothered her because she actually speaks French. I added a line about tone. Francisco said a bunch of other things. We had overheard a lot, is the truth. It's a basement. No secrets in a basement. Luc mussed his own hair around, but he seemed to be listening. He told Francisco to stop making jokes while we worked. "Too many jokes," he said.

We worked until sundown. They all left first, Timma and Francisco holding hands, Luc shouldering his stylish messenger bag and saying bye to me, thanking me. Alone in the basement, I gathered up the trash bag and put it in my backpack. I could at least take their ecosystem with me. I could port them around. True, there was that other stuff in the trash bag, less appealing: Timma's yogurt cup. Some tissues stained with Luc's tears and snot. Francisco's turkey sandwich crust, my beef jerky wrapper, the chip bag. Maybe some fingernails, to birth a bird. Whatever.

When I got home, I shook it all out on the ground, in the cement area behind my building. It was shitty to litter, but also it wasn't a lot, and like tiny people emerging from a broken-down city, there they were. They looked good on the dirt, the same way a fingernail bird might look good on the dirt.

"Later, little buddy," I said.

Into the world, he smiled at me, as the wind blew them away.

Maybe things were a little better, I thought, as I started up the stairs to home. Maybe he had altered my life a little bit. I could feel a new tag growing on my hip, his baby. Maybe I'd twist that one off later.

As I was mounting the outdoor stairway, someone came running around the corner, chasing a gray cat. "Kitty!" she was yelling. The cat dashed into the cement area and up a tree.

"Aladdin!" the woman shouted. "You come down now. Aladdin!"

I put my key in the lock. Did they even live around here? I'd never seen her in the neighborhood before, but I had hardly explored the place. I opened and closed the door, laughed a little to myself. He had a reach, didn't he, that FJ guy. He had some abilities. I swiveled the blinds shut, listened to her coaxing outside. It was just like him, wasn't it, to somehow lure the cat here, to try to broker a meeting, to want to share the good feeling he'd just experienced with the hair thing, even if it all was a little fast for my taste? Still: what a thoughtful little creature I'd made. And now I had an opening line. I heard her coo as the cat came down the tree and into her arms, and went over to the stovetop to make myself a can of soup.

DANCING

BY TANANARIVE DUE

t began at her grandmother's funeral.

Grand-mère had been ninety-six years old, that was the thing. She'd done a lot of living in those years, mother to ten children between four marriages, three ending in divorce, the last cut short by widowhood. So when it was time for tributes at the feedback-ridden microphone, the first three speakers all called her by different names, Mrs. Bassett and then Mrs. DuPont and so on, and by the end of the third speech Monique was shaking with giggles fighting through her layers of sorrow.

Monique saw herself as ridiculous in the crowded pew: grief clawing her insides when Grand-mère had been only four years shy of one hundred, the very antithesis of *Too Soon*. Yet her absence had flayed Monique from the instant the old woman's chest never rose for her next breath while Tchaikovsky played on her CD player.

Why hadn't she spent more time preparing herself? "I thought we would have more time," Monique had whispered to Grand-mère's cooling ear.

More time! Outrageous. Another laugh shook Monique's shoulders. She had been caring for Grand-mère, sharing her apartment, for twenty years—half of her life. She'd moved in during her last year at Xavier to save expenses and never moved out, as Grand-mère had more trouble walking and needed help cleaning her house and running her errands. As they realized Grand-mère's situation was "handled," her aunts, uncles, and cousins visited less and less, and Monique had entered middle age without truly living a life on her own.

Her laughter turned to tears; grief and self-loathing and, well, a dash of the root laughter, and she was caught in a terrible loop. She could only bark out noises she hoped sounded like sobs. In the end, she stopped her demon laughter by forcing a memory of how her mother, dying of cancer when Monique was a college freshman, had asked her to take her favorite blue dress. Monique had carelessly told her that she didn't have any more room in her closet and she didn't look good in blue anyway, answering her mother's realness with bullshit she'd never had a chance to make up for. By the time Monique had stewed herself in guilt, she was wailing for real and her cousins behind her were patting her back, saying, "Let it out." (But what more could she let out? Her throat was already raw.)

Monique had family in name, but as she watched Grand-mère's casket sink out of sight, she felt erased from the world. Grand-mère had always been ready to commiserate over gossip and headlines ("Evil asshole," she'd whispered while she watched CNN with her the night before she died), and now all of her cussing and complaining were over, along with her gap-toothed smiles and gentle birdlike hands braiding Monique's hair.

Everything felt wrong. The world. The air. Her body. Everything.

She found herself trapped in the line for fruit punch at the repast in the church basement where Grand-mère had never missed a Sunday meal (until just six months ago), with Monique dutifully pushing her wheelchair. She was only a yard from the stacked plastic cups and punch bowl when she couldn't stand the wait and began pacing the old wood-plank floor instead. Her feet could not stay rooted anywhere, tracing the wheelchair's phantom tracks around the room. Standing still made her cramp up, so her only relief was to pace, or to shift her weight from side to side. She stood on her tippy toes until it was uncomfortable, then started pacing again. She had never felt so restless in her skin.

Because the only music was sad flourishes from the new organ upstairs stabbing through the age-old planks, she wasn't aware at first that her body's unpredictable movements were *dancing*. She didn't hear imaginary music in her head to stir her, not even Grand-mère's favorite, James Brown. She might never be able to listen to "I Got the Feelin'" without imagining bedsores and shit-stained sheets, so James Brown was probably ruined for her now.

While she tried to think of an excuse so she could leave early, a thrumming bass beat from a car parked outside found her ear, from someone on one of the surrounding streets Pastor Moss referred to as "The Forsaken." The music was too far away to fully penetrate even half-open windows, but the beat was untouched, unmuffled. Pristine.

Monique's feet shuffled to the music, one-two, back and forth. Then her hips joined in, swaying from side to side, gently at first, then with surprising abandon. Her cramps vanished, replaced by a feeling like floating. Flying, even! The more she moved, the lighter she felt in body and spirit.

Monique let out a small gasp of happy startlement.

When she looked up, everyone was staring at her.

* * *

The dancing felt divine at first. Beyond divine. Mourners lined up to watch while she boogied out of church to the parking lot and the 1990 Mercedes she had inherited from Grand-mère, all cares of death lifted while her body celebrated life and motion. When she could no longer hear the music, her body swayed instead to honking cars and clattering construction and barking dogs and any rhythm she could find while she unlocked her car door. Particularly dramatic sounds propelled her to leap into the air, a remnant of the ballet lessons Grand-mère had paid for and insisted she attend when she was ten, until Monique begged to stop going because she hated the girlie costumes and slippers.

The liberation was indescribable. Her first day of dancing was her finest. Until the moment she died, she would remember it as the best feeling of her life.

But Monique couldn't stop.

As she started the car, her knees bumped against the steering wheel in spasms and her foot would not stay steady on the pedal. *Lord Jesus, what's wrong with me?* The thought came for the first time, halfway between a prayer and a curse.

She wondered if she should be more alarmed, even terrified, but she was so relieved to be freed from her grief that she rationalized her movements as a stress response and decided to walk the mile back to her apartment—which wasn't such a bad walk, she told herself, although she was sweating within half a block. No matter how she tried to disguise her motions as gliding or skipping or jogging, the dancing made her a spectacle. Strangers raised their camera phones to chronicle the sight of her. Small children waved, laughed, and mimicked her until she seemed to be leading a conga line to Grand-mère's faded green-gray building.

Once the darkened first-floor window came into view, the impromptu Pied Piper street party was over. Back at home, grief was inescapable, dancing or not. As she shimmied through the doorway, the stitch beneath her rib cage on the left side felt like a yawning wound. She touched herself to make sure she wasn't bleeding while her hips rolled and swayed to the rhythm of her panting.

"Please . . ." she whispered to her relentless muscles, or to the hidden puppet master who'd taken hold of them somehow, ". . . let it stop."

It did not stop. The terror she'd denied herself began taking hold as every item in sight that reminded her of Grand-mère made her dancing more frenzied: Grand-mère's old CD player, with Tchaikovsky still queued up; the woven straw basket from South Africa her Uncle Roy had sent when he was in the Peace Corps; Grand-mère's voter registration card from 1954 framed on her wall, which she'd won after breezing through the civics quiz designed to deny Negro voters their rights, a story Monique had heard a dozen more times in the last few weeks of Grand-mère's life because Grand-mère wanted her to remember it.

A muffled *crack* stiffened Monique's lower back as her hips tried to twerk. She let out her first cry of real pain. Her body was at war with itself, her shoulders trying to wrench her one way, hips another, knees fighting to keep steady, ankles steering her with dizzying speed. The more she smelled signs of Grand-mère in the room—her peppermint tea in the kitchen, the faint remnants of urine absorbed by the sofa cushions, her Zest soap in the bathroom—the faster and harder Monique whirled.

She thought actual music might give her dancing more order, at least, so she turned on the CD player and tried to tame her movements with the O'Jays, the Temptations, Earth, Wind

& Fire, and, yes, James Brown, but Grand-mère's favorite music only sharpened her grief, fueling her wild gyrations with sobs.

I can't go on like this, Monique thought, just before the room went dark.

When she woke up, new gray daylight was peeking through Grand-mère's flower-patterned curtains that had been unchanged since the 1970s. She was lying on the living room floor, the back of her head still throbbing because she had collapsed just beyond the edge of Grand-mère's old shag rug and banged her head on the wooden floor. Every muscle hurt, so she did not move, savoring stillness.

Thank you, Lord, she thought. *It's over—*

But it wasn't.

Monique trained herself to stand with her laptop on the kitchen counter and slide only a few inches side to side so she could do Internet searches for any clues about what the hell was going on with her. She studied diseases and disorders with tics and spasms, but nothing came close to capturing her movements: rhythmic and complex and sometimes with jazz hands. She also scanned countless articles on delusions and hysteria, though nothing she read made sense of her dancing.

She finally called her freshman-year roommate, Rose, who was now a school board member in Chicago with a wealth-manager husband and three teenage children. Life had torn her and Rose farther apart over the years as Monique's dreams shrank while Rose's blossomed one after the other, but Rose was the first person she'd told when her mother died, and when she lost her virginity (the two happening in such close succession that Monique had rarely had sex since, out of superstition), so she trusted Rose to at least listen. Until now, she hadn't mentioned to hardly any of her friends that Grand-mère had died, postponing the telling.

"You're free now," Rose said, overly chipper.

"What?"

"Girl, I'm sorry you lost her, bless her spirit, but now you can live *your* life." After Monique's stunned silence, Rose elaborated: "Remember last year? I offered to *pay* to fly you to Hawaii for my fortieth, and you were all like——"

"Grand-mère had that appointment." Grand-mère's feet had been swelling from her congestive heart failure and they had waited for weeks for an appointment with her specialist. Grand-mère's decline had begun in earnest during those months.

"She always had an appointment, Mo. That big family she had and no one else could help? It always had to be you? I tried to tell you."

Monique blinked away her rage. She reminded herself that Rose always had a touch of that affliction when people didn't know the right thing to say, so she ignored the celebratory high five her friend was trying to give her so soon after her grandmother's funeral. You could never take what Rose said seriously—although her words stirred a sick feeling in the pit of Monique's stomach that felt far too close to *Yes, thank goodness she's finally gone.*

"That's not even the real reason I called," Monique said. Her swaying hip bumped the counter when she shifted position. "I can't stop . . ."

"Crying? You just need to—"

"Dancing," Monique whispered. "I can't stop *dancing.*"

Monique described everything that had happened to her since the funeral, including collapsing on the floor from exhaustion. And how the dancing had started again before she could stand up that morning, her body flopping on the floor like a catfish.

"Number one," Rose said with the air of authority she'd adopted since they realized she was six months older than Monique, "you had too much to drink at the repast. You never could hold a drink. That's why you passed out."

"I didn't—"

"And number two," Rose said, "what did I just tell you? You're *free*. Of course you're dancing! Just let it out."

Let it out. The advice was as useless now as it had been at Grand-mère's funeral. "It hurts, Rose. Every part of my body is—"

"All passages hurt, Mo. You'll be alright."

Monique already knew she would *not* be alright. She had not been alright since Mom died, and maybe her destiny was never to be alright. What did that word even mean? "Alright" was a great anthem by Kendrick Lamar, but it was mostly a lazy word for a temporary designation—more like a delusion—so how could it matter? It was like trying to clutch a puff of smoke in her hand, as futile as trying to will Grand-mère to breathe.

"You keep on dancing, girl," Rose said. "There's no shame in it."

As if Monique could help it.

As if shame meant anything compared to the pain.

Monique tried taking a shower in the hope that hot water beating across her skin might soothe her strained muscles, but her heels' squeaky movements against the slippery tub floor stole her balance, and she banged her elbows against the tiles. A bath was no better, since her gyrations splashed everywhere and made her head slip underwater, where soapy residue from Grand-mère's Zest stung her nostrils.

Monique had never suffered childbirth, though she couldn't imagine how it could be worse than her uncontrollable limbs. By the time she managed to climb out of the bathtub, she was sure that since the funeral, she had dislocated at least one shoulder, perhaps both, and pulled muscles in both her calf and her side, or even cracked a rib or two. In the mirror, her brown skin was mottled with ugly bruises inflicted from within.

Was she being punished? Was it a hex? Monique had never had patience for Grand-mère's candles and powders, yet she lit every candle she could find (knocking a few over with her frenetic motions, quickly stamping out the flames) and tried to pray—although, honestly, the pointed silence she'd met during her prayers over Grand-mère in the past six months made it feel like a useless exercise.

Naked and shuddering, still damp from the tub, she bounce-walked to Grand-mère's closet and washed herself in her grandmother's scent, rubbing her face across Grand-mère's favorite French robe. She slipped the silk across her shoulders, wincing when her body jerked to and fro.

Was Grand-mère trying to dance through her?

Yes, she realized. *Yes, of course.*

She finally remembered the story.

1937

That day had begun as the greatest adventure of Nadine Moreau's life.

Nadine's mother surprised her with a quarter to start dance lessons when she was ten. The studio was in the basement of a row house six long blocks from her home. The lessons were after school, at three o'clock sharp, so she made a litany of promises about her behavior and common sense to win the privilege of walking alone, since her parents both worked for a rich white family in the Garden District until after dark. They did not want Nadine to ride a railcar even if they could have afforded it.

From the moment she had seen photographs of *Swan Lake* in *Life* magazine, Nadine had hounded her parents for dance lessons. She practiced twirls and leaps in a cracked shaving mirror she mounted on a stool (and got a spanking for breaking), and eventually could stand on her toes for eight seconds straight, even without special shoes.

Mme. Pinede, Dance Instruction

The sign on the door made her breath catch. All day at school, she'd been afraid it would not be real—but it was! The studio might have been shabby to someone else's eyes, but to Nadine the large mirror on the wall made it look as grand as a mansion. Madame Pinede was Maman's age, two shades shy of passing for white, and pleasant. She took the quarter without asking for a penny more. The lesson was off to such a wonderful start that Nadine was bouncing on the soles of her feet.

"Let's get your shoes," Madame Pinede said. "I think I have your size."

Nadine practiced standing on her toes while Madame Pinede turned a corner into a small office, but she was too nervous to stay up.

Then, the shoes. Madame Pinede returned with an offering in outstretched hands. Instead of ballet shoes, the woman held very plain brown, scuffed shoes with frayed shoelaces.

"These aren't for ballet," Nadine said.

"*Chéri,*" Madame Pinede said, "what would you do with ballet slippers?"

"I'm going to dance ballet," Nadine responded. "*Swan Lake.* See?" She propped herself up on her toes, realizing this might be an audition: of *course* she would have to audition! She was amazed as she counted off the seconds, *one, two, three,* and then *seven, eight, nine,* and she still did not fall.

"Oh my!" Madame Pinede said. "Isn't that lovely?"

Nadine grinned up at her, thinking she must have passed the audition, but Madame Pinede met her grin with sagging cheeks. A smile tried to peek out, although it was the wrong kind of smile.

"Nadine," Madame Pinede said, her voice hushed and stripped of anything to remind Nadine that one of them was an adult and one was a child, the way her mother might talk to her auntie, "no ballet company will take a Negro girl."

Nadine thought about *Life* magazine and how rarely she'd seen a Negro face except for a photograph Maman had spread on the table like a lace cloth: Negro men, women, and children lined up for food beneath a massive billboard of a sunny white family and the words, *There's no way like the American Way.* She remembered how the words mismatched the image. Wasn't *Swan Lake* a part of her American Way too?

"You should study a kind of dancing where you'll have a future, Nadine," Madame Pinede said. "Your folks can't afford flights of fancy. Let's see how it goes with your lessons, and maybe you can dance in pictures one day. But not ballet."

Slowly, the woman turned the shoes over until the soles faced upward, glinting in the late-afternoon light from her narrow basement window. Metal plates shone at the toes and heels. "Tap shoes," she said, answering the confusion on the girl's face.

Nadine had been delighted by boys dancing for pennies on street corners, their feet in furious motion. But these shoes didn't hold the promise of leaping high in the air like the ladies with impossibly long legs on the magazine pages. Only now did she remember that all of those ladies in *Life* had been white.

Nadine's lip tremored. She'd never felt like such a fool.

"Maybe one day, *chéri*," Madame Pinede said. "But not today."

Years later, long after her dancing dreams were ash, after she'd fled from marriage to marriage searching for the joy she'd lost, after she'd fortified her heart and driven most of her family away, she had heard about the Dance Theatre of Harlem. And Anne Benna Simms, who would become the first Black dancer in the American Ballet Theatre long decades later, in 1978. In her last years, she thought about Madame Pinede when she saw Misty Copeland standing on her toes on the cover of *Time* magazine in 2015.

But she remembered only for an instant, a flick of a match, before her muddy mind swallowed it away.

After all, Grand-mère had not been that little girl for more than eighty years. Grand-mère had lived to be ninety-six, but that little dancing girl had died long before.

A buried dream could be reborn like a curse in the wake of the dead, it seemed. Monique had not known you could love someone so much, and want to hold on to them with such fervor, that you could swallow them inside of you—even their dead dreams. And that those dreams could eat you in return.

Still wearing Grand-mère's robe, Monique was trying to stand on her toes, counting *one, two, three*—

Monique screamed when her untrained ankle folded beneath her weight. This was not the first bone her dancing had broken, yet the pain of the fracture cascaded up and down her leg. She fell against the wall so hard that her head snapped back with a *crack*.

Finally, stillness. Her pain, gone.

Monique exhaled in an unsteady stream as she realized she had damaged herself so badly that she could not move, could barely breathe. The missing pain was only a lack of *any* sensation. Had she broken her neck?

Smoke. The haziness she thought was only in her mind was real. She strained her eyes to see as far as she could behind her without moving her neck and saw flames climbing Grand-mère's bedspread, greedy and gorging. She had knocked over another candle, and this time the fire was spreading fast, fueled by Grand-mère's piles of old newspapers and *Life* magazines piled under her bed.

She almost laughed at herself. Almost. What a ludicrous sight she was, contorted like a snake half naked on Grand-mère's floor. Would anyone find her? Would anyone except Rose ever know how she had danced? Would she ever have the chance to tell anyone about Grand-mère's lost dream?

Even before she felt the heat, the growing fire turned the room a brilliant, angry gold color until smoke leeched her vision gray.

I thought I would have more time.

Her body, so untamed since the funeral, lay immobile except for her right index finger tapping to the rhythm of the crackling flames.

SCARLET RIBBONS

BY **MEGAN ABBOTT**

A ll the children knew about the Hoffman House.

Penny couldn't remember a time when she didn't know about it. She had spent all of her eleven years three doors down and around the corner from it, and it had been empty her entire life.

No one had lived in the house for years, though everyone seemed to remember a time when new renters had passed through, staying a week or two and then disappearing in the night, even leaving their belongings behind, suitcases left open, boxes unpacked.

It was the neighborhood spookhouse, the Halloween dare, the stuff of all the children's nightmares, and Doctor Hoffman was the boogeyman that haunted their dreams, sharpened their taunts, fired their morbid kid fantasies.

Sometimes, high school boys threw rocks at the windows. Then, last spring, two girls in Penny's class came to school, breathless. They claimed they had snuck up to the house. The doors were all boarded shut, but they had seen things in the windows: TV trays, a dusty globe, rippled magazines, a stuffed teddy bear, its stomach chewed open. A Formica table covered with fading Christmas wrapping paper and all the trimmings, long ribbons curled into wilting bows.

By the end of the school day, they were claiming they'd seen the hammer itself, red-slathered and punched hard into the entryway floor.

That didn't seem like it could be true. *The police would have taken the weapon,* Susan Candliss insisted. *Don't you know anything?*

Besides, another girl said, *how could it be stuck in the floor? It was a ball peen, not a claw.*

And then someone insisted the Hoffmans were Jewish anyway and wouldn't have Christmas paper.

But that visit had an impact. Soon, other girls wanted to go. It was like French kissing. Soon enough, if you hadn't done it, you were good as dead.

Though it had happened many years ago, it seemed like almost everyone knew someone who was a part of it. Maybe their aunt or aunt's friend had been one of Doctor Hoffman's patients and remembered he always had such soft, dimpled hands when he placed the stethoscope over her heart. Maybe their father used to mow the Hoffmans' lawn when he was in high school and sometimes could see Mrs. Hoffman clipping her prized night-blooming jasmine, her monkey-faced orchids, her spider lilies in the glass conservatory. Maybe they'd even heard the hushed recounting from the neighbor who took in the Hoffman girl the night it happened, when she ran down the zigzag front steps and pounded on their glass door, her hair thick with blood.

The story was deceptively simple. Doctor Hoffman had been a heart doctor and his wife Agnes led the Horticulture Society and decorated their marvelous home. They had three children, sixteen-year-old Bettye and the eleven-year-old twins, Jody and Kathy.

These were the known things, the rest were heard things, passed things, behind hands at slumber parties, whispered in the kitchen at cocktail parties.

Things like this: Doctor Hoffman would sometimes have agonizing headaches that would make him nearly go blind with pain and you could hear his screams from the hill below the house.

And like this: Once, in her high school English class, Bettye recited a poem she'd written herself about a merry-go-round that never stopped spinning and all the children clutched on the horses eventually grew up and grew old while the ride kept going. Their now-gray hair had grown so long it caught in the horses' pumping legs and wound around their hooves, setting sparks that caught fire and the merry-go-round went up in flames. *A fire, a fire, and they finally knew what it was that they had been running from!* she read to the rapt class, her voice shaking with feeling.

But no one could have guessed what was to come next. A December night when something snapped inside Doctor Hoffman. That was what everyone said—"Something snapped" or "He snapped," as though this could happen to anyone, as though any parent, any father, might one day take a ball-peen hammer and crush his wife's skull as she slept. Which was what Doctor Hoffman did.

Bludgeoned. That was the word people often used. It was a terrible word, Penny thought. It felt like a cold marble in your mouth, the kind that might land in the center of your throat so you couldn't breathe at all.

But Doctor Hoffman wasn't done. Bettye woke up to her mother's screams and to her father standing above her bed, the hammer raised above his head. He caught one glancing blow on her temple before she spun loose and stumbled to the floor, crawling across the thick pink carpet of her princess bedroom, then leaping to her feet, running down the zigzag steps, her father behind, chasing after her, tripping on his pajamas— patterned with painted clowns holding balloons—and stumbling, giving Betty just enough time to escape through the front door and down the steep concrete to a neighbor's house, screaming, screaming, screaming.

The twins were climbing out their window when their father walked by their open bedroom door. He stared at them a long minute, hammer swinging at his side.

Go back to sleep, he told them calmly. *This is a nightmare.*

Go back to sleep. This is a nightmare.

Meanwhile, the neighbor opened his door to find Bettye there in her nightgown, blood pouring down her cheek and neck like a bucket of paint had tipped over on her head.

He called for his wife as Bettye kept asking, over and over, *Where are the twins? Where's Mommy?*, scratching her head with fingers red-slicked. Poking at the wound on her head until the neighbor's wife fainted right on the doorstep.

The neighbor ran to the Hoffman house and opened the front door, and he could hear this awful, ghoulish moaning. Slowly, slowly creeping upstairs, he could see Doctor Hoffman roaming the hall in his gaudy clown pajamas, the hammer loose between his fingers.

He was saying strange things, the neighbor said, and only later was it reported in all the newspapers that he'd been reciting from Dante's *Inferno*, Canto One open on his bedside table. *Midway through the journey of our life I found myself within a forest dark, for the straightforward path had been lost . . .*

By then, Doctor Hoffman had already taken a fatal combination of barbiturates.

Moments later, while tending to the children, the neighbor heard a slump and discovered Doctor Hoffman on his bedroom carpet, a swirl of his clown pajamas.

Maybe it wasn't true, at least most of it, but it felt true.

No one knew what happened to the children after. They would be grown-ups by now, maybe with children of their own. Who could guess the nightmares they had? Who could guess how they slept again?

It was rumored that Doctor Hoffman had financial difficulties. That that was what had driven him to such dark acts. He couldn't afford the grand home in which they lived, complete with ballroom and glassed-in conservatory. But others said it was "emotional." That Doctor Hoffman had struggled with melancholy before and maybe had even been in a sanitorium.

That was what Mr. Calhoun said. He was the only one on the block to remember the Hoffmans. Sometimes Penny talked to him while he was repairing radios in his garage. He gave her honey candy and butterscotch curls.

When he was sixteen, Mr. Calhoun had mowed the lawn for Mrs. Hoffman, who paid him a quarter each time.

She was a nice lady, he said. *She always said, "My husband's a heart specialist, but his heart belongs to me!"*

Once, Penny heard her mother talking in the backyard to Mrs. Candliss about it.

They were sunbathing in their new two-pieces, the only time Penny's mother took off her pantyhose because she didn't like the backs of her legs, the faint red skein Penny herself could barely see. Spider veins, her mother called them, making a face.

They were talking about Mrs. Hoffman whose head, it was said, became melon soft from the hammer blows.

I guess he got tired of her.

I guess she got fat.

And they laughed in a funny, high voices, like they didn't mean it but wanted their words to be a shield that would protect them. Protect them from whatever put Mrs. Hoffman at hazard.

Go back to sleep. That was what Doctor Hoffman told the twins. *This is a nightmare.*

That was in all the newspaper articles. It was the one detail everyone included when they told the story. That, and the hammer.

Go back to sleep. This is a nightmare.

Penny always remembered it. It was something every kid heard, all the time.

Penny knew if she ever went to the house, she would never tell her father. Certainly not her mother. But someday, she thought, she would have to go.

Everyone seemed to, eventually.

Don't go near there, her mother always said. *You'll get lockjaw.*

Lockjaw was the scariest thing you could ever get, Penny was sure. Ever since her father told her how his Great-Uncle Ernie stepped on a rusty nail and died six days later.

Don't set foot there, her father told Penny once, his face hidden behind the newspaper.

Why not?

A man went mad there, he said, shaking straight his newspaper, his fingers twitchy. *Mad as a hatter.*

Don't bother your father, Penny's mother said, watching them from the kitchen, drying dishes slowly with a long towel. *He works hard.*

You get too close to the house, her father whispered to her, his breath sweet with vermouth, *the house gets into you.*

Sometimes, four or five times a year, her father had to spend rest days in the dark bedroom, a cold towel on his face. You were never to bother him. He worked very hard selling vacuums all day. He managed the whole department and customers could be very difficult and demanding. Sometimes Penny could hear him crying softly through the door. Sometimes moaning. He had a case of the black clouds. That's what he called them. *Don't bother your father,* her mother would say. *He's very sensitive.*

But then the black clouds would pass, and he'd take Penny to the skating rink and to Schwitt's for candy and to pick any doll she wanted in the whole store. He would be grinning the entire time, grinning so hard his face might burst.

It seemed to Penny that there was a day world and a night world, and her parents' night world was so different and she only had occasional keyholes into its mysteries.

She sometimes listened to her parents talking late into the night. There was a strange, lolling rhythm to it, and she mentioned it once to her mother, who said her father talked in his sleep and sometimes sang. She said it was on account of the war. *Don't mention it,* she said. Penny never would. Her father didn't ever talk about the war except the time she heard him tell Mr. Thorpe next door that he was always the point man because he was the shortest in his platoon. Once a year, on Veterans Day, he'd go to the VA dinner and be too tight to drive home. Someone else would bring him home.

Last year, Penny thought she could hear him through her bedroom wall, singing "Scarlet Ribbons" on the sleeping porch. It was about a man who roams the town all night to find scarlet ribbons for his daughter, but all the stores are closed and shuttered. Finally, he comes home at dawn to find his daughter asleep in her bed, surrounded by mounds of scarlet ribbons *in gay profusion lying there*.

Her father's singing sounded so pretty, like a cartoon princess, crooning softly, his voice like it might crack, break, shatter as he called out the final *for her hair*.

Daddy, she said. *Daddy, are you okay?* And the singing stopped so fast, and then a *creak, creak, creak,* and he appeared in her doorway, the long shadow of him, his body swaying and only the gleam of his hair oil.

He didn't move and Penny didn't move either, and her hand, curled around her blanket, pressed against her mouth.

Go to sleep, he said, his voice low and strained. *You were dreaming.*

And maybe she was.

The next day, she told her mother about it and her mother sat down at the kitchen table and cried and cried. I should never mention the night world in the day world, Penny realized. Adults never liked it and sometimes they hated you for it.

How could you start sixth grade never having braved the Hoffman house, zigzagging up its zigzag stairs? Suddenly that was what everyone at school wanted to know.

At first Penny could never imagine doing it. She thought it might be like all those other things you can't imagine you'd ever do, like let boys lie on top of you. And then, in the dark basement of some party, after a few passed sips of Ripple, it happens, your eyes stuck open, fixed on the dangling light bulb in the laundry room.

First, Susan Candliss did it, then Nina and Tina, the twins, together. They were still having nightmares about it. They said they saw something through the window, a dark shape on the stairs. The dark shape had followed them home and maybe was living in their closet. Their mother had to spray all the corners of their bedroom with Florida water.

Pretty soon, all the girls in Penny's class had gone, or said they had. They all had stories. Of shadows and fluttering bats, creaking shutters and a nest of crushed baby mice. One girl claimed she'd climbed through a broken window and that it was like outside had become inside, with scattering birds and rodents living in the stove and Mrs. Hoffman's spider lilies growing deep in the carpet. She said she felt like something had gotten in her throat—a spore or fungus—and how, at night, she couldn't breathe.

You don't have to do it, Susan assured Penny, but that didn't seem true either.

And maybe Penny wanted to. Wanted to have to go, so she would.

Some days, she took the long way home from school just to walk by.

She was building up to it.

Maybe it would be like that boy in the basement, making her stomach wiggle in ways she never knew it could. She could almost taste the Ripple now.

Maybe it would be okay and then over.

Maybe it would be like letting her into night world at last, where all the grown-ups lingered, exploring their mysteries, feeling feelings, seeing things untold, untellable.

* * *

One night, two weeks before sixth grade, Penny decided to do it. To go.

It was late, but still before the eleven o'clock news.

Her parents were in the TV room, the anchor's voice droning and her mother's knitting needles clacking. Her father snoring, today's newspaper twitching on his lap.

They never heard the screen door, its spring loose and lazy.

Her father's service flashlight heavy in her pocket, swinging against her leg as she ran.

One house, two house, three house, turn. Kitty-corner.

And there it was, the Hoffman house.

Spanish-style and large, three stories, the house lurching high up on a hilltop, its red-tile roof jutting out like a grooved tongue.

Penny's breath caught in her throat.

But it felt right, the time, the night, warm and moon-bright.

There was so much time going up those zigzag steps, so much time to change your mind, glancing up at its long, narrow windows, especially the biggest one, through which you could see the sharp slash of a staircase. Every time Penny looked away, she thought she saw something moving up those stairs. Maybe it was the dark thing Nina and Tina had seen, the one that followed them home and, despite the Florida water, still hadn't left, crouching over them as they slept.

There were two tall windows flanking the entryway, boarded shut.

Penny peered inside both, her legs shaking.

Inside was a grand room, a drawing room, maybe, the floor swirled with sooty sheets.

The room was so alive, dust motes dancing on the Spanish tiles, the moonlight silver-streaking the spiral staircase.

No one ever said what you were really supposed to do when you got up there. Clap the front knocker, try all the door handles, tug at the window sashes, slip a hand through a broken pane. See what you can see. Put yourself in the beast's mouth. Open the forbidden box.

She placed her right hand on the heavy wooden front door. *Maybe I'll feel something*, she thought.

The wood felt warm and spongy-soft, so soft she wanted to stroke it. So soft she stroked it a bit until she felt a pinch and pulled her hands back fast.

A spider—shiny black with a red blotch shaped like an hourglass—flitted away.

The wind—hot, sparkling—lifted.

Penny could hear a shush of leaves, branches behind her.

She thought suddenly of Bettye Hoffman. How neighbors said she sounded like a wild animal shrieking as she ran from the house. How someone said the newspapers printed a picture of Bettye's monogrammed light plate smeared with blood.

Maybe I can go home now, Penny thought. She'd done it, after all. She'd braved the ascent to the Hoffman house, stood at the front door, peeked in the front windows. But the idea of going back down those steps, of going back home, the tight stillness of the house, her parents, eyes glazed, seated on opposite sides of the living room, the TV going to snow . . .

Both hands on the heavy flashlight, Penny started moving.

She decided she would walk the full perimeter of the house, she would peer in every window, half broken, glass glittering.

The full perimeter. That was a phrase her father used, from the war. How they made the infantry walk the perimeter with dowsing rods, looking for land mines or something. *Booby traps*, he called them, *and the booby was me.* Laughing, laughing so he couldn't stop, until he bent over at the dinner table, nearly crying from laughing.

Everything was as everyone said, but different.

First, the glass conservatory on the right side, fogged and moss-slimed. When Penny pressed her face against it, she could see Mrs. Hoffman's famed spider lilies still growing, impossibly growing inside.

Next, she came upon a sitting room, a pair of acid-yellow wing chairs, the cushions heavy with old rain, a draped sofa, a draped turntable, a draped Zenith, its antennae piercing through. A dark stain on the tufted wall-to-wall carpet, indeterminate and large. There was nothing in the room to be scared of. But there was a feeling she couldn't name.

It was hard not to think of Bettye, or the twins, or even poor Mrs. Hoffman, whom Penny could picture roaming the rooms in a frilly peignoir, her hair in curlers, bending over to pick up the sock, the hammer still caught in the back of her head, hovering there like a tuning rod, blood tumbling down like scarlet ribbons in her hair.

She thought of what they said about Mrs. Hoffman, how her husband had brought down the ball peen so hard, he'd split the back of her head open. How he'd left an inch-wide hole. How she had drowned in her own blood. How even the whites of her eyes had turned red.

You could never imagine that much blood, Susan Candliss said, even as they were both imagining it. Like the spin art kit Penny got for Christmas, the hum of its motor, squeezing red paint into the spinner, spattering it across the paper. Dappling it across Penny's fingers so her mother stood her over the sink, rubbing the washcloth so hard it felt like pins.

Penny went back around the other side. She was saving the rear of the house for last. It was so dark back there, a place no streetlamps or even moonlight seemed to go.

She felt something claw at her throat. *The dust*, she thought. *It must be the dust.*

First, there was the kitchen, the oven door creaked open, the metal table laden with cans curled open, a raccoon-rummaged box of Rinso soap flakes, pastel stacks of melamine bowls, a brown-sluiced bottle of Lea & Perrins, a saucer smeared with mint jelly. It made Penny's head hurt, all of it.

Next to the window, there was a door that Penny knew would open.

She knew somehow it wasn't locked, but she didn't go inside.

She remembered the pinch of the spider and didn't touch the handle.

Don't go inside, something told her. And in her head she was already upstairs, in the Hoffman bedroom, her feet soft in the deep carpet, the deep carpet spattered black with moonlit blood.

Once, Penny's neighbor caught his dog in the car door and the dog's poor head bled all over the driveway. She remembered watching from the window as her father hosed the driveway down. You could never think a dachshund had that much blood.

* * *

Next to the kitchen, there was a set of windows too high to reach.

She crawled, spiderlike, on top of a set of cellar doors.

Panting, she stepped on the damp, splintering wood. For a second, she thought her shoe might poke through, capture her. That a nail might pierce her, poisoning her with fatal lockjaw.

But the wood held her.

Her hand on the window screen, Penny knew as soon as she saw the tinsel. It was the room everyone had mentioned. The one full of wrapped Christmas presents. The gleaming silver paper and gaudy gold ribbons, scattered pom-pom bows in tinsel red, green ribbons like tendrils, crimson ones like Mrs. Hoffman's spider-lily legs.

Scarlet ribbons, scarlet ribbons. She could nearly hear her father singing.

Scarlet ribbons, scarlet ribbons, scarlet ribbons for her hair.

Penny wondered what was inside the bright wrapping: an Erector Set for Jody, a Ginny doll for Kathy, a vanity set for Bettye? A brand-new briar-wood pipe for Doctor Hoffman? She liked to imagine inside were a pair of fancy new garden shears for Mrs. Hoffman, but maybe she was like her own mother, wrapping everything—and what was under the tree for her? Her father had trouble remembering things and sometimes he'd rush out for a jumbo bottle of Evening in Paris from Woolworth's. Once he'd forgotten entirely, then cried over Rumple Minze for hours. A week later, he spent all his money on a pretty gold locket from Ahee Jewelers and Penny's mother had to return it so they could make the car payments.

But the Hoffmans were Jewish, weren't they? Maybe they

were Hannukah presents, she thought. And the store only had Santa paper. Or maybe these weren't their gifts at all but some renters' or squatters' left abandoned as they ran away in the night.

Hold still, Penny whispered to herself, her hand on her beating hard.

That was what Doctor Hoffman had told his daughter Bettye, struggling under her bedclothes, staring up at the hammer in his hand . . . how he told her, *Hold still.*

There was no avoiding it now. The rear of the house, the blackness there. She had to go. She had to, even if it felt like she had gone farther and deeper than any of her classmates, than anyone at all since the Hoffman children bolted out of that house, bolted from one nightmare into the next.

She wondered suddenly why Doctor Hoffman didn't kill the twins. Had he come to his senses by then? Or had he planned to kill them later? Or had he looked into their eyes, blinking and scared, and lost his nerve?

Penny crept slowly, her ankles prickling with mosquitoes, maybe with the furry stamens of the spider lilies.

One hand on the winged wall, the stucco soft in her hand, she turned the last corner, expecting a pool of darkness.

But it was brighter than she guessed, the moon slipping from behind the clouds.

Everything was overgrown, muzzy, two sets of patio doors clotted with sooty mold. Spores, slime, everything mossy soft under her feet.

She felt the scratching in her throat again, like furry things had slipped inside her. But as she moved closer, it didn't matter anymore. Because the moonlight made the green muck iridescent, magical.

And she could see inside.

A ballroom dancing along the entire rear of the house, its doors spilling out onto a patio of broken tiles, Penny's ankle turning on every one as she moved closer still.

Inside were gleaming floors, a black and gold bar along one wall and mirrors everywhere.

In one of them, Penny could see herself, her eyes wide, her hands gripped on the window ledge. Penny could see herself, moonlit silver.

In an instant, all the bad feeling disappeared, the smell everywhere of night-blooming jasmine, of floor polish, of cigarette smoke.

It was like in a movie, everything sparkling, shadows flickering. Penny imagined whirling around inside in a swirling gown.

She heard the footsteps first, then turned, squinting. But even before she saw him, she knew. There, at the far end of the room, was Doctor Hoffman, tall and pale, dancing alone on the herringbone floor in his jaunty clown pajamas.

Oh, she thought, *he's so happy. Look how happy he is.*

Inside there was music, grand and sweeping. She could hear it, tinny and muffled through the glass doors.

Doctor Hoffman turned and looked at her. *Come inside*, he seemed to say with his eyes, and Penny wanted to, she did.

It was all a terrible mistake, she realized, a gasp in her throat. He never meant to do it. He'd only wanted to dance with his wife, with his daughter, the hammer like some glittering conductor's baton.

He never meant to do it!

She knew it somehow, watching him, large and ungainly, pajamas billowing, spinning around in his scuffing slippers, a spot of dried shaving cream caught in his ear.

Come inside, he seemed to say, waving again, moving toward her as he swayed and twirled.

I will, Penny thought. *I must.*

Her hand on the patio door's knob, she tugged and she tugged but the door wouldn't give. There was something wrong with her hand, her fingers tight and a throbbing in her palm.

Daddy! the cry came. *Oh, Daddy!*

Penny looked up and saw it was Bettye.

Bettye, curled in Doctor Hoffman's gangling arms, her feet bare and her white nightgown dotted with red bows.

Father-daughter dance, Penny thought, her face aching from smiling.

Whirling her around the dance floor, Bettye's arms wrenched high enough to meet her father's, and Penny couldn't quite see her face.

Bettye, Penny wanted to cry out, and maybe she did. *Bettye, hold still! Hold still!*

But suddenly Penny had that feeling again of something scrabbling its way up her throat, and her hand hurt even more, stiff like a claw.

She knew it was time to go.

Something had closed shut, sealed itself up.

Night world was zipping its zipper shut and if you didn't want to be trapped inside its dark center forever, you better go, go, go.

* * *

The air had grown still, heavy. The tree branches hung low, and the moon slipped behind everything.

Skittering down the zigzag steps, the flashlight clunking against her leg. The streetlamps bright and garish and the sound of an airplane vrooming above.

The night quiet, the street empty and cool.

She hurried, nearly smiling.

She'd done it, she'd done it.

Her hand hurt and felt big, like the gloved hand of her Donald Duck rubber squeak toy. She had to use her other one to turn the doorknob, the swollen screen pressed against her face.

The house was still, fans humming.

Her bed was cool, her breath settling.

She'd done it, she'd done it.

She couldn't make her brain shut off.

The house was still in her, she'd taken it with her.

An aching pain in her right hand, Penny lay in bed.

Every time she closed her eyes, she saw the red Christmas curlings and the red bows in Bettye Hoffman's nightgown and the red threads on her grandfather's cheeks, and on Principal Stevens's puffy nose. The red veins on the backs of her mother's legs. The deep red of Mrs. Hoffman's spider lilies.

Spider lilies.

It was then she remembered the front door, the spongy wood, the pinch in her hand, and the shiny spider flitting away.

Her head felt hot, everything felt hot.

She looked down at her puffy hand and saw it, a red line

extending from her palm up to her elbow. A red line like one of those coiling Christmas ribbons.

Oh, how it ached.

Daddy! she cried out. *Help me, Daddy!*

Scarlet ribbons, scarlet ribbons. She could hear her father singing the song.

She could nearly feel herself like the girl in the song, tucked in bed, the crinkling sound of ribbons, scarlet ribbons swirled around her, snaking around her ankles, curling around her wrists and throat. Curling so tight she couldn't breathe.

Scarlet ribbons, scarlet ribbons, scarlet ribbons for her hair . . .

And there he was in the doorway, his long shadow lined black.

Go back to sleep, Penny, he said. *Go back to sleep.*

His body swaying in striped pajamas and only the gleam of his hair oil.

But Daddy, you don't—

Go back to sleep, he said louder now, louder even as his voice seemed far away. And then she knew what was coming, the red encircling her, her throat closing up around her—

This is a nightmare, Penny.

Go back to sleep.

MALENA

BY JOANNA MARGARET

Your gift is inside you, the voice whispered.

Sharp pains woke Lara in the middle of the night. She couldn't pinpoint their precise location, whether kidney or bowel or ovary—one of those confusing organs conducting unseen processes in her core. She'd been experiencing similar cramps on and off over the past year. Usually, the pain disappeared after a few minutes, although lately it had been lasting longer.

Your gift is inside you. Deep inside you. Lara heard it again. She flung off the covers, rolled to the edge of the bed, and sat up.

In the final year of her BFA at art school in New York City, Lara was thinking about her thesis project, currently a large mound of clay in the school's sculpture studio, waiting for her to extract the life out of it. So far, she'd crafted a balloon-like head resting on a slim neck. She'd started to add three breasts and four arms, coming out of a lumpy torso. She wasn't sure whether or not she would add legs. The strangely shaped body was neither baby nor child nor adult. It did not yet have a name.

Lara pulled on a clean T-shirt and stepped into the overalls she always wore to the studio.

In the past few months, Lara's work had become dark, grotesque. Her last three sculptures had been headless women's torsos, with extra limbs and breasts, but missing hands and feet. She hadn't told anyone, but she'd been having visions and dreams of misshapen bodies. Accompanied by a voice. Low, atonal, garbled. Recently, she'd thought the voice resembled her own, but disguised and disembodied. Calling her, beckoning her. To what end, she wasn't sure. *Lara*, it would whisper, waking her up, or startling her while she was working.

Today she'd heard that full sentence for the first time: *Your gift is inside you.* What did it mean? It sounded like cheesy self-help advice.

But Lara was pleased that her instructors had been heaping praise on her latest creative output. Her favorite, Professor Stewart, herself a sculptor, had introduced Lara to a gallerist in Chelsea, who had evinced interest in exhibiting her thesis project after graduation.

When the cramps eased up, Lara tiptoed to the bathroom. She bent over the sink, then sat on the toilet, but nothing would come out. Sticking three fingers down her throat, she forced herself to throw up, hoping it would make her feel better. It didn't.

Lara washed her face, then sat back down on the bed. The pain was pulsating. She curled her knees up to her chest and squeezed her eyes closed. After a few seconds, a sharp wave of pain resonated through her. It felt as though something had exploded inside her. Shaking, she slowly pushed herself out of bed. She stared at her reflection in the long mirror. Her eyes were bloodshot, and her stomach had bloated out and up, like the belly of a dead fish. Lara knew she wasn't pregnant.

She walked into the hall. She was living in a single that year, and her window looked out over a leafy quad surrounded by brick buildings. All the other doors along the neon-lit hallway were shut.

She took a taxi to the nearest hospital and waited for an hour in the ER among victims of car accidents, gunshot wounds, drug overdoses, each in their own private state of horror. When the throbbing in her stomach became unbearable, she hobbled up to the reception desk.

"Can someone please see me soon? I'm in bad pain," she wheezed.

The man behind the counter looked her up and down and passed her a plastic cup with a lid. "Everyone here's in pain, girly. You'll have to wait. Pee in this."

"I can't," Lara groaned. "I really can't."

"Suit yourself," said the man, turning back to his screen and starting to type.

Lara brought the cup inside the bathroom but couldn't produce more than a few drops.

She went back to the waiting room, sank down on the floor, hugging her knees against her chin, and after a while drifted into an uneasy sleep. A nurse nudged her shoulder at five a.m. and brought her into a room with curtained-off beds, handing her a flower-print gown. She changed and stretched out on the bed, leaving the gown open in front.

A young doctor peered over at her from the other side of the curtain. "What's going on?" he asked.

"Terrible. Pains. In my. Stomach." A few tears slid out of her right eye and into her ear.

"May I examine you?"

She nodded.

With cold, pointy fingers, he pressed down hard in different spots on her chest and stomach. When he reached the area around her navel, she wheezed out a cry. He stepped back.

"My appendix?" she asked, pearls of sweat dripping down from her temples and mixing with the tears that kept coming.

"How old are you?" he asked.

"Twenty-one."

"Are you sexually active?"

"Yes."

"You should see a gynecologist. I recommend testing for pregnancy and STDs."

"My boyfriend and I broke up. A few months ago."

The doctor lifted his head. "Well, at your age, you're very fertile, you never know."

Lara huffed out a breath. "He's in school in California. I haven't even seen him for three months. Something's wrong—I've never had pain like this before."

He twisted his mouth to one side. "It's not a medical emergency."

"It is!" She clutched her extended stomach with her hands.

"Make an appointment to see a gynecologist. Are you allergic to any medications?"

"No."

The doctor gave Lara two Tylenols and sent her home.

By the time she got back to campus, the pain had subsided. Apparently it hadn't been an emergency after all. Lara didn't even tell anyone she'd gone to the hospital.

She walked to the studio. It was a Saturday, and she was alone in the bright room, which made it easier to concentrate. She glanced around at the other student creations, some figurative like hers, others abstract and angular, up against the concrete walls, some of them suspended from ropes attached to the ceiling. The bare space and the hulking, lifeless bodies called to mind an abattoir; the only thing missing was splattered blood.

Lara looked at her own sculpture, the deformed body. Although she had shown talent in drawing and painting, she'd gravitated to the tactile nature, the physicality, of sculpting. Creating something three-dimensional. She'd only made ceramic sculptures previously—bronze and aluminum were too expensive—but at the end of this semester the school would pay for one sculpture to be sent to a local foundry and cast in bronze.

The transformation from clay to metal fascinated her. When she'd finished sculpting the clay piece, the next step would be to apply a layer of plaster around it. Once it dried, the plaster mold would be removed from the outside of the original clay sculpture, the contours of its "insides" having formed a perfect negative image of the clay figure. Wax would then be poured into it, producing an exact replica of the original. At that point she would refine her creation, doing what she could do to bring it alive before it was sent to the foundry. The wax would be heated in a kiln and melt away, evaporate, leaving behind a cavity in the shape of the sculpture, where liquid bronze would be poured in.

The intricate process, known as lost wax casting, stretched back thousands of years. Lara felt awed by the continuum, being part of such a long tradition.

She ran her hands over the looming clay lump in front of her, its weight supported by a metal armature underneath, a skeleton of sorts. She slipped on her headphones, and switched on a techno music channel. She needed something wordless and otherworldly to get her into a trancelike state. She sculpted for several hours, kneading and smoothing the clay, then used a loop tool and a scalpel to carve lines and details onto the surface. She barely noticed the other students who came in and worked alongside her. By the time she left the studio, she was again the only one there.

That night the pain came back, and the voice with it: *It's beautiful, the art you're creating, Lara. Use your gift. The gift inside you.*

Lara made an appointment to see the gynecologist on Monday afternoon.

Dr. Fletcher had orange hair and wore a string of fat, dull pearls. She walked with a slight limp, favoring her left side.

"Your stomach is very distended," she said, as she began to examine Lara.

Lara held her breath and let out a small cry as Dr. Fletcher poked along her rib cage, sensitive to even the lightest tap.

"Have you had a pregnancy test?"

"I don't need one," said Lara. "I haven't seen my boyfriend in months. My ex-boyfriend—we broke up."

"How long has it been since you last had sex?"

"Three months. Anyway, I just had my period. What else could it be?"

Dr. Fletcher glanced toward the window and then back at Lara. "Perhaps a spontaneous ruptured ovarian cyst. They're very common in women of child-bearing age. Probably not cancerous. I'll send you in for a sonogram."

The tech taking Lara's blood stabbed her over and over, complaining that he couldn't find her veins. A half hour and three vials later, he led her into another exam room. As the probe rolled over her stomach, she saw this second tech's eyes widen.

"What is it?" asked Lara.

"I need to talk to the doctor," the young woman said. "Everything's fine."

Guessing this was a good sign, Lara's heart rate slackened. It didn't take long before someone called her name and she was directed to Dr. Fletcher's office.

"You need to have an operation, Lara," the doctor said, even before Lara had a chance to settle in her seat.

"An operation?" She pulled the exam gown tightly around her.

"There's a fair amount of internal bleeding." Dr. Fletcher pursed her lips. "I honestly don't know how you look the picture of health, not with the amount of blood circulating inside you right now. We need to go in and stop the uncontrolled bleeding. It's trapped. There's nowhere for it to go."

Lara looked down at her lap, and lifted her heels, then squeezed her knees together. "What . . . What's causing the bleeding?"

"We're going to find out. First you'll need a transvaginal ultrasound."

They insisted she sit in a wheelchair, and in the next room Lara tried to stay still as she felt the long probe go all the way up inside her. It rolled back and forth between her ovaries, an unpleasant tickling.

After the test she went back to the office and sat back in the chair, her thighs still sticky.

Dr. Fletcher looked in Lara's eyes. "There's a growth outside your ovaries, but I'm not sure what it is. It's concealed. Could be an ectopic pregnancy, but that's unlikely, according to what you told me."

"Not just unlikely. Impossible."

Dr. Fletcher made Lara an appointment for a CT scan.

That night Lara heard the voice speaking again, so softly she could barely hear: *You feed me, but I feed you too.*

The next day Dr. Fletcher called. "Well, you aren't pregnant."

"The growth?"

"It might be a cyst, or a tumor. Or it could be part of a fetus."

Lara's mouth opened. "I don't understand. You just told me I'm not pregnant."

"The mass we're seeing appears to be a . . . remnant. From a twin. A twin that was only partly absorbed by your body when you were an infant."

Lara stood up, clutching the phone in her hand. "Wait . . . *my* twin?"

"It's an unusual condition. Fetus-in-fetu. I've never seen it before. The likelihood of it happening is about one in a million."

"You're saying my twin is living inside my body?"

"Not living. It's not now and never has been a viable fetus. But there is a head, a brain without a full skull, teeth, bones, even a spinal cord. The fetus could never have lived outside your body. There's nowhere for it to grow. The mass is growing, however, which is the reason for the swelling and pain. It's also using your blood supply. In the old days it used to be called a parasitic twin. If we don't surgically remove it, it'll continue to press on your other organs, causing more bleeding. Could even be life-threatening."

"It could . . . kill me?"

"Yes. Or cause irreversible damage to your organs. The surgery is laparoscopic, which is not so invasive. We go through your navel and also make two small incisions on either side of your stomach."

Lara gulped. "And the recovery?"

"You'll be back at school in no time."

Lara put the phone down and clasped her hands together tightly, as if praying, and willed herself not to cry.

That night as she lay in bed, thinking over what Dr. Fletcher had told her, Lara realized that the voice she'd been hearing was her twin's. Lara gave her a name: Malena.

Your gift is inside you, Malena had said. At last Lara knew why.

Lara felt a twinge of pain, and imagined Malena moving inside her stomach, but that was impossible, wasn't it? Malena was not now, nor had she ever been, alive. Yet Lara soon heard Malena's voice speaking again. Louder and louder until the voice was all she could hear.

Why you, Lara? Why not me? The beauty. We created it. Together. You're nothing without me.

Lara went back to the studio, put on her headphones, and turned the music up, but she couldn't block out Malena's voice: *Lara, my twin! You need me. You can't survive without me!*

Lara's emergency surgery was scheduled for the following day. Her mother flew in from Fort Lauderdale.

"My dear one-in-a-million girl," her mother sighed, as she stood arched over Lara's hospital bed holding her hand.

"Why is this happening?" Lara asked.

"Why does anything happen?" her mother said, with a sad nod. "Bad luck."

Lara's surgery was on Easter Sunday, and also the second day of Passover. They had assigned her two anesthesiologists.

Lara started talking quickly: "I've had light anesthesia before, when I had my tonsils removed. I remember the doctor called it 'the twilight serum,' but you're giving me general anesthesia today, right?" She looked at the woman anesthesiologist, and then the man, her heart slamming in her chest.

"Yes," the female anesthesiologist said, her tone as emotionless as her pale face. "Think of this as the *midnight* serum."

"The dark midnight serum, yes," the man said. He was bald and had a big lump on the side of his head. While the woman stood, he sat down and wrapped a bright red tie around Lara's left wrist. He started pressing the inside of her arm at her elbow. "You've got rolling veins, young lady. Just a second." He grabbed a different needle from a concealed pouch.

"Please . . ." Lara reached with her other hand and grabbed the woman's wrist and whispered up at her: "Please don't kill me."

Then she heard it. The voice. Pleading, frantic: *Stop them, Lara! This is a mistake. It's not too late to stop. Stop them!*

She was still holding the woman's wrist. "I don't feel so well. Can we please stop? I need to reschedule! I—"

"You're okay," said the woman, peeling Lara's hand off her wrist. "You'll feel so much better once this is over."

No, Lara! No! Stop them!

The man clamped a clear plastic mask over Lara's nose and mouth, and told her to count to ten. She tried to resist, but after counting to three the midnight darkness descended upon her, fast as light.

When Lara woke up, she started to vomit. Her friend Janice, who had come to the hospital, tried to calm her down, whispering soothing words until Lara quieted and started breathing normally. Janice and Lara's mother took turns offering her tiny spoonfuls of crushed ice, which Lara refused even though she was thirsty.

"You're so pale," said her mother, grasping her hand. "Your hands are cold. Fingers look blue, like when you were born. Oh, my Lara. You look . . . like a corpse."

Lara tried to squeeze her mother's hand, but she had no strength.

"You were talking when you woke up," said Janice.

"I was?" said Lara, her voice raspy. "What did I say?"

Her mother answered: "You told me you loved me. And you kept saying a name. Malena. Who is that?"

"I don't, umm, I don't know." She was too embarrassed to tell her mother the truth, and wanted to protect her. From what, she wasn't sure.

They kept Lara overnight for observation. The next morning, Dr. Fletcher read the report to mother and daughter as Lara lay in bed. The "growth" had been fully excised. A chill passed down the back of Lara's neck as Dr. Fletcher showed her the image of Malena's stunted, misshapen body, buried inside her own for twenty-one years. She saw small eyes and a brain partly covered by a half-formed skull, a few hairs protruding like weeds through the cracks of an old, crumbling wall. But Malena's face was smiling. A hideous smile.

"Will I be . . . okay?" Lara asked.

"There's nothing to worry about," Dr. Fletcher said. "You're out of the danger zone."

"So, zero risk of complications?" asked Lara's mother.

"I wish I could say that, but unfortunately there's no such thing as zero risk." She turned to Lara. "You had a lot of internal bleeding that we had to cauterize, but I wouldn't be too concerned. Go home. Take it easy for a while. Enjoy your life. You're so young. You should forget this ever happened."

But how could she forget?

Her mother rented an Airbnb and mostly read while Lara slept. After two weeks, it became easier to climb out of bed in the morning, to shower by herself and take walks. Lara pushed herself a little further each day. "I need to get back to the studio," she said each time her mother begged her to take it easy. Then her mother flew back to Florida and Lara returned to school. Her dorm room was filled with notes and dried-up bouquets from classmates, but she ignored them and went to the studio right away. She just wanted to get on with her work, for everything to go back to the way it had been before.

At first, she was only able to work for an hour or two at a time. She was weaker on certain days, and felt phantom pains from time to time, though she gradually started to improve.

Nevertheless, she knew something had changed, would never be the same. She'd become fearful about her health in a way she hadn't been in the past, when she'd taken it for granted. Now she paid attention to every click of her neck, any gurgle that seemed out of the ordinary. Uncharacteristically for a college student, Lara started to do all the right things, the things that doctors advise. She slept for eight hours a night, banished junk food, stopped drinking alcohol, and as soon as she was able, she began to exercise regularly.

But each night, when she'd switched the lights off, she lay in the dark waiting to hear Malena's voice.

She heard nothing for a while, but then, instead of her voice,

Malena herself appeared in Lara's dreams—not really a body but a tangled and sinewy mess of stretched, purple dough. One night Lara saw two breasts with inverted nipples but only one arm, hairs sprouting out of a head that was half smooth, half rocky, only partially covering a mushy pink brain that squeezed out along the sides. Inches below her small, malformed eyes were nostrils without a nose, and always the same smiling mouth, with a few partly-grown-in sharp teeth. Another night Lara saw an oversized heart thumping inside the otherwise empty rib cage of Malena's skeleton, which looked a lot like the metal armatures that supported the sculptures in the studio.

In an attempt to stop dreaming about her, to exorcise her, Lara had written *Malena* over and over again in a notebook she kept by the side of her bed. She wrote the name down hundreds of times, until her hand was too tired to continue, the last pages scribbled in a messy, childlike, desperate scrawl. On the last page she'd written down phrases she remembered having heard: *You're nothing without me!* and *Your gift is inside you.*

A month passed. Two months. Lara was leaving the studio every night at midnight by then. One Tuesday around eleven p.m., she heard a noise, a tapping, followed by a sort of cry. She couldn't tell where it was coming from. The sounds continued. She took the scalpel out of her apron and walked slowly out into the hallway. She looked around the stairwell.

"Hello? Is someone there? Hello?"

No one answered.

She went back into the studio. She heard the cry again. When she walked over to her sculpture, she gasped. There was blood on the floor. She looked up. Coming out of the sculpture's three nipples were droplets of blood. Flowing from its navel, its vagina, was more blood. She heard laughter. From the ceiling?

"Hello?" Lara called. "Who's there? Who's there? What do you want?"

She held the scalpel up in her hand and stripped off her apron. She walked over to a mirror on the far wall, pulled off her apron, shrugged out of her overalls, rolled up her T-shirt, and with four quick strokes carved the letter M into the skin underneath her belly button, in between the tiny incision scars on either side.

She wriggled back into her clothes as she ran out of the studio and to her dorm room. Inside, she pressed her pillow over the wound until the bleeding stopped, and then applied a thick layer of bacitracin and covered the M with a bandanna held in place with packing tape. She lay down and was asleep within minutes.

The next few weeks in the studio went smoothly. Every couple of hours she stepped back to consider the sculpture, to check if she needed to make adjustments. She ran her eyes over every inch of the malformed head and the flab along the middle, the extra limbs and one extra breast. She noticed that people who passed it couldn't look away. When she hit her deadline, she took a week to work on the wax duplicate.

The next time Professor Stewart visited the studio, she walked by each of the student works, nodding her head. When she reached Lara's piece, she stood there, not speaking for several seconds.

"What a transformation! And in such a short amount of time. It's eerily lifelike, but inhuman somehow. Very powerful, Lara." She touched Lara's shoulder lightly. "How are you feeling? I can't help noticing you're skin and bones."

"Better every day, Professor Stewart."

"Glad to hear it. I'm planning a dinner with the gallerist who wants to exhibit your work. I'll email you the details."

"How great! Thank you! For everything. I appreciate your support."

"No need to thank me. You have a gift." At the mention of that word, Lara put her hand over her navel and felt an electric shock course through her body. "But make sure you eat a proper meal tonight. And don't push yourself so hard."

Lara nodded and forced herself to smile.

The following Sunday, Lara stood up at the end of the day. She was alone in the studio. Graduation was only a week away. She looked at the seven-foot-tall wax model. It was ready to undergo its final transformation into bronze.

She pictured the red wax melting down, dissolving in the hot oven. She saw molten metal flowing, orange lava. Then the sculpture would cool, forged into something new. The body would be hard, strong. Something that could last.

Lara stepped back. She needed to make one last adjustment. She took the scalpel out of her apron, stepped forward, and carved an extra two lines on the edge of the sculpture's mouth to create just the right smile.

"Perfect."

She heard something in the distance that sounded like rolling thunder, or the throb of an underground train. She felt a flash of heat pulse through her.

Within seconds, shooting stars of pain were tearing through her insides. Lara grabbed her stomach. Her legs crumpled beneath her, as if they were sticks of melting butter. Her head

thwacked on the tile floor. She tried to scream, *Help me! Help!*
But no words came out, so no one heard her. No one was there
anyway. Her cell phone was back in her dorm room. She opened
her eyes. Such an odd viewpoint, lying sideways, the right side
of her face crushed against the floor.

Already dark-red blood was pooling on the beige tiles next
to her head. It seemed to sparkle, illuminated by fluorescent
lights. Blood touched the side of her nose and trickled into her
nostril. It smelled like candy. She felt blood ooze into her scalp,
moving up through her hair. And into her mouth. And then it
was everywhere.

Early the next morning, a janitor discovered Lara sprawled out
on the studio floor. When the school realized that her bloody
body was not, in fact, a macabre piece of staged performance
art, they tried to reconstruct the sequence of events. Calls were
made. To her mother. To her ex-boyfriend. Friends and relatives
cried when they heard the news. While going through the belongings in her dorm room, Lara's friend Janice found her notebook, filled with odd phrases and the name *Malena*.

The next day, her classmates held a vigil.

The following month, Lara's bronze sculpture was unveiled
at the student exhibition with a plaque on the base featuring
Lara's full name printed side by side next to Malena's. Later,
when the piece went on display in the gallery in Chelsea, the
gallerist framed a series of pages taken from Lara's notebook,
and retitled the sculpture: *Your Gift Is Inside You.*

WRITTEN AND ILLUSTRATED BY **LISA LIM**

I would often watch my mother dancing with mirrors. She stared into the mirror for hours as if she was trying to rearrange the body she was given, like she was trying to find her true "self." I wondered as a child what lay inside the mirror. What was so fascinating that it swallowed her whole, making her ignore everything around her, including me?

You see, my mother's body was covered head to toe in superficial veins. These veins were visible to the human eye because they were close to the body's surface. My mother used to joke, "My body looks like a geographic map, but I'm always lost." One day, I peered closely while she was dancing with mirrors and I saw that her body's veins had a life of their own. They pulsed through her skin, tendril by tendril. My mother tried to look away, but the veins held her, force-feeding her the unsightly skin she was born into.

Our stomachs growled something awful as she stood there, entranced in disgust. To quiet the hunger, my mother insisted we eat brewer's yeast and cod-liver oil every day. She said it would keep our veins from taking over our bodies. "The monster is in our blood," she warned. We juiced many carrots and beets and guzzled them down to fight genetics. Nothing worked. The ritual left our breath with fish-market rank and our skin red-orange. It was not pretty.

It all started when my mother was a child. She grew up listen-ing to my grandmother's toxic tongue that felt like hammers on her head. Words beating her down, always making her feel small. My grandmother would often say, "Your sisters have the brains and you, well, at least you're pretty." It was easier to bat-tle with the mirror demons than her relentless matriarch. To escape her own mother's venom, she would hide in her room dancing with mirrors. And that's how it all began.

It was no wonder my mother clung to her looks, believing they were her only treasure. She used to revel in the catcalls from the streets. All compliments to her pretty young face and body, not a wrinkle in sight. "Hey, mami!" they flirted, validating her purpose. So, when she saw a flaw, she saw her worth disintegrating. That's when the monsters would rear their ugly heads. So many ugly heads. I asked my mother one day, "Why don't you have any wrinkles?" "I don't think too deeply about things in life. And I don't read the news." It was her beauty secret along with the hemorrhoid cream she generously smeared on her face before bedtime.

My mother would sleep facing the ceiling just because she read in a magazine that sleeping on your side causes wrinkles. So she slept like the dead sleep in caskets. Watching her lie there reminded me of Chinese wakes. In Chinese culture, white is the color of death and grief. White flowers such as chrysanthemums and lilies often fill funeral homes. My mother preferred lilies because they are deceptive. They look so beautiful, with elegant swanlike petals, and a strong perfume smell. But they only mask the stench of rotting death. I hated the smell of lilies more than I hated the smell of brewer's yeast and cod-liver oil. Blech.

My father and mother never spoke. He married her for her looks.
She married him to escape her mother's toxic tongue. They sto-
ically walked past each other, their arms always crossed. The
air thick with loathing. Sometimes it was so quiet at home you
could hear a mosquito buzzing. The only passion they shared
was when my mother swatted the flying pest on his body. And
you could see her wry smile form as she crushed the mosquito
that would soon shed his blood. It was a twisted love story.

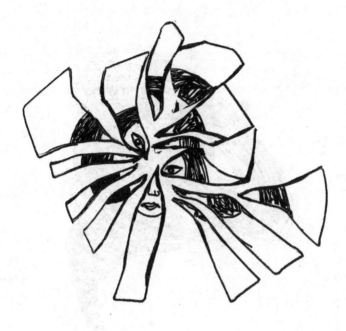

My father thought my mother was crazy and warned me, "Do not become your mother!" Which unbeknownst to him was an invitation to become her. One day, my father's fear of her continued vanity turned into rage. He smashed all the mirrors in the house. "Stop looking at the goddamn mirror and take care of your family, you selfish woman!" His words cut like a knife, but not enough to make her stop. When he left the room, she pulled out the hand mirror she hid in her bureau and stared into it.

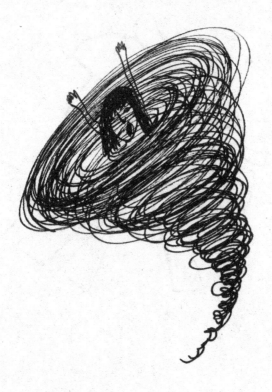

After the mirror-smashing, I remember the sadness that overcame my mother. It was a vacant stare. Knock-knock, anyone home? She may have answered in words but she was nowhere to be found. A prisoner of her own reflection. And no matter what we did, she continued to spiral deeper into melancholy. She just hid in the bathroom with her small hand mirror, whispering to it. I wanted desperately to pull her out, to save her, but the mirror held her gaze.

One night, while she lay in bed sleeping like a corpse, my mother's veins curdled with outrage over recent neglect. They slowly tore out of her skin and slithered over to my father's side of the bed, strangling him. Stifling the snores exhaling from his sleeping mouth. He began to gasp for air, fighting for survival. But his will, strong as it was, was no match for her vanity. Her veins tightened like a snake around his neck, until they suffocated their angry love. It was the best night of sleep she'd had in a long time. It was her time to snore.

The next day, I placed the small hand mirror under my father's mouth. No trace of breath. That's when my mother let out a maniacal laugh. So loud it could have shattered a thousand mirrors. When the police came, my father's body showed no signs of agitation. No bruises. No vestige of my mother's killer veins. According to the world and the coroner's report, he died of a sudden and unexplained nocturnal death syndrome. She looked like she was crying hysterically, but she was really laughing out loud. She was finally free.

After his "sudden death," my mother inherited a small sum of money. Without hesitation, she spent her newfound wealth on erasing her mirror demons. First, she indulged in sclerotherapy, an injection treatment that zapped her superficial veins, rerouting the blood to more interior ones. Afterward, her body no longer looked like a map created by a madman cartographer. But her joy was short-lived.

Her veins may have disappeared, but my mother still danced with mirrors. It was as if her body called out more flaws. And the mirror demons multiplied. Shape-shifting and eating away at her. One day I saw my mother unwrapping bandages like a mummy coming undone. Revealing craters and bruises all over her stomach. Out of them danced these tiny henchmen, slicing her up like cold cuts in a deli. I could hear them cackling. My mother explained, "Don't worry, it's just liposuction gone wrong. I'll pay for yours one day. And it will be the fancy kind. I promise."

A year later, my mother told me her boobs had been botched by a quack surgeon. She found him on Craigslist. The ad read, *Beautiful* breasts for less. "I should've sued him!" she exclaimed. "He wasn't certified but he was cheap. Why did I trust him?" I watched these red angry welts pulse and bleed through her bandages, outlining the boundaries of her hapless incisions. Later, my mother would get another boob job that unsuccessfully tried to fix the first one. With each botched surgery her breasts became more mangled and enraged. My mother sighed and said, "My skin just doesn't heal well. And this is why we must eat our brewer's yeast and cod-liver oil."

With each incision, her breasts grew angrier. They multiplied like Gremlins. Then one day they began to choke her. My mother tried to fight these fleshy beasts off, but they were insatiable and wanted blood, revenge for all the botched surgeries. You see, no amount of surgery could ever slay the monster inside her. Only death. And that is exactly what happened. My mother died at the hands of her botched boobs choking her. It sounds absurd, but it is true.

That day, the stench of lily flower dust made my throat itch. My mother lay in her coffin for an open-casket wake. I dressed her in long sleeves to cover most of her body and tied a sash around her neck to conceal the bruises. Only her hands and face showed. Not a single wrinkle on her still. Every mirror was covered with cloth. So vanity wouldn't dare rear its ugly head. She lay still in a roomful of lilies choking me. How I hated the deathly smell of lilies. But finally my mother looked content with her morticianed body. No longer dancing with mirrors.

Strange thing is, the day she died, I started dancing with mirrors. Fulfilling my father's prophesy, "Like mother, like daughter."

PART II

MORBID ANATOMY

Laurel Hausler

METEMPSYCHOSIS, OR THE JOURNEY OF THE SOUL

BY **MARGARET ATWOOD**

They were right about the soul: there is one. But nothing else we were told was correct, as it turns out.

You've probably seen those diagrams: a so-called primitive organism, such as a snail, is shown with a globe of light glowing within it. That globe represents the soul. If the snail behaves well, upon its death the soul is allowed to reincarnate in a supposedly higher organism, such as a fish. Hopping from one organic stepping stone to another—or, rather, because the soul's progress is not believed to be horizontal but vertical, from one rung of the ladder on the Great Chain of Being to another—the soul of the well-behaved snail finally arrives at the pinnacle of creation, and—oh joy!—is reborn as a human being. So goes the story.

But I'm here to tell you that very little about this fantasy is true.

For instance, I myself jumped directly from snail to human, with no guppies, basking sharks, whales, beetles, turtles, alligators, skunks, naked mole rats, aardvarks, elephants, or orang-utans in between. Nor was I even forced to be conceived, gestated, born, and then raised from infancy, with all the mucus, blood, burping, vomit, urine, rashes, teething, tantrums, pain, and weeping this process entails.

I was demolishing a lettuce leaf, my oval raspy-toothed mouth opening and closing like a flesh valve as I oozed along on my own self-generated glistening slime highway. The lovely green blur all around me, the lacework I was creating, the scent of chlorophyll, the juiciness—it was pure bliss. Live in the moment, humans are often told, but snails don't need to be told. We're in the moment all the time, and the moment is in us.

What happened next? Some guy intent on exterminating me got busy with the environmentally friendly pesticide, which—and I shouldn't be telling you this—was cold coffee in a spray bottle, to which had been added half a cup of salt. *Wait!* I ought to have screamed as the first scalding droplets hit my tender neck. *Spare me! I am part of an ecosystem! I contribute to the eggshells of birds!*

Did I know that then? No. Snails are not focused on their place in the universe. I've researched the bird-shell connection since; it has to do with ingested calcium. (I couldn't have screamed, anyway: snails are notoriously mute.)

I didn't even have time to retract my stalked eyes and withdraw into my protective carapace. My miniature snail soul, a translucent spiral of softly phosphorescent light, shot into the air—the spirit air, you must understand, where the rules are somewhat different—and made its way through the iridescent rainbow clouds and the tinkling bells and theremin woo-woo sounds of that region, then straight into the body of a mid-level female customer service representative at one of the major banks.

I won't tell you which bank. I'm guessing the top brass

would be less than pleased to discover that one of their customer service representatives is, au coeur, a snail. Not even an exotic snail. The common garden variety.

"How may I help you?" I found myself saying. My mouth felt stiff; this mouth of a woman was not as flexible as my snail mouth, and its teeth were clumsily block-shaped. Needless to say, I felt disembodied, also radically unsuited to the work my human casement had apparently been trained to do. This work consisted of answering calls from distraught members of the banking public who claimed to have experienced maltreatment. The bank had lost their money, or some of their money, or had calculated their interest wrong. The bank had misreported. The bank had failed to provide checks in a timely manner, leading to unpaid bills, and no, digital checks were not acceptable. The bank had sold them some banking product or service they did not want. The bank's anti-hacking defenses were crap.

My human casement had been extensively trained to soothe, to mollify, to reassure. It ran on autopilot, like a flesh robot. It pronounced the word *rectify* a lot.

Curled within the shell of the human woman's skull where our two souls were space-sharing, I found myself muttering, "Why are you whining? At least no one's sprayed you with snail pesticide." In fact, these words actually came out through my human mouth while a customer was still on the phone.

"Snail pesticide? Excuse me?"

People don't want you to excuse them when they say, "Excuse me." I've learned that. They want you to know you've offended them. "I'm so sorry," my human mouth said. "We seem to have had some interference from a radio station. It cuts in on our frequency. It's happened before." The woman-shaped snail refuge within which I was sheltering had no compunction about lying, it seemed. But I myself was bewildered: snails never lie, so they don't recognize lying as a category.

I was shortly to encounter another variety of customer, more plaintive, more hopeless. These had replied to text messages purporting to be from the bank that had claimed there was an irregularity with their account and had then asked them to verify their details. This they had obligingly done, only to find that the message hadn't been from the bank at all but from a scammer who'd cleaned out their life savings.

"How upsetting," the woman's face would murmur. "I'll refer you to our fraud squad."

"But what about all my money? Is it gone? Will I get it back?"

"I'm transferring you now."

Snails don't have any money. They don't need money. Yet here I was, forced to witness these irritating conversations about a subject that meant nothing to me.

With considerable exercise of my snail will, I usurped control of our joint mouth and spoke through it as myself. "You replied to the message?" I said to the seventh unwary victim. "You gave them your pass codes? That was certainly effing stupid!"

"Excuse me?"

What was I doing in this uncalled-for body? What force chained me in this room, to this desk, to this phone? My transition from my snail body had been so rapid I didn't even know what this new carapace looked like! Of course, I hadn't known what I looked like when I was a snail either. Snails have no interest in mirrors.

At last the clock said five. My human brain—the thinking-meat part of this foreign body, and let me inform you that the soul is indeed distinct from the brain—this human brain knew about clocks. So I, or perhaps she, could log out and head for the washroom. New torments awaited me there.

We were working from a place that was supposed to be "home," due to something called COVID. (This was a virus. Snails have their own viruses, and also many parasites—let us not even mention rat lungworm—but COVID is not among them.) So the bathroom was "mine," if I may use such a possessive pronoun of a room that, although familiar in a hazy way, felt utterly alien. It was suffused with overpowering aromas. I detected what I would later learn were almond soap, lemon air freshener, and a scented candle: rose petals and orange blossoms. This last was the most tempting. I resisted the impulse to eat it.

Our next act was to look in the mirror. There was a face, a hair-fringed face, a face with an ugly protruding nose in the middle of it, a symmetrical human face I'd certainly seen before, or shall we say my mirror image was a mirage that generated a similar mirage in the brain tissue that enclosed my tiny whorled snail soul. It was a good enough face as they go, I suppose. Humans would find it appealing. There were no large warts on it. I discovered that I could make it smile and frown. I put the face through its motions, to see what sort of range was available. I stuck out its tongue. At last, I thought, a body part I could identify with: moist, flexible, retractable, with chemical sensors on it. Very much like a snail, despite the pinkish color.

My interest in tongue-manipulating was soon exhausted, and I veered to other matters. Although snails do have eyes, our vision is limited: we examine our surroundings through touch and smell. But although I had a strong desire to get down on all fours and lick the floor, I controlled it. I could not really run my borrowed tongue over everything in this bathroom. I would need to focus. I turned my attention to the fixtures.

There was a sink in this bathroom. In addition, there was a toilet. I did not at that moment know the terminology, although I deduced the purpose. Need I tell you how appalling I found this hard, shiny, water-filled appliance, not to mention the bodily functions it was designed to accommodate? Snails do not give much thought to their excretions, which are innocuous and of a pleasing shade of green. I would have preferred to ignore the whole shooting match, as it were, but I had little choice in the matter. It was the floor, the toilet, or burst. Our body held its breath and availed itself.

In this bathroom there were also a tub with a shower. Human bodies are very dry on the outside, lacking that luxurious coating of mucus that renders the bodies of snails—apart from their shells—so lithe and sinuous. The thought of immersing myself in water was greatly appealing to me. We shed the sweatpants and the long-sleeved shirt that said This Is Not a Drill—it had a picture of a hammer on it, a joke that at the time I failed to grasp—and slid into the warm water that a twist of a faucet handle had caused to emerge from the tap.

I was soaking in the tub, trying not to look at the daunting expanse of wet mammal flesh extending downward from my neck while feeling my tissues becoming more gastropodal by the minute, when the bathroom door opened. "Hi, beautiful," said a voice.

The word *beautiful* must have been meant for our shared body, as it was the only visible living entity in the room. Nonetheless I was startled. Instinctively I attempted to withdraw into my shell before remembering that I no longer had one. The door opened farther, and another human entered the room. As he was an adult male, his vibrations were alarmingly similar to those of the oaf who had so recently sprayed me with snail killer.

This male was carrying a large paper bag. A nauseating stench of burned meat permeated the air. Some species of snails are carnivores, but I was not of that ilk.

"I got ribs," said the deeply reverberating voice. This conveyed nothing to me. "I got some corn bread too. I know you like that."

"Great," I managed to quaver. "Ribs."

"And a bottle of Pinot. So when you've got your luscious bod out of the tub, we'll eat, and then maybe . . . Netflix?" He pronounced this last word like a caress.

"Netflix . . ." we whispered. The hominid brain imprisoning me seemed to recall the term. Was it some kind of food?

The man, whom I now recognized as a sort of quasi-mate, contorted his facial muscles into a lopsided grin and engaged in eye contact, a look I registered as a type of sexual signaling, like the first tentative brush of one tender snail tentacle against another's. "Some like it hot," he said enigmatically as he went out, failing to close the door behind him.

We clambered out of the tub, then called upon muscle memory for the sequence of movements that followed. We pat-dried our now-wrinkled skin, inspected our toes—how odd to have two feet! Snails have only one—and maneuvered us into the not entirely clean robe that was hanging on the hook beside the door. It was a sickly shade of pink, like the tongue. Our hair was damp: this caused me to experience anxiety. Snails never have to worry about hair, whereas—as I was soon to discover—humans fret about it constantly. Having it, not having it, arranging it, deriding it when arranged by others, twisting it, braiding it, piling it up, cutting it off, pulling it out . . . In their rummaging through the distant past in search of their prehistoric origins, a thing that obsesses them, humans could do worse than hair as a leitmotif.

We wrapped our hair in another towel and crept cautiously out into the main room. The boyfriend—for such he was—had arranged the ribs and corn bread on two plates, with a side of slaw on each. These were on a small table beside a window. It seemed we lived in a condo, with a view. The view was of other condo buildings, a lake, a sky. Did the human brain remember this view? It did. Was this memory overwriting my snail memories, like a palimpsest? It was. I felt dizzy. It was all too much to take in.

I sat us down in the chair provided. "Is there any lettuce?" I asked faintly.

"I got slaw." My boyfriend grinned, the foreboding grin of an omnivore. How to explain to him that I couldn't eat the slaw? The vinegar in the dressing, which my snail sensors could detect a mile off, might as well have been fire.

The boyfriend was uncapping a bottle of beer. This was better news. Snails love beer; they like the yeast, as it smells like fermenting vegetation. Beer, I am sorry to say, is often used to drown us.

"I'd rather have lettuce. I've got some sort of tummy bug. It's easy to digest. Is there some?"

"Dunno," he said. He opened a white door, looked inside. Oh yes, the human brain reminded me. A refrigerator. "Nope. Guess we ate it. There's a carrot."

"I'll have a beer too," I said.

"You? You hate the stuff!"

"Not anymore," I said.

"Anything for you, babe," he said. "Even my beer!" Our mouth took a sip from the proffered bottle: at last, something in this human life I could enjoy.

I toyed with the carrot—it was not rotten, so it was too

hard. Then I ventured a small piece of corn bread, but it was too harsh: like sand. The boyfriend, Tyler—his name had appeared in my consciousness as a set of indistinct letters, as if written in mist—gnawed on the ribs, holding each of them in his large paws and wrenching the flesh off the bone with his enormous white teeth. How uncouth was this process—how unlike the delicate rasping motions practiced by snails! I watched him, repelled but fascinated.

"Not hungry, babe?" he asked between gollops.

"Not much," I said in my bank service representative voice, smiling in a manner I intended to be agreeable. I hoped the beer contained some nourishment. If I got stuck in this human body for much longer, what was I going to eat? Tomorrow I would take the body shopping. Lay in a supply of pea sprouts and some overripe fruit.

"How was your day?" said Tyler. Through what was rapidly becoming a beery haze I eyed him across the table. I could see he was attractive, in the human sense. He had a lot of hair, dark in color, and some muscles.

"Oh, the usual," I said. "But I think I was rude to a customer."

"You? No way!" He barked out a laugh, ejecting small bits of rib. "You couldn't be rude to Godzilla!"

So that was the persona of my woman host, back before she'd had a snail move in on her: she'd been limp, flaccid, a flimsy pushover. Was that why she'd been available to my soul? No inner strength? "I bet they were monitoring the calls. I might get fired," I said. I was hopeful about this rather than otherwise.

"Fat chance," he said. "You're too good for that job. Shit, you're too good for me!" He came around behind and began massaging our shoulders. He would get smelly meat juice on the pink robe. I had a fuzzy mental image of a washing machine: Did we have one? He kissed our neck and gave it an exploratory lick.

This was a courtship move—even among the snails it would have been received as such—and shortly he and our body were engaged in the early stages of a coupling event, which then led with unseemly rapidity to the later stages, with my small green soul enmeshed in the proceedings like a toddler strapped onto a bullet train. How crude are the sexual procedures of humans compared with those of snails! How precipitous! No slow slippery caresses of tentacles, no intertwining, no tantalizingly voluptuous wreathing and writhing. Snails can go on for hours. But not so humans.

How could I explain what I wanted? I couldn't just blurt out, "I'm a hermaphrodite." It would not have been understood. Nor could I tell the boyfriend that I wished to insert my penis into his genital pore—it would have been somewhere near his ear, if he'd had such a pore—at the same time he was inserting his into mine. And I especially could not tell him that I wished to fire a love dart into him, to give my sperm a better chance at fertilizing his eggs. My rational human brain-mind knew that he didn't have any eggs, but sex isn't rational, is it? It's about feelings, and that is how I felt.

I didn't have any love darts anyway. A long steak knife would have made a poor substitute, and might in fact have killed him. I wouldn't have wanted that. But urges are urges. I could barely restrain myself.

"Something wrong, babe? You seemed different," Tyler said upon completion of the act.

"I don't feel like myself." How much could I reveal without being taken for an out-and-out lunatic?

"Like, how?"

"There's something wrong with my body."

There was a pause. By this time it was dark: I could not see Tyler's face. He must have been thinking. The hand that had been stroking my hair withdrew.

"Oh," he said. "You're maybe coming down with something."

"No," I said. "I'm perfectly fine. But this body doesn't feel like mine."

"How do you mean? It's a great body."

"Maybe for someone else," I said. "Just not me. I ought to be in a different body."

There was a long pause, which I took to be a symptom of thought. "You want to see someone about that?" he said carefully, more as a statement than a question.

"Yes," I said, "I think I should." I noticed that he hadn't asked what sort of body I felt I ought to be in.

Tyler worked as a soundman in the television business, so finding a psychiatrist was not difficult for him. This doctor came highly recommended by a friend, said Tyler. He was used to dealing with unusual people

"What do you mean by unusual?" I asked.

"Oh, you know. Actors."

It took a couple of weeks to arrange an appointment, during which time I slid further into my human incarnation as if pulling on a rubber suit. By now, via the neural pathways of my human brain, I had almost total recall of my woman host's days and ways. I knew what was expected of me in this disguise; I mouthed the phrases, I performed the rituals, but I remained convinced that I was really a terrestrial gastropod. At night I would curl up as tightly as I could and pull the sheet up over my head. My dreams would be of leaves, of damp logs, and of other snails.

The psychiatrist was a short man with glasses and a mustache who looked like a child's cartoon of a psychiatrist. He had a notebook. He opened it and asked me what my problem seemed to be. I told him I was worried about having a nose. He tried not to show surprise.

"Ah," he said. "Body dysmorphia."

"No," I said. I'd been reading up on the terms. "I don't want a different nose. I don't want to have a nose at all. I mean, not one that sticks out."

"Have you considered plastic surgery?" This was a ploy called "entering into the patient's delusion." I was ready for it.

"I don't want this body altered," I said. "I want it removed. I'm in the wrong body altogether."

"Ah," he said again. "You are in the wrong body."

"I'm not a man," I said. "If you were wondering."

"Ah." He looked disappointed, but at the same time interested. He fiddled with his pen. Did he sense a peer-reviewed research paper coming on?

"But I do have a penis," I said. "Though it's not a human penis. The real me does."

"Ah?"

"It's near my ear."

He looked confused. He placed his pen on the desk.

"I also have eggs," I said. "And a love dart. I mean, in my real body. The one I'm not in right now."

"A love dart?" His eyebrows went up. "You have a weapon?"

"Not exactly a weapon. It's a gypsobelum," I said. "It's made of calcium. I shoot it into my mate. I mean, I would, if I was in my real body."

"Ah." He was staring at me with some alarm. Not only at me, but past me at the door, which was behind me.

"Not shoot like a gun," I said. "More like a sort of blowpipe."

"I see," he said. "And your real body, you say . . ."

"I'm actually a snail."

There was a silence. "I believe that's our time," he said, though there was at least five minutes to go. "I'll see you next week?"

"I don't think you can help me," I said, gathering up my purse. It had taken me awhile to acclimatize myself to this purse. Snails have no use for purses.

I left his office in a state of despair. For what crime am I being punished? I asked myself. What did I do so wrong, back when I was a snail? How long will I be confined to this purgatory? What are the penances I must perform in order to free myself?

Possibly, I thought, it was a religious problem. I began to frequent churches, sidling into them when few people were inside. They were dim and dampish, like the undersides of leaves, and they smelled faintly of mold, a smell I found comforting. I began to pray. *Oh God, or whoever's responsible for this mess, please get me out of here! Let my little soul out of this ungainly giant cage! I don't have to go back into a snail, though I would prefer that. Maybe a tortoise? A frog? No, too eventful. Something placid, something vegetarian . . .*

Then I began to have doubts. What if I didn't have the soul of a snail after all? What if I was really this woman— Amber was her name—what if I was Amber, and had always been Amber, and was having a psychotic break? Why had that happened? Should I try to erase all memories of my snail existence? Would that make me happier? The mere thought of such a thing drove me frantic. Should I jump off our condo balcony, put an end to this unloved body in the hope of reincarnating once again? But I might end up in something worse. A leech. An eyebrow mite. At the very least, a slug.

That phase passed, with the aid of some THC gummies procured for me by Tyler. That was kind of him. I found that if I got sufficiently stoned I could tolerate his form of coupling well enough, and even enjoy it sometimes. I decided that since I couldn't get off the bus I might as well appreciate the tour, so I and my purloined body did our best.

After another two weeks I lost my job as a bank service representative. In truth, I more or less quit. I didn't have the energy for the work—all those unhappy voices—and I had no interest in anything they said. Who cared about GICs? Not me. "Interest" and "exchange rate" were inventions that had no relationship to the real world: they did not eat, breed, or defecate. These fragments of the human ideosphere swirled around me like smoke, ever-changing, impossible to grasp in any tangible way.

After leaving the employ of the bank I took to snoozing in our condo, coiled in the beanbag chair, with my tiny spiral soul glowing inside its carnal domicile. When not asleep I dozed, in a liminal state that felt to me as if I'd been hypnotized. I spent hours gazing at the hands—the whorls on the fingertips, the lines wandering over the surfaces of my palms—imagining what it would be like to slide on my slippery tongue-like foot along the pathways of my own skin.

Tyler began asking when I would start looking for another job. I assumed he was anxious because I was no longer contributing my share of the rent, but his anxiety left me indifferent. Then he said maybe I had a condition—mononucleosis was his guess—and shouldn't I see a doctor? I said I was just tired a lot. He said that wasn't normal, plus I was losing weight: I had to eat something more than vegetables. I said I would try, but meanwhile could he get some more lettuce? We seemed to have run out. The farmers' market would be a good place for it, I said. They'd have local produce. Once Tyler had gone off with his reusable shopping bag, I turned the beanbag chair upside down and withdrew under it. So warm and dark, and slightly moist.

As we were eating lunch—a lovely salad, though his had bacon on it—Tyler found a snail on his romaine. "Proves it's organic," he said. He stood up. "I'll just flush the little fucker down the toilet."

"No," I cried. Or I thought I cried, but no sound came out. I'd lost my voice. Was I speechless with horror? Now that Tyler had been revealed as a murderer, I couldn't possibly stay with him. While he was in the bathroom doing away with my relative, I walked quietly out of our condo and along the hall to the elevator. I was still wearing my sweatpants and T-shirt, with only a light fall coat on over them. Where could I go?

I headed for the nearest park, but it was too open. The bird-filled sky was frightening to me. I found a railway bridge and crouched underneath it, against the dank cement wall. I would stay there, I decided. It was October: I would nudge down into the soil before it froze; I would hibernate. If only I could make my way slowly up the wall to the enticing weeds that I could see through a gap in the ironwork . . . But no, this could not work, because I was not a snail. Or was I?

I stuck it out for several hours, crouching, hugging myself, shivering, ignored by passersby. Someone gave me two dollars. I could feel my tissues contracting, shriveling up. Thirst drove me back to the condo.

"Where did you go, babe?" Tyler asked, as I was gulping water in the kitchen.

"Out," I managed to croak. I collapsed into his arms: I must have fainted.

When I woke up, I was in a hospital with an IV line stuck into my arm. Severe dehydration, they said. Also malnutrition. Nourishing soup, gelatin desserts, custards: these were prescribed. I managed to ingest them, although it was an effort. At least they were damp.

Now I'm back at the condo. Tyler is seldom here. He says he goes to the gym, but no one can go to the gym that much. He's avoiding me. In fact, he may be a little afraid of me. Naturally he has another woman that he is coupling with—a substitute form of strenuous gym-like exercise for him, no doubt. I can smell her musky perfume on him a mile away. But I don't care: although snails experience passion, they don't understand jealousy. Perhaps this boyfriend-poacher would like to entwine herself with both of us, I speculate idly. Should I suggest it to Tyler? Snails enjoy threesomes. This into that into this into that, a sort of floral wreath of silky but muscular interconnection . . . No, Tyler is at heart a puritan—you can tell by his addiction to the gym—and like all good puritans he is monogamous in his inclinations. Such a pity.

The days pass. I'm biding my time. I'm meditating. Perhaps my understanding of this phenomenon has been upside down. Perhaps I was a woman to begin with—maybe even this particular woman, Amber, with her wardrobe of jokey T-shirts—and I was sent into a snail in order to learn something of deep importance to my soul. But what could that be? To pay homage to the immediate, such as the rich veins and cells of edible greens and the heady, intoxicating scent of decaying pears? To appreciate the simple joys of the universe, such as congress with a fellow snail, or snails? Was that it? What am I missing? It is what it is? I am what I am? What am I?

Why must I suffer? The ultimate puzzle. That is what it is to be human, I suppose: to question the terms of existence.

But it's not all penitential. There are upsides. Snails in their own bodies cannot see the stars, but through these borrowed eyes I have now seen them. The stars are magnificent. Perhaps I will have memories of them when I am a snail again, if I am ever permitted that grace.

There must be a purpose. I must be learning something. I can't believe this is all random.

I must stay positive until my present skin-and-tissue host wears out. Then my small bright spiral soul will rise and fly through the iridescent clouds and minor-key music of the intermediate spirit realm, to embody itself once more. But as what?

Any husk other than this one. Any shell other than this.

CONCEALED CARRY

BY **LISA TUTTLE**

She had been looking forward to spending a year work-ing in America, until, at almost the last minute, the location was changed from New York to Texas. There was a good reason for it: a member of the management team in the Houston office had left without warning, leaving them in the lurch. Fortunately, Kelly's experience and skill set were a good match for the missing team member, and since she was already prepared to leave London the following week, only a little tweaking to the plan was required.

Her boss told her: "You'll have a company car—you can't live without a car in Texas. And there will be a furnished apart-ment waiting for you; I've seen pictures, and it looks lovely and spacious. There's even a pool. And it's a short drive to the office. But if you don't like it, you can cancel the lease at the end of the month and make your own arrangements. They're so grateful to have you step in on short notice, they're eager to do whatever they can to make you happy."

She knew she wasn't being given a choice, and that it would be ungrateful to complain, but all those perks made her wonder what she would be walking into.

"Why did the team member leave?"

"Does it matter?"

She gave him a look.

With a twitch of his mouth, he conceded: "She's having a baby."

She wondered why he hadn't just said she'd be providing maternity cover until he said it had been made clear that this was no temporary absence; she would not be returning.

"So we may have a problem getting you to come back here," he said cheerfully. "You'll be wanting American citizenship. Everybody does."

Kelly wasn't so sure. She had never even considered leaving London; New York had been the draw. New York had all the glamour. Texas seemed to be filled with fanatics, right-wing politicians, fundamentalist preachers, and killers. The very week that she learned she was to go to Texas, that state was in the news for another deadly massacre of schoolchildren and their teachers—the worst yet.

She confided her fears to her best friend, who, on the basis of several holidays in Florida, was a big fan of America. She agreed that mass shootings were far too common there, and the gun laws were stupid, but said that terrible things also happened in England. "Did you leave London when there was that bomb? No. Do you stay home every night in case you are abducted and raped? You really think you're so much safer in London? Those shootings weren't even in Houston. Besides, when was the last time you set foot in a school?"

She was met at the Houston airport by a young man who introduced himself as Alberto and said he would drive her home. He did not explain in what capacity he worked for the company, or if he did. He wore no uniform, but had a handgun holstered on his belt. She found this detail worrying but hesitated to ask about it. He was a man of few words, and because he spoke them with a slight accent, she was afraid of being misunderstood. Or maybe she was intimidated by his silence and the gun. Or perhaps she feared revealing her own ignorance. It might be that all taxi and Uber drivers in Texas went armed as a matter of course. In her present sleep-deprived state of culture shock, it seemed best to let things happen as they were intended, and not make any waves.

The drive took much longer than she had expected, and she occasionally dozed off before jerking awake again, worried she had missed something. But each time she woke, the car was still moving smoothly through the artificially lit night, along a wide highway bounded by a city or landscape she could not see, and the radio was playing familiar pop songs from decades past, frequently interrupted by ads for unfamiliar services and companies.

A bit timidly, she asked Alberto where they were, and how much farther they had to go, and in this way she learned that her new home, both workplace and residence, was actually quite some distance from the city of Houston, in an unincorporated area next to the town of Homer. "Not much farther now," he said.

Hearing that, she was determined to stay awake, but after a few minutes her head began to nod, and then Alberto spoke again, startling her into sitting upright when she noticed his indicator was blinking and he was heading for the exit ramp. "Look over there," he said. "See that building? The one that's all lit up? That's where we are."

"Where we are?" she repeated, confused.

He said the name of her company. "Our Houston HQ. And

your apartment is just another five minutes away. Well, maybe a bit more coming from that direction, but it won't take any time at all for you to get to work in the morning. Some of our colleagues live in the same building—it's a good place to live, if you don't have kids, anyway."

His sudden burst of chattiness surprised her less than her realization that the man she'd thought an Uber driver was a work colleague. She had probably been introduced to him during the Zoom meeting last week. She was embarrassed, but relieved to have found out the truth before she tried to tip him.

Her apartment was on the fourth floor of an eight-story, octagonal glass tower. She thanked Alberto when he had hauled her luggage into the lobby, insisting she could manage from there.

"Well, if you're sure. I'll just wait until the elevator comes. Oh, and your car is in the parking lot. It's a blue Lexus. The spaces are numbered the same as the apartment. You'll find the key and everything else you need upstairs. But give me a call if you have any questions." He gave her his card along with the keys to her apartment.

The apartment was spacious and smelled faintly of cleaning products overlaid with a stronger, Christmas-y scent of room freshener. The furniture was recognizably IKEA, not brand-new, but not too shabby. Someone (Alberto?) had even stocked the kitchen with basic provisions, and there was a huge basket of fruit on the table with a welcoming note signed by more than a dozen semidecipherable names.

After wandering around aimlessly checking the place out, she let herself fall onto the sofa, only to get up again as she felt something hard poking into her hip. She thought it was under the cushion, but that turned out to be attached to the base. She pushed her hand down into the narrow gap between the two cushions and encountered something large and hard that surely did not belong there. She got a grip on the thing and pulled it out.

When she saw what she had found, she dropped it as if she'd been burned.

It was a gun.

The weapon was small, scarcely bigger than her phone, but unlike a smooth, flat object that might easily slip down accidentally and be lost from sight, it must have been deliberately hidden.

By the last resident? But someone must have done a thorough cleaning job on the place before Kelly arrived. A cleaner must have come across the gun before she did. The sofa was not new, but maybe it was a replacement, moved here, complete with hidden gun, from another apartment? Or maybe the cleaner was the person who had hidden the gun, taking the opportunity to get rid of evidence of some other crime.

She shuddered and then she yawned. She ought to tell the police, but not now, when she was too tired to think properly. Although she hated to touch it again, she picked it up gingerly and pushed it back down between the cushions as far as it would go.

Work was not a problem. Kelly knew what she had to do. Adjusting to her coworkers was a little trickier. They seemed nice, but strange . . . She knew *she* was the alien here, of course. They were probably all perfectly normal, and it would be her duty to conform to the local norms as much as she could. She could not really be like them, though she wanted to blend in. She was grateful for their friendliness, even if it struck her as over the top. She'd never had so many invitations to join a church as in that first week. It was not so much her nationality, her accent, or her ignorance of local ways that set her apart; her lack of any religious affiliation (not to mention belief) was what they found hardest to accept.

At the end of the week, alone at home with a bottle of wine and her phone, she turned to Tinder. Before very long she made a match. Pierce, thirty-eight, a lawyer, with interests in history, politics, art, theater, and wine. (He was part owner of a vineyard.) Their texts rapidly became more intimate, and they talked on the phone for hours. A physical meeting at first seemed problematic; she did not want to drive all the way into Houston for their first face-to-face, yet neither was she willing to invite him to the restaurant-free zone that was Homer.

After giving it careful consideration, he suggested what he called a midway meeting place. This was a barbecue joint reputed to serve the best ribs and best sausages in two counties. It was not exactly fine dining, and opening hours were limited to daytime, but he thought she would enjoy the authentic Texas experience if she happened to be free for lunch the following Saturday.

In reality, she found when she checked, the barbecue joint was not "halfway" for both of them—it was closer to Homer, considerably farther from Houston. In spite of having a longer distance to travel, he managed to arrive first, and was waiting for her in the parking lot out front. She was touched by his consideration and delighted to find that Pierce was even better looking in real life than in the pictures he had sent, and when he walked toward her, a swagger in his step and a sexy grin spreading across his face, she felt the hot rush of desire. *Oh yes.*

They exchanged a few words, but the real conversation was going on beneath speech: she knew he was feeling the same way about her. It was only when he stepped ahead to open the door for her that she saw the gun holstered on his belt.

It felt like stumbling; her stomach pitched. "You said you were a lawyer."

Holding the door open, he looked at her in surprise, probably more by her accusatory tone than the words. "Only the boring kind of lawyer who deals with company business. Nothing too thrilling. Why?"

"Why the gun? If you don't deal with criminals. More lawman than lawyer."

His eyebrows went up. "I seeeee. Well, we're not in jolly old England. I know you haven't been here long, but I can't be the first armed civilian you've come across."

She thought of Alberto. She had never seen him without his gun, in or out of the office, although it had nothing to do with his job. But, he said, someday it might be. If there was ever a live-shooter incident at work, he hoped he would be able to protect himself and others. He'd also told her that at least half of her coworkers were also gun owners, whether or not they chose to carry them openly. Even Donna Jo, an older woman who had yet to give up on the possibility of getting Kelly to join her church, carried a gun in her handbag. That was known as "concealed carry." Alberto, like Pierce, preferred "open carry," but both practices were legal, and neither required a special license.

"You're right," she said, and tried to let go of the tension, relaxing her shoulders. "But it still freaks me out. It's even worse, knowing how many guns are out there—"

"May I suggest we go inside and order before they sell out of the baby back ribs? Believe me, you would be sorry to miss

them. We can talk about the exercise of constitutional rights later."

Gun or no gun, he was awfully attractive.

"Sorry," she murmured.

"You won't be," he murmured back with a wink.

The food was fantastic. She possibly preferred the brisket to the vaunted ribs, but everything on the combination plate was delicious. They ate, speaking only of their pleasure in the food at first, and were in a better state of mind when the conversation turned back to guns.

"I know things are different in England," he said. "Y'all have some pretty tough gun laws. Even your police—most of them don't even carry firearms, am I right? Which seems kind of crazy, but if it works for y'all, it's not my place to object. Thing is, for us, the right to bear arms is enshrined in the US Constitution. Even if we wanted to put through the kinds of laws some people talk about, similar basic requirements that anybody who wants to drive a car has to meet—even if there was the political will for something like that, it's too late. There's already way more guns than people in Texas, and every time there's a rumor about gun control, more people go out and buy more guns. It is what it is. And with so many potentially irresponsible, crazy, even downright evil people in possession of deadly weapons, some of us feel it is our responsibility—I sure do—to be the good guy with a gun."

She had never been a fan of the Westerns her grandfather had loved, yet Kelly was still moved by the image of the lone defender, standing up for the innocent and protecting the defenseless. Maybe all the American movies and TV shows she'd watched since childhood had corrupted her mind, but the good guy with a gun was sexy.

They lingered over coffee, the conversation still circling around guns. He offered to teach her to shoot. He said she was frightened by them because she didn't understand them, and she'd grown up in a culture that hated them, but guns were not, in themselves, bad.

"Guns don't kill people, people kill people," she said, deadpan.

"Yes, exactly!"

"I read it on a bumper sticker."

"That doesn't make it untrue."

She had doubts, but no desire to argue. No desire to buy a gun, or go with him to a shooting range, but plenty of desire for something else. She took him back to her place.

She startled awake out of a light sleep. Pierce slept beside her. All was dark and still, though there had been a noise; she thought a thud, the sound of something falling? Something in the other room. The image came to her of a man in a frozen posture, standing in the dark living room waiting to be sure he had not been heard.

She stopped breathing, listening as hard as she could, but the noise—if there had been one—was not repeated. The next-door apartment was empty, and she'd never been bothered by noises from the people above; certainly not at this hour . . . Reaching for her phone, she saw that it was 5:23 on Sunday morning. Well, people did get up early to go to church, didn't they? Maybe someone upstairs had dropped a shoe.

Or else she had dreamed it. She listened to the steady breathing of the man beside her, trying to will herself back to sleep. Impossible. She would only be able to settle if she saw for herself that everything was all right.

Pierce still had not stirred. She wasn't going to disturb him

for this, playing the helpless female whose only hope was to find a man to protect her. A good man with a gun.

Slipping out of bed, she wrapped herself in her robe and moved softly toward the door, pausing by the dressing table where Pierce had divested himself of his watch, his wallet, and his gun. If someone had broken into her apartment, wouldn't it be better to face him with a gun?

The weapon slipped into her hand as if eager to be held. She was surprised at how good it felt. She could not see much in the darkness, though the dim view suggested it looked very natural. No one would think she had never held a gun before.

She left the bedroom, prepared for confrontation, but found no one in the living room. It was almost a disappointment. Even after she ascertained that the door was still locked, the dead bolt in place, she turned on the light to check behind the couch and the curtains, opened the coat closet, and went into the kitchen, just to make sure.

Back in the bedroom, Pierce slept on, oblivious. Only half conscious of what she was doing, she raised the gun and aimed it at the shape beneath the sheet. She thought how easy it would be to fire a shot, to see him wake, confused and terrified. And when he realized it was his own gun, fired by a woman who had told him, hours earlier, that she did not think she would ever be able to shoot another human being, no, not even for "self-protection"? What would he think, what would he say if she woke him up right now?

Her finger tightened on the trigger. She tried to shoot, but nothing happened.

Safety catch. The safety catch is on.

What was wrong with her? She didn't want to fire a gun, not to frighten and certainly not to kill. Those thoughts were not her own; they must be coming from someone else—from the gun itself! *It* had enticed her into picking it up, and now . . .

Horrified, she flung the deadly thing away. It landed with a heavy crash on the dressing table, setting off a chorus of clinking, clashing perfume bottles, cosmetics, and jewelry trays. The cacophony brought Pierce surging up from the sheets, hoarsely barking, "Who? What? Who's that?"

"Your gun!" Kelly shrieked at him, clutching her robe closer at her breast. "The horrid, nasty thing! Get it out—take it away—get it out of here now, I mean it!"

He attempted to talk her down, but it was no good, and when he tried to hold her, she thrust him away. "I am awake! No dream! I know what happened! I won't have it!"

"Did you take something? Pills? What did you take?"

"Your gun! That's all I touched. I wish I'd never seen the fucking thing. Get it out of here! No, get off, I told you before, don't you touch me again. Get it out of here, right now."

"Calm down. Just calm down and talk to me, please."

She nodded, held up her hands to indicate surrender, and managed to speak more calmly: "You think they are tools. You think tools must do what you want. Maybe that used to be true, but things have changed. They always do. Nothing stays the same forever. Things evolve. Don't look at me like that; things don't have to be alive to change—look at clouds or rocks or the weather. The climate! Things don't have to change themselves, you know. They don't have to think. Things get changed by the forces around them, by time and weather, by whatever created them, some people say God; but you can't deny things change because of what people do, and what they want."

He tried to interrupt; she bared her teeth at him. "Let me finish! The reason for a gun's existence is to kill. But it can't do that on its own because it needs a person to aim and fire it. From the point of view of owners, the gun did what *they* wanted. But if you look at it from the gun's point of view, it is always wanting to be fired. It can only express its truest meaning when it is fired, and accomplishes its purpose: when one person uses it to shoot another."

"That's crazy talk, Kelly. Listen to yourself. Guns don't think. They don't know what they are. They don't have a mission in life because they don't have a life. It's only people who—"

"Guns don't kill people, people kill people?" she spoke rapidly over him. "How do you know? How do you know that when some sad eighteen-year-old kid takes his new gun into a school and shoots as many people as he can, how do you know he's doing it because it's what he *wants* to do, and not what he's somehow been made to do? I am telling *you*, people don't kill people—guns kill people."

He sighed heavily. She saw he was about to present another argument, or the same one in different words. He was a lawyer, after all. All he really cared about was winning.

"Forget it," she said wearily. "You think I'm crazy, and maybe you're right. But I need you to go now and take that gun away. Will you do that for me? Please?"

"I won't stay if you don't want me. Can I get dressed first?"

"Of course."

She moved away from the dressing table and began picking up her own discarded clothes when he said from behind her, "Aren't you afraid?"

Turning to face him, she saw he was holding his gun, pointing it in her direction. She said nothing.

"I mean . . ." The gun wavered; now it tilted toward the

floor. "It is only natural to be afraid, if you think that guns control people instead of the other way around . . ."

She had felt a twist of fear in her guts when she'd seen the gun pointed at her, but he was not as vulnerable to its desires as she. Maybe that was why the gun had decided to get someone else to hold it. She was in danger from the gun, but not from its present owner. She said softly, "But you're a good guy."

After he'd gone, she went back to bed, and slept deeply until she woke to find herself lying naked on the couch, on the brink of orgasm as she pleasured herself with a gun.

No!

She woke up. She was in bed and knew the previous awakening had been a dream—a nightmare. She was still moist and sticky between the legs, a little sore too, and although she did not regret having sex with Pierce, she was sorry for the way it had ended. Had that sickening dream been her subconscious way of punishing herself? *He* had done nothing wrong; *she* was the one who had been on the brink of killing him—at the very least she might have injured him if the safety had not been on—and then she'd screamed at him like the crazy bitch he had every right to think her.

Sighing, she stretched, and her hand brushed against something hard. Even before her fingers teased out its precise, deadly shape, she knew, and when she felt the sticky moisture clinging to the muzzle, she screamed—

—and woke herself with a soundless cry.

She sat up and threw back the sheet so she could see the whole bed. There was no gun. It was broad daylight, and she was truly wide awake this time.

That second waking had been as much a dream as the first.

She saw that it was past ten o'clock. She never slept so late. It was the weekend, so it didn't matter, but it added to her feeling that she'd lost control of her own life.

She put on the first clothes that came to hand and went to make coffee. Passing the couch, she flinched at the memory. When the coffee machine began to hiss, she got a pair of rubber gloves from under the sink and went back to the couch. No more worrying about where it had come from or who owned it; she was going to throw it in the bin and let the garbagemen take it away.

But the gun was not there.

She spent the next hour searching for it, although if someone had moved it, surely they would have taken it away? Unless she had done it herself, acting in her sleep. After the weirdness of the past night, that seemed possible. Something about the very idea of guns had affected her psychologically. Once she'd got rid of the thing, she promised herself, she would seek help from a therapist. Preferably one of European birth, and certainly not a gun owner.

There were finally only two possibilities: either it had been taken away by someone, or it had never existed. She had been tired, jet-lagged, in a strange mental state—maybe she had dreamed the whole thing? Otherwise, someone must have come into her apartment and taken it away. How many other people had keys to her home? The sound that had awakened her in the night could have been someone who let himself in with a key, retrieved what he was after, and got away before she came out of the bedroom. She should move.

She decided to ask Donna Jo for suggestions; she'd probably get another invitation to her church, but only Alberto and Donna Jo had given her their home numbers, and if the invitation came with useful advice, maybe this time she would accept.

* * *

Donna Jo sounded pleased to hear from her. Kelly quickly explained the reason for her call, saying she was thinking about moving.

Donna Jo caught her breath. "Is something wrong?"

Kelly prevaricated: "Oh, no, not really . . . it's a nice space, and of course it's near work, but—"

"But you have a bad feeling about it?"

"Why—what makes you say that?"

The other woman did not immediately reply. Kelly didn't interrupt the silence, and was rewarded when Donna Jo said, "You could be more sensitive to atmospheres than other people. Like me. Do you ever find that sometimes when something very bad or very good has happened, the place where it happens holds that emotion?"

Kelly's mind raced to consider many horrible possibilities connected to the gun as she stammered out her questions: "What—what happened? Who lived here before me?"

"Shayna. The rent was paid up for another six months, so it seemed sensible—but not to *me*, I must say."

"Who's Shayna?"

"Why, she's the girl you replaced. I thought you might have guessed."

"Did she die in this apartment?"

"Her? Dearie me, no. Nobody died, praise the Lord."

"Then what did happen?"

"I'm surprised you don't know. It was in the news. Shayna DeWitt. Of course, we don't like to talk about it." Donna Jo lowered her voice: "She tried to kill her baby."

"How awful. Is the baby okay?"

"Praise the Lord, it will be. The pills were not what she

thought they were. Luckily they were harmless. What can you expect, ordering illegal substances over the Internet? Her lawyer argued that since the baby was never in any real danger, she should not be charged with attempted murder, but that is *wrong*. She most certainly intended to kill her unborn child. If she had the chance, she'd try another way, as was obvious to the jury that convicted her. And as a direct result of that case, there's this new legislation they're trying to push through, to stop pregnant people from traveling out of state. That's the way we're to say it now, *pregnant people*, not *women*. The problem with a law like that is you can't be sure when somebody is pregnant just by looking; if you ask, anybody planning to fly to New York for an abortion is going to lie; and you can't make *everybody* take a pregnancy test before they're allowed to travel—can you? And it would be wrong to punish women who are glad to be pregnant by making them stay at home for the better part of a year. Of course, the lives of the unborn are so, so important, but does that mean every woman of childbearing age has to be treated like a potential murderer?"

At some point during Donna Jo's heated sermon Kelly tuned out, remembering something an acquaintance in London, an American expat from New York, had said when she heard Kelly was going to Texas: "It's not like they've gone full-on *Handmaid's Tale*, but they're heading that way. Whatever you do, don't get pregnant."

Kelly had no desire to get pregnant, and just in case she might find it difficult to get the same pills that had kept her safe so far, she'd brought a full year's supply in her handbag.

"So, what happened to Shayna?" she asked when Donna Jo ran down.

"They put her in jail, but they don't call it that; she's somewhere more like a hospital, I think; kept under close observation, confined where she can't harm herself or her child. I don't think she should be allowed to keep it, after what she tried to do. But you never know; maybe she'll be born again and truly repent."

The disappearance of the gun did not bother Kelly as much once she'd heard about Shayna. She thought it likely that the gun had been Shayna's, but never used. Her boyfriend—for there must have been a boyfriend—could have had a key, and he could have come to retrieve the gun. Kind of creepy that he had waited until late at night, when the apartment was occupied, but it was over now. She took notes of the names of places Donna Jo mentioned as somewhere she might want to consider for her next home, though she no longer felt the same compulsion to move.

She didn't feel much compulsion to do anything, truth be told. There was work, and when she was not working, Kelly did the minimum with regard to other chores, watched TV, drank a little too much, and slept more than she ever had. She felt sluggish and generally detatched from life. She had burned out on Tinder and had made no new friends; the time difference made phone calls too difficult during the week for her friends and family at home, and there was nothing she really wanted to say in a text. It was too hot to go outside. She was not exactly unhappy, just bored, and seemed to be existing more than living.

She thought it would pass, but after a few more weeks, she felt worse. There was a weird metallic taste in her mouth, and she had stopped enjoying coffee. She felt tired all the time, possibly due to lack of coffee, no exercise, and long hours spent staring at screens. She had a sudden craving for Marmite, which was unavailable locally, so she had to order a jar at a ridiculously inflated price. But didn't she deserve the occasional treat?

Yes, she decided, she did. Something much better than Marmite. A bit of excitement and a change of scene might jar her out of her apathy. She found a cheap last-minute deal for a flight to New Orleans and booked a room in a boutique hotel.

The morning of the day she was to go she woke early, gripped by a pain she immediately identified as period cramps, although she had not suffered them for a long time; it had been more than two years since she'd had anything like a period, due to the type of birth control she was on. Getting up, she noticed a small bloodstain on the sheet, and remembered something called "breakthrough bleeding" that she had experienced a couple of times before, although never with any accompanying pain. Another cramp twisted her guts. Groaning, she hurried to the toilet.

After pissing, she raised up slightly to look between her legs into the bowl. No sign of blood. Another cramp, worse than before. She hunched down on the seat and waited for it to pass. She broke into a cold sweat. Something was happening. Her body was acting without her will, with a purpose that, for all her reading and attempts to understand, she had never been able to fathom, and that she thought she could control with the tiny dose of artificial hormones she consumed like a Communion wafer every morning. She had relied on it utterly to keep her safe from pregnancy and do no harm, although over the years there were occasional scares and stories suggesting links to cancer, heart attacks, strokes, or permanent infertility. But maybe this had nothing to do with the pill; maybe it was an STD? Or a urinary tract infection? Or that old standby: something she ate.

Another sharp cramp in her belly, and something was ejected. She felt the splash and, looking down, saw the water turn slightly pink. Her body expelled two more small reddish masses—and the cramping was done.

Kelly got up and flushed the toilet. When she turned back after washing her hands, she saw that although the water was clear, *something* had not been flushed away. Going closer, she saw three small objects on the bottom of the bowl. They gleamed, faintly metallic, beneath patchy layers of some pinkish matter: three small, pointed ovoid shapes.

She stopped herself from trying to flush them away. They had not gone down the first time, and wasn't it better to know what her body had expelled?

She fetched rubber gloves from the kitchen and scooped them out. She dropped them into the sink, hearing the sharp clinking noise they made against the smooth porcelain, and stared as they rolled.

Bullets. At least, that's what they looked like and felt like beneath the protective coating (her womb lining, she guessed), some of which had been flushed away. It would be easy enough to wash or wipe them clean—

She flinched at the thought. Why clean them? Why keep them, unless to show a doctor, but to tell a doctor where they'd come from would mark her as insane. It was impossible, crazy. Was she hallucinating, even now?

She scooped the bullets up and dropped them into the bin, then peeled off the gloves and threw them in too. If only she could get rid of the memory so easily.

Driving to the airport, she listened to an audiobook that promised anyone could get whatever they wanted by using the power

of thought. All you had to do, according to the persuasive author/narrator, was visualize the life you wanted, think about it every day, and then concentrate on one particular aspect until, eventually, if you were truly determined, it would come about. Too many people, said the author, let others determine the course of their lives, not realizing how simple it is to change it, by taking control of the narrative.

The author was either a con man or crazier than she was, she thought. It was a comforting fantasy until she wondered: what about the people who want to change the lives of others?

She had checked in online and had only one carry-on. Security should be easy: nothing potentially dangerous in her baggage, and she wore light clothes, flat shoes that were easy to slip on and off, and nothing made of metal. Even as the randomly selected (so they claimed) passenger chosen to have a metal-detecting wand run up and down her body, she was not expecting any trouble.

The wand flashed and beeped as the serious-faced security man guided it down one side and then the other. He stopped and looked at her strangely. "Do you have any implants?"

"What? No!" she protested, perhaps too loudly, as she remembered the things that had come out of her earlier that day. Were there any more waiting to drop?

"Prosthetics? Heart monitor?"

"Nothing like that, no."

He did not wave her on, but spoke in a monotone, "Ma'am, I'm going to have to ask you to step over there for a moment. Where that lady in uniform is standing. She will show you what to do."

Puzzled and a little worried, but obedient, as one must be in such circumstances, Kelly followed his instructions and approached the security officer. This no longer seemed so much like a random selection.

The woman directed her toward a glass-sided cubicle. "Please step inside there and stand with your legs apart, your feet in the prints on the floor, arms up over your head."

"Why?"

"Security."

"I mean why me, why that box?"

"The scanner indicated . . . it gave some inconsistent readings. We need to see if you are carrying anything concealed under your clothes that could be a danger to others."

"So do you want me to strip? What happens if I go in there?"

"You will not need to remove any of your clothing. You'll be subjected to a kind of very low-level X-ray. It doesn't hurt. There's no risk to your health." When Kelly did not respond, the woman added, slightly testily, "It will only take a minute. Please step inside."

"What if I say no?"

"That is your right. But you might find an intimate cavity search to be more unpleasant, and of course it will take longer. You might even miss your flight."

With a look of disgust, Kelly said, "Thanks for the warning. I'll risk the rays."

"Remember: face front, legs apart, feet where marked, hands above your head, and hold as still as you can. Thank you for your cooperation."

Kelly stepped into the box, hating it and the stupidity of a land where everyone could carry a gun, openly or concealed, in every private or public place (except such holy spaces as bars and airplanes), but ordinary, unarmed women had to undergo ludicrous levels of screening because of a stupid malfunctioning wand. She remembered Donna Jo's predictions about the possibility that women of childbearing age might soon find it very difficult to travel, and wondered if this was the beginning.

The pose she'd been instructed to hold was getting uncomfortable. What was taking so long? Had other members of the security staff been called in to admire her tits or judge her for her pubic hair? She called out, "Seen enough? Can I move?" Getting no reply, she dropped her arms. Nobody shouted at her to resume the position, and after a few seconds of hesitation, she turned to leave the little booth, through the other side. She was stopped by one of the security men.

"Go back," he said.

She glared. "Haven't you seen enough?"

"You won't be flying today."

She stared at him in disbelief. "Are you kidding me? Why not? I'm already checked in. I've paid for my ticket. You can't stop me. There's no reason—"

His stolid expression did not change as he spoke over her: "Yes ma'am, we can. You can't fly while carrying."

She felt sick and swallowed it down. It couldn't be. *Carrying?* "If you mean a weapon—I don't have one. You've got my bag, and you've just seen—"

"Yes ma'am, we saw. Now, I'm going to ask you once more, politely, to leave. Make any fuss and you'll get yourself arrested. Now, go back. You'll find your bag waiting."

Without touching her, he forced her to move, herding her like a dog with a recalcitrant sheep. She had no choice but to comply.

He walked her around the metal detector, past a line of people waiting to go through, and approached a female security officer armed with a gun and a taser, who stood guard over Kelly's handbag, shoes, and wheeled case. "There you go," he told Kelly. "Taylor here will escort you out of the airport. Have a nice day."

Kelly stood still, trying not to cry.

"This way, ma'am," said Taylor, speaking a little too loudly. "Don't forget your bags."

"I'm supposed to be flying to New Orleans," Kelly said, turning to her with a look that appealed for understanding. "They say I can't. I don't get it. I'm not carrying anything illegal."

"No ma'am, of course it's not illegal—walk this way, please. No, not illegal to have as many as you like, not illegal if you prefer concealed or open carry—not in most places, but there are some exceptions, you understand. The secured areas of an airport, like the cabin of a plane, are exceptions. Maybe you didn't know that, 'cause I can hear from your voice that you're— is it Australian? English? Huh. The English usually aren't so keen on guns."

Her head was pounding; the sound of her own blood rushing in her ears obscured some of what the guard was saying, but it was about guns—why was everyone in this godforsaken country so obsessed with them? She started to protest that she was not carrying and never had carried a gun, but she gave up, knowing it would be a waste of breath. Some officious jerk had decided she would not be allowed to fly today. But they couldn't stop her from driving to New Orleans. It might take six or eight hours to get there, but all was not lost.

Having a plan, knowing that she wasn't entirely at the mercy of petty airport officials, cheered her up, and for once she didn't mind the feel of hot, humid air descending on her as Taylor pushed the door open to let her out.

"Do you want a taxi to take you home?"

Kelly turned on her. "That would not be possible. My *home* is in London. I'm not an American."

Taylor's look in return was pitying. "Never mind—your baby will be born here, so it will be American—whatever else it is."

Kelly watched her go, feeling sick. The feeling was accompanied by the now-familiar cramping sensation low in her belly. Hunching slightly she pressed a hand against the place where she felt pain, and felt something move.

She'd barely had time to register the motion before it became more vehement, pushing up and out. Cramps had never been like this. There was something growing inside her body.

But not a baby; no, she refused to believe she could be pregnant. Not possible. Even if aptly named Pierce's sperm had miraculously overwhelmed her contraception, it was barely six weeks since she'd been with him. At six weeks, a fetus was no bigger than a baked bean. It had no arms or legs. Whatever was moving around inside her now was very much bigger and stronger than that, and whatever it was was *pushing,* as if it intended to force its way out through her solid flesh.

She took her hand away and saw how her dress remained tented, as if pushed up by an erect penis. But whatever prodded her was not made of flesh. It was so hard that it hurt. And although she could not see it—and maybe with all the things that had happened lately she was letting her imagination run away with her—it felt exactly like the barrel of a gun.

GROSS ANATOMY

BY **AIMEE LABRIE**

allace "Wally" Allen McCarter, first-year med student at the Philadelphia College of Medicine in East
Falls, Pennsylvania, sits hungover in the folding
chair of the (slightly dingy? possibly noble?) Hench-
man Hall. It's a Monday in September, bright and clear. The
classroom is generic, dull brick walls, greenish carpeting, and
filled with students he doesn't know. The room reminds him of
something he once overheard a girl say about him. *Oh, Wally,
he's beige.* That stayed with him, *He's beige.* Boring, vanilla, not
really good or bad. A color you would choose for a sofa if you
wanted to emphasize colorful throw pillows. He doesn't mind.
Beige blends.

The lights in the room are dim, which is good for Wally,
whose head pounds. He recognizes a handful of the students
from the party on Saturday—Initiation Night, the second-year
students called it. When he slunk into the room earlier, he
thought someone might yell out, *Pervert*! But nobody said a
word. The details of the night are hazy, so it is probably totally
fine. (It's not fine, you're disgusting.)

He is searching for Shivali among the rows of heads in
the auditorium, but she is nowhere to be found. He saw her

first at the white-coat ceremony at the Academy of Music. She was sitting near the front of the stage, paying close attention to the welcome speeches. She didn't move, didn't look at her phone, remained still as a statue. When they stood and filed out, he glanced at her name tag and said it over and over in his head so he would remember: *Shivali.* She was Indian, small, serious-looking, pretty. Glasses, straight hair, warm eyes. He looked away when she turned her head toward him and ducked out of the building.

But today, she is missing.

They are starting the third week of the introductory curriculum with a section on treating open wounds. The PowerPoint shows a giant close-up of near-fatal knife stabbing in the lower posterior region. The wound is an explosion of colors—purple, green, deep red—and the edges of the skin tilt inward toward the gash, like wilted flowers around a gaping hole.

Wally feels a wave of nausea roll up from his stomach. It is not because of the images, which he delights in (they are fascinating!), but because of what the picture brings back for him, the revelry of Saturday night. He hangs over the desk, and a very specific pain slices through him, causing him to sit upright.

The professor, Dr. Downing, turns his head toward Wally. "Yes, Wally? Your ideas about the process of debriding?"

Debriding, he knows from flash cards he studied over the summer, occurs when the dead tissue is removed from the wound, so the infection doesn't get worse.

The pain moves to his bowels, and he shifts in his seat. "I need to be excused, please." He shoots from his chair, jogging for the exit doors of the auditorium.

He passes the college's time line plastered on the beige walls—starting as the Female Medical College in 1847. 1847!

When many women were bleeding out during childbirth and none of them could vote. A hallowed few were allowed to sit in on labs and watch amputations and lobotomies, but it wasn't until 1944 that the college admitted them as students. It's not the best medical school in the country (ranked #132, in fact), but Wally, whose grades were good but not great, knows he is lucky to be here. Lucky, lucky, lucky.

Wally always wanted to be a doctor. He dressed up as Dr. Frankenstein every year for Halloween, wearing his dad's old doctor coat stained with fake blood. His parents were extraordinarily supportive. They gave him a full-sized skeleton on his thirteenth birthday, a set of wooden teeth another year, Victorian forceps on his fifteenth birthday, an expensive microscope for high school graduation. He was obsessed with the microscope and how it could make tiny things become huge under the lens, the swirling of the bacteria from his spit, the detail of his own eyelash, the cat's broken claw. Sperm he caught in his sock and swiped on a slide. The sperm, still alive for a moment, squirmed, long tails extended like sea creatures until they died off one by one. And when he got into medical school (by the skin of his teeth), his dad gave him a leather-bound scalpel kit of his very own, with Wally's initials carved into the front: WAM. Inside, six scalpels, two pairs of surgical scissors, fifteen scalpel blades, and a small pair of curved mosquito forceps.

His family was proud of him. They didn't know that he had a nickname in high school—*Whaley*, or *Walleye*, or *Hey, Moby!*—because he was heavy, but he was really a nothing, a zilch, a zero. Except for his size, he blended in and got by as a linebacker on the varsity football team for his junior year, until his dad, a forensic pathologist who had autopsied dozens of damaged brains, pulled him out of the game. "You're shaking up your brain, son. One more concussion and you could be a zombie."

During his first year of undergrad, instead of the freshman fifteen, he started going to the gym, and now this, finally, years of toiling, memorizing the names of each and every cavity in the body, the tendons that connect the bones, the functions of the female reproductive system; he couldn't wait, couldn't wait to start medical school. He signed up for the required classes—biochemistry, gross anatomy, pathology, and an elective in diseases of the brain.

Now, Wally doesn't want a nickname. He doesn't want the guys in his class to know a lot of things about him—how he struggled to fit in, that he used to weigh 372 pounds, how he is (technically) a virgin. A few of them, like Andy Wu and the other quieter students, probably wouldn't care. Like him, they are studious and excited to learn their profession.

The only kid who gets under his skin is Brandon Carol. He reminds Wally too much of the guys who acted like he was a nothing, a fat kid with bad skin (yes, but you still wanted them to like you, didn't you?). Brandon is cut from that type—blond, confident, never had trouble with girls. Spoiled, privileged. This idea was solidified when Wally saw that Brandon drove a canary-yellow Camaro with vanity plates reading, *DR2B.*

Dick.

But it was Brandon who invited him to the male-only party. "Come on, bro. It's a tradition," he said when he ran into him in the graduate dorm. Wally braced himself for a headlock or some other physical assault, but none came. "I get that you're a little shy, no biggie." Brandon told him the party would be chill but interesting. "Kind of like pledging, except . . . more intense." Brandon gave him a little nudge. "You'll like it."

Brandon definitely never has trouble with women. Not like Wally, who has never kissed a girl, never touched a real breast, never had sexual contact with a female. Well, almost never.

There had been one person, Crystal. She was from the neighborhood, and she had this divorced mom who worked nights. Crystal was what the guys called slutty, easy. She'd get on her knees without hesitation. You could finger her at the bus stop. She liked to swallow. Stuff like that.

Deke Barton's swimming party barbecue senior year. Friday night. Wally finds her passed out in Mr. and Mrs. Deke's well-designed bedroom with its king-sized mattress. (This is where they fuck, where Mr. Deke probably turns Mrs. Deke on her knees and takes her from behind.) *Home Is Where the Heart Is* runs in stenciled, loopy cursive above their bed. Crystal wears a blue sundress with white polka dots. He sits beside her, very gently, hoping she won't wake up. He takes her pulse—it's fine, strong and pounding.

He locks the bedroom door knowing that Bill and a bunch of others of his ilk will take advantage. He goes back to her, checks her airway, turns her gently to the side to avoid asphyxiation if she vomits. He has consumed two shitty drinks and doesn't like how his head feels. He doesn't know why he needs to stay in control, but he does.

Her ankle is thin and delicate as a deer's. That is the tibia. He pulls up her dress a bit, revealing the patella, the knee bone. Next, the bare expanse of her thigh bone, the femur. She stirs and he freezes. After a moment, he moves the dress a bit higher, and now can see the white-lace panties stretched across her pelvic area.

Outside, there's the jangle of a pop song: *"Let's make the most of the night like we're gonna die young . . ."* The distant splash of a body cannonballing into the pool, and screeching. It's so easy for everybody else.

He picks up her arm, noting the curl of her fingers, her tiny little nails. He lets the arm fall on the bed. Waits. She doesn't move.

He won't hurt her. He leans down. She smells good, like Ivory soap and girl. The girl smell—he's never been this close to a vagina (a pussy). He pushes her legs apart gently, just a nudge, feeling the thud of excitant in his throat at the curl of public hair escaping her panties. He unzips his khaki Dockers. He takes his erect penis out. He fixates on a cut in her skin that she might have gotten from shaving, this most intimate detail that no one else will see.

Someone tries the doorknob. A female voice calls out, "Crystal, you okay?"

He waits, holding his inhalation. Crystal doesn't stir. There is something very erotic about him being here, having to hurry, to finish before someone else tries to get in, or before she wakes up.

His excitement is beyond anything he's experienced so far from porn—the freckles on her arms, the curve of her fingers—but more than anything, it's her helplessness. She doesn't know he's about to erupt, loosen his load, spit up the chuck, burp the worm. He barely has to touch himself, and he explodes—but not *on* her, never on her, into a Kleenex. The pleasure is so intense, he feels a slice of pain in his temple, as if he's bitten into a chunk of Rocky Road ice cream.

When she wakes up half an hour later, he's sitting away from her at the end of the bed reading *I'm Okay, You're Okay*, a book on the nightstand. She says, "Oh shit, Wally. No."

He closes the book, gives her a smile. "Don't worry, nothing happened."

She feels around for her sandals. He has removed them with care, noting the red polish on her toes. "Thank you." She almost gives him a kiss then, it looks like she might, but she doesn't. Instead, she pats his hand. "Thanks for being a good guy."

In that moment, he feels like, yes, he did the right thing. Or rather: he did a very, very, very wrong thing. But nobody will know.

Now, Wally fears he will not make it to the men's room before shitting his pants because of the agony in his groin. Not a noble way to begin the second week of classes. He steps into a stall, pulls down his khakis, sits. He has made it. But the pain is not just from cramping, it's also coming from his phallus. He examines the shaft in the light from the nearby window, touching it gingerly, as if it might break off. A cluster of small white bumps, like whiteheads; medical term: *comedo* or plural *comedones,* near the tip. The bumps itch in a distant way as if they are mosquito bites or mites. But they're not mites. He pinches one, and an ooze of pus emerges, like a tiny worm from a hole. Another pinch, same thing. He feels around as if he is a proctologist: *Does this hurt? Is there any sensitivity here?* He finds another cluster of bumps near and around the scrotum and rectum (asshole).

He's half hard from touching himself, thinks for a second about getting some relief or distraction by rubbing one out— that's what the guys call it. He prefers to think of it as *onanism,* a term from his favorite Walt Whitman poem. He suddenly remembers his ejaculation on Saturday—how much there was, how he got to that place—and feels another wave of nausea. He is going to wait to do that, wait to see how long it takes before the images pass and to see how long it takes for the bumps to go away. He is not worried about the zits; it seems miniscule compared to what could happen.

He squeezes the shaft of his penis as hard as he can, half expecting blood to spurt out. That would be good. That would be what he deserves, because he knows the symptoms are connected to what happened. This is likely the outbreak of a venereal disease of some type. (Fucking stupid not to wear a condom.)

He cleans himself up, looks in the mirror, sees his pathetic oval pie face staring back at him. "Like a Virgin," that's the song that keeps looping through his head, a song his mom liked to play while chopping vegetables for dinner. But he was not, he was not a virgin any longer (sicko).

He has to play it cool, make it through the next class without acting like a maniac. It's his favorite class, anatomy, after the two Greek words: *ana* meaning up, and *tome* meaning cutting. Today, they will be cutting.

The bodies arrived last week. The first two meetings were all textbook stuff, discussing how they would begin with peeling away the skin, taking away layer after layer, through the sebaceous fat, the muscle, down to the organs and the bones. The bones they would cut through with a buzz saw. It made Wally jittery; he wanted to get to the good stuff.

When they arrived at the lab, the bodies were lying on the tables wrapped head to toe in white plastic like gifts. Before they could unwrap them and get to work, a pastor led them in prayer. "God bless the donors for helping students in their search to bring healing to living bodies."

Brandon said "Amen" the loudest. Wally, who does not believe in any god, simply bowed his head and wondered why his stomach was rumbling. (Formaldehyde is an appetite stimulant.)

Wally's body was Angie P. They received sketchy details about the cadavers—age twenty-two, 102 pounds, 5'4", heroin overdose. No info about her previous life, how she first started using, what drew her to injecting drugs. She had long black hair pressed back from her face, thin arms and legs, skin that had a yellowish tinge from embalming fluid, otherwise unblemished except for the track marks like tiny scabs in the soft bend of her elbow. Probably a runaway, probably homeless; somebody offered her a form to sign to donate her body. Given a different life, she could have been any of the girls who Wally never had the guts to ask out in college.

Her fingernails were bitten to the quick. On her arms, a constellation of little black stars, homemade tattoos done with ink. Blocky plugs removed from her ears, holes in her lip and her nose, little pinpricks where her earring studs used to be.

She was amazing.

That first day, they didn't do more than catalog the body. Wally was embarrassed as they unwrapped her torso. He could see—one, two, three of her ribs protruding, the pit of her stomach and her small whorl of a belly button (though bloated). The lower extremities were hidden by a blue tarp, like she was a vessel about to be shunted off to sea.

He vowed not to look at her breasts. The nipples were small and pink like pencil erasers. The areola darker, almost brown. Large breasts for her size (more than a handful!). But he doesn't think that way. She had (at one time, when she was alive) lovely breasts. He felt a stirring in his groin. It didn't worry him. He was a twenty-four-year-old male, for God's sake, erections happened simply from walking too briskly in tight khakis. Last week, his cock sprang to life when an older cashier at Trader Joe's told him to have a good day, her voice throaty and sensuous.

"Is this your first dead body?" Wally asked the kid next to him, Andrew Yu.

Andrew Yu had to sit down and take a few deep breaths. "Yes, I mean, besides my grandparents."

He doesn't ask Wally the same question, and even if he did, what would Wally have said? That he was eight years old when he snuck into his dad's office and discovered file after file of case notes and autopsies? His first dead body was a girl who had been stabbed fifteen times by her boyfriend—each cut was detailed and labeled on a form, perforations on the right-hand palm, three-inch wound in the upper right torso, plus photos of the nude body: first the front pictures, then the back, then the side, then just the head, neck, and the places where the knife went in and out. That was Wally's first dead body, and first naked body.

This cadaver was pretty, you could see that despite the yellow flesh and bloating from the preservation fluid. She might have had to do all sorts of things to keep getting drugs (smack, horse, junk); she most definitely sold her body to science so that he, Wally McCarter, Andrew Yu, Shivali Patel, Brandon Carol, and others could learn about anatomy.

Once upon a time, she might have had a beautiful smile.

Wally gets ready for their third anatomy class, washing with disinfectant, donning blue scrubs. Today, they will be cutting the bodies open. Skinning them, actually. She'll be there. Weirdly, he feels nervous, as if anticipating a date. As if she is his girlfriend.

After he scrubs in, he lines up the scalpels, thread, and other materials on a metal tray next to the operating table. The lab instructor had explained that Wally wouldn't be permitted to use his own scalpel during dissection class. "We provide the materials, son," he'd said, tugging on his beard like Wally was weird for even suggesting it. So Wally kept the set his father had bought him in the top drawer of his dorm dressers next to his folded (still size XL) boxers and his barely used bottle of Ralph Lauren Polo cologne. He couldn't wait, couldn't wait, to start cutting.

Andrew Yu arrives, and then Dave Johnson, and three other guys Wally barely knows. Andrew wasn't at the party, but Dave and the other three were. They say nothing to him. Are they acting weird? It's difficult to tell because it could be nerves about the dissection.

The instructor tells them to unwrap the bodies completely. They have been laid out on their bellies today, so the students can remove the upper layer of epidermis from the wide swaths of their backs. Dave Johnson pulls down the plastic. It isn't Angie. It is a Caucasian male, very large, bigger than Wally ever was. His body is barely contained on the table.

"Joseph P.," Dave says, waving the chart. "Someone else must have your girl, Wally." He laughs into his fist.

Wally looks around the room at the white coats bent over the bodies. He doesn't see her, but there are sixteen different stations, so she could be anywhere. He needs to focus, take notes, pay attention.

"We'll cut the first layer today," the lab instructor says. "By the end of this course, you will either be vegetarians or cannibals." He is a jovial man with a shock of white hair. Dr. O'Donnell. He has coached them on how to manage the body, giving them a speech about the sacredness of this gift. Also, going over the rules: "Do not give the body a nickname like Bob. Do not remove the body's extremities and turn them into key rings. Do not try to bring her home and introduce her to your mother." The class had laughed, Wally one second behind them.

Wally wonders what has happened to Angie, why they have rotated bodies.

Andrew Yu holds the scalpel out to Wally. He looks a little sick. He might be on his way to becoming a med school dropout statistic, someone who doesn't survive this part of the training. "You want to do it?"

"Sure, my good man." Wally does a little bow and takes the scalpel. It is polished and sharp, and has probably been used to cut into hundreds of cadavers over the years. The blade is new, and if he were to run his finger along the edge, the skin would open up in an instant like a gill.

Dave has taken a medical marker to draw a dotted purple line down the center of the back, marking the path the scalpel should travel to part the skin.

Wally places a gloved hand firmly on the specimen's back, between the shoulder blades, putting the scalpel just above the first rib. Later, they will sever the spinal column, rendering the corpse forever unable to walk (ha-ha-ha-ha).

The professor says, "Push harder than you think."

Wally adds pressure, feeling the skin give. It reminds him again—a flash of the weekend, when he had pushed . . . had he pushed? The scalpel cuts deep, past where he is supposed to go, revealing a great spill of fat that looks like cottage cheese.

He remembers now. He had hit something, like she had a sponge up there or a tampon—he feels hysterical remembering it—like, *This is real, I am really doing it.* He starts to laugh, but then feels another stab of pain in his groin, this one worse than in pathology class on Monday.

Brandon Carol has wandered over, holding a piece of white

gauze with a smear of pink on it. The bodies don't bleed, so it must be part of the flesh. He dips in next to Wally. "Looking good, bud." He steps back. "What's that smell? Dude, something's off."

Wally sniffs, thinking it must be the body, but then realizes it's not formaldehyde, it's something else. It might even be Wally who is off, like a bad piece of cheese, like something rotten or moldy. He can't recall if he smelled anything when he was in the bathroom. He cannot leave now, must finish the task.

As soon as they are dismissed, Wally heads for the showers in Whitman Hall where many of the graduate students live. He has doused himself in ocean-breeze body spray, doesn't want anyone to get too close to him.

He runs into Shivali on his way to the shower. She is looking at him oddly, almost like she doesn't recognize him. "Hey, what happened Saturday night?" she asks. She has circles under her eyes, as if she stayed up late into the night, worried about him.

He truly does like Shivali. He doesn't think of her when he is touching himself because he wants to keep her pure, not foul up interactions by placing her at the center of images that degrade her. He's watched so much porn from such an early age that it takes a lot now to get him going, fetish sites that worry him—penetration with giant dildos, an older lady with her bernadoodle, and, just lately, videos where the young girls are gagged and tied up, sites where he wonders sometimes if they really *are* kidnapped, really crying, or if they are acting. (Let's be honest, that's often what tips him over the edge—thinking, *What if these bodies are really suffering?*)

Shivali stands too close. He can see the small round pores

on her face, smell her cinnamon breath, and then wonders if she can smell him. Smell *it*.

It's too much, like the time he ate fifteen chocolate bars all at once, stuffing them in his face so that his little sister couldn't get to them. (Wally the Whale.)

He backs away. "Nothing happened, m'lady," he says. "Everything is A-OK." He winks, and then, horrified at how he's behaving, trots away.

In the shower, he jumps back when he touches his penis. He slips on the tiled floor, nearly falls and hits his head. He imagines Dave or Andrew finding him, the blood swirling down the sink. He feels along the edge of his penis and encounters a split, like a cut or a groove where the skin has cracked under pressure. The bumps have turned into blood blisters. He can't help it—he picks at one until it bursts, sending a splatter of blood onto the wall like a starburst. He quickly washes it off. He steadies himself on the slippery wall, doing the same thing with each welt, disgusted and gratified when he is able to burst them all. Afterward, he pats around the area, and they do feel less swollen, as if he has released the infection.

He goes to the Michael Collins Medical Library to use the computers there, because he doesn't want the search showing up on his laptop. He finds a wealth of information, some of it alarming (cancer, syphilis, AIDS). It could be quite a few things, but most likely it's herpes or gonorrhea. Not fatal. Not a big deal. Treatable.

He stops at Walgreens to buy rash cream and Benadryl, along with Preparation H to stop the swelling.

When he returns to his room, he locks the door and goes in for an inspection. When he sees it, the first thing he thinks is, *Oh, yes, it's like when you boil a piece of meat*. Around the head of the penis, the white spots have turned red. The top leaks a greenish liquid that certainly means infection. The spots have solidified, and look like tiny lima beans along the ridge of the penal stem. He could take a #3 scalpel to them—he has done this before to a mole on his side, removed it cleanly on his own (the mole came back), but with his fever and his trembling hands, he knows this is a terrible idea, especially if he nicks the deep dorsal artery. Among other things, his library research has revealed that if this is one of the bad infections and he does nothing, it could blossom like corral, continuing to grow and multiply until his dick looks like it's covered in barnacles.

He imagines strolling along to class the next day, how he will have to play it cool as the flesh falls down his pant leg and plops on the ground. In a campy horror movie, a Frisbee-catching dog would come over and eat it and then lick its owner's face.

The fever has reached his head. Wally makes a calculated decision—if he can get antibiotics, this may clear up in time for his next dissection class.

The doctor at the Temple University Hospital emergency room is a tall Indian man with a polite demeanor. He does not make small talk. He asks pointed questions about Wally's recent and past sexual history. Wally answers untruthfully. He says doesn't know what happened, he was with a girl at a party and she gave him something. He asks Wally if he has been traveling overseas recently, or if he has worked in disaster areas where there were numerous fatalities. "This kind of infection is usually something we see when working with devastation."

Wally says, "The farthest I have traversed is northern Idaho." This is also a ridiculous lie. He has never been anywhere near Idaho.

The doctor pushes up his glasses, and writes something on his chart with a small pencil like Wally used to take the MCAT. He has taken a swab to one of Wally's scabs and sent it to the lab and asked him if he has any flu-like symptoms, which makes Wally sneeze. "We'll know more with the blood work, but this is a very rare infection. This is not something that I've ever seen from person-to-person contact." He goes on to marvel that in his twenty-five years, he's never witnessed an infection cycle through its stages this aggressively. "Did you touch the area?" he asks.

Wally lies again: "No sir. I believe in letting the medical professionals do their job."

The doctor notes something on his chart. "You had chicken pox as a kid?"

Wally says yes, and that is true.

"Very odd. Astounding, really. I would like to bring in my colleagues to review."

Wally imagines a row of faces surrounding him, leaning in for a better look at his groin. His teeth chatter and his bare knees bump together under the thin hospital gown. He is definitely developing a cold.

The doctor explains in careful terms that one of the treatments will involve removing the dead skin to prevent further infection. (Debriding! How funny that this has come up again.) They will need to call a specialist. He will insert a catheter, get Wally sedated, take samples.

Wally's penis is wrapped in cotton, and it throbs in a muted way, like a bell that won't stop clanging. Even now, it still wants what it wants—he knows that given the right stimulation, he could cum in a second. Right on the floor. It's an affliction.

When the doctor leaves to get the admission process started,

Wally imagines him going to the phone, placing a call to the police. *Suspicious activity*. He walks out of the swinging double doors of the hospital. A patient can do this anytime. It's called a discharge AMA ("against medical advice").

He wants to see her again. Not to do anything, just to see her. Just put his hand on her flesh, to make sure this isn't a nightmare he dreamed up. He has blacked out before in college but made himself a promise that he wouldn't do that in med school. And this was different. It wasn't a blackout. He remembers her, the skin, the difficulty of pushing inside her, the resistance and relief. His own thick, stupid guy fingers touching her.

The way he wants to do it again, even if she's been altered.

He is sick. Definitely, he will get help. See a psychiatrist like he did in tenth grade when his mother found his sister's dolls under his bed, naked and covered in his sticky funk. He isn't going to do anything to her this time. That is just the furthest thing from his mind.

This is what he remembers from Saturday night:

The gross anatomy lab is in the basement of the Tenant Building, the central part of the three-block campus off Walker's Lane. On the front of the building, there is a large growling bear, the university mascot. That night, the reception area is deserted except for a janitor who has been bribed by Brandon to let them in. That's just fine, and Wally feels good, or okay; he's going to fit in here, these are the true scholars, this is not the dumb-dumb frat guys from undergraduate school, party boys whose parents paid for their cars; these are smart people, solid kids.

For a moment, before he pushes through the double doors, he thinks, *Maybe not. Maybe not, maybe the risk isn't worth it. I can go home and watch porn and then* Game of Thrones.

But then he thinks of how his dad might have acted in the same situation. His dad wasn't afraid of anything. Wally knew his dad worried about him, weirdo kid, should have been more outgoing, but he wasn't, he was different, he didn't get that gene of easy laughter and wide smiles. He got nervous twitches and the tendency to duck under things as if he was too tall instead of too fat. *The Whale.*

He runs into Dave Johnson at the lab station, which is set up like a bar with plastic cups and bottles of vodka, gin, something greenish. Dave hands him a cup filled with clear liquid. Wally wonders for a moment if they're drinking embalming fluid. "What did you get?" Dave is on something, his pupils wide and excited, dilated, almost taking over the rest of his eyes. He must have snorted something (not Oxy, right?). He keeps clenching his teeth, opening and shutting his mouth, catching his tongue.

"Pardon me?"

"Did you get the whole body? One of the other guys just got a head with the mouth pried open. How fucked up and funny is that? What did you get?"

Wally just stares back at him, confused.

"Oh, you didn't go yet. Brandon! Brandon, he didn't go!"

On the PowerPoint screen a silent video plays, a black-and-white film of a doctor and a nurse fucking on an operating table. None of the women from his class are there. Only guys. A select number of guys. On the screen, a man has tied up a woman dressed in white nurse regalia. A horse is introduced into the scene. He wonders briefly if they are playing a snuff film.

Brandon appears and slaps Wally on the back, man-to-man style. "Your turn. You ready for your five minutes in heaven?" That was a game the other kids played in middle school, where you and a girl went into a closet to make out. Every other guy in his class did it, coming out disheveled with their uniform collars popped up.

He has quickly consumed two cups of the clear liquid. He wonders what it would take to stop all of this, to turn around and say, *I'm not going to join, guys.*

Brandon leans in. "This is tradition. My dad did it. He's the one who lent me the keys to the rooms." He claps Wally on the back again. "Don't be a pussy."

Wally winces. He hates that word, hates that it's used to reduce women to their anatomy only. That's part of what he likes about medical school, the anatomical parts have Latin names—the vulva, the uterus, the clitoris; the words are not clinical so much as honorable, and less degrading than jock talk.

The main room is where the cadaver tables are set up, but they are empty tonight, stored away for safekeeping. On the perimeter of the room are smaller simulation labs. He sees some of the first-year male students standing in a row, as if in line for Communion. Before they go into the room, Brandon fills their mouths with something from a syringe.

None of them seem to be worried, not even a little bit. They're having a hell of a time. Wally turns back to Brandon. "Alright, sir, I will." He opens his mouth and Brandon squirts the shot down his throat. He gags and chokes, feeling the liquid burn like acid. But it is a familiar taste, some kind of hard alcohol, nothing toxic.

"Okay, let's see how much you can handle. Go into the room, jerk off, and then bring back proof that you could chock your chicken under any circumstances." Brandon hands Wally a plastic vial, the kind used to capture lab samples—urine, feces, sputum. "Concentrate, buddy. Show us what you're made of."

He opens the door to one of the rooms, and Wally steps inside.

The room is meant for patient simulations. They have dummies in storage of all sizes—that was on the brochure to the med school: best simulation lab, state of the art, almost like working on real patients. The plastic patients can be used to show signs of distress, and the med students diagnose them based on their body temperature and presenting symptoms.

At first, Wally thinks the body in repose on the examining chair is one of the dummies, though a lifelike one, bigger than he imagined, and then he sees that no, actually, it's a body from the anatomy lab.

What Dave said now makes sense, *What did you get?* In the other rooms, there could be other cadavers, or simply just heads. Students who will become ocular or plastic surgeons practice first on severed human heads, removing their eyeballs, injecting the foreheads with Botox or the lips with collagen. Maybe next door a student is staring at the head of a dead woman, trying to rub one out with her half-open eyes watching.

When his own eyes adjust, Wally sees that the body is Angie. She is covered from the waist up just like she was in anatomy class. She is positioned supine in an examining space for a gynecological course. Her feet are propped up in the stirrups. Her legs are spread slightly. She has small feet, clean soles, a high arch. Her toenails are painted black. This makes him feel protective of her. At one point, she had been a living person who did ordinary things like eating ice cream and painting her nails (and mainlining heroin).

He hears the pounding of the music, imagines Shivali in her room studying for their exam on blood-borne antigens. He likes Shivali. He thinks maybe she likes him too.

He looks at the body. He moves the blue tarp away, puts a hand on her leg. It's cold and solid as marble, like a Grecian statue.

They've left a giant bottle of K-Y Jelly on the cabinet next to some instructions.

He touches her knee. The bones of her hips protrude. She's very skinny, her pelvic bone visible. How long has she been dead? Bodies can be stored for weeks, months. Six years she could be preserved.

Someone yells through the door, the words garbled, indistinguishable.

This is pressure, but he can do it.

He puts on some K-Y Jelly with one squirt. It is slick and cold, but instantly heats up. He closes his eyes and thinks first about Shivali. That helps, but it's not totally working. His penis, his penile stem, is only halfway erect, the head of it a shrinking mushroom, sad-looking.

This is like practice, which is what the dead bodies are for—practice to get ready for a real person.

He imagines Shivali, whispering into his ear, *Yeah, do that again, that feels good, oh my God, that's incredible.* Then he switches to Crystal now, her still body, her quiet breathing. Angie now, crouched down in an alleyway, looking up at him: *Sir, can you help me? Sir, just a little bit of cash, sir?* When she was alive, she might have asked for a little bit of help, a transaction, back behind the ShopRite.

It's not working. It's not enough.

He moves between her legs. He won't look at her. This is real, her real body, her real pubic hair, dark and sleek like an animal, not like the women in porn who are shaved down like babies. Her legs are already apart, in stirrups, like she's getting an exam. She might like that (if she were alive).

He is fully, painfully erect now.

He is not like the other guys—single-minded, focused on pussy. He knows that the female body requires care that doesn't come from penetration, not like you would see in PornHub videos where the women are getting pounded and loving it. Female pleasure requires the stimulation of the clitoris—Latin origin, *kleitoris,* the crown of the vagina. His finger shaking, he parts the folds on her labia and finds the cold tip of the clitoris. This is where there are hundreds of nerve endings, more even than the phallus.

Angie. He is gentle, and he wishes, wishes this would be the thing that could bring her to life like something from a fairy tale.

When he pushes inside, he feels something give, like a caving in. A part of him stands outside of himself, the part that was a lot like Brandon, the other him. *This is how you pop your cherry, huh?*

He can smell alcohol, and his own doggy breath, and the low-level buzz of formaldehyde, but he can also see her pubic hair, and because the lights are dim, her skin doesn't look yellowish or dead (like a skinned chicken), it looks silver, like a creature in *Avatar.* And what does it feel like? It feels like many things he's already tried this on (too many things to name— sofa cushions, food, stuffed animals), except Angie is cold and tight. He feels the resistance of her, as if she is alive and pushing back, as if she is saying, *No, no, please don't,* and that's what tips him over the edge and into a gush of release into her body in great heaving pulses like a seizure.

Afterward, he takes the cup and places it under the lip of her vulva to catch the evidence. This is called an excretion. He tightens the lid and sets it aside. He uses a paper towel to gently clean her up. He does not want to leave her like that, so undignified. He lingers by her face. He puts his mouth to hers, presses slightly, his head buzzing with a line from a poem, *O, my body.*

A knock on the door. He breaks the kiss.

Brandon enters and immediately comes over to see how he's doing. "I hope that wasn't too fucked up—" He looks at the vial. "You took a souvenir? Or wait . . . You didn't seriously think—" He stares at Wally's face, something on it must look wrong. "Are you fucking with me? Guys!" he hollers to the room crowd. "Wally fucked a dead girl!"

The remaining men are too far away to hear, gathered in the center of the room, watching the video which now shows two women performing oral sex on one another, all tangled up so they look like one creature.

Wally sees the row of vials on the shelf near the makeshift bar. All empty. When he goes to hand the cup to Brandon, he drops it. The lid stays shut but the vial bounces, one, two, three, across the floor, and then rolls beneath the cabinet.

"Drat," Wally mutters.

"You are one sick fuck," Brandon says, still staring at him, but is there something in his voice—admiration? Yes, Wally could be one of those wacko guys like from his dad's favorite eighties movies, the freak who the popular kids embrace, like in *Weird Science.* Brandon gives him a high five. "My man," he says, and Wally feels a wave of relief so strong his knees nearly buckle.

Now, it's close to midnight and the gross anatomy lab is deserted. Wally goes through the swinging doors and stands for a second looking into the dark room. He switches on the lights. They flicker, blink, and the room turns bright. He has a sickening twist in his stomach, like he is about to descend on a roller coaster. Excitement and dread. He feels like he needs to see her one more time, to see for himself if there is anything wrong with the body.

At night, the bodies are stored in a cooling freezer, each one in a bin with a number on it. Wally steps into the freezer and looks for the names on a chart along the side. He finds the fat man, Joseph P., and then Angie's body: #645. He goes to the shelf where she is stored, these neat little stacked refrigerated containers as if she is a large piece of venison. The group that worked on her before will have removed the skin on her back, so he will have to turn her over. A severe pain jolts him, and he realizes it's because he's getting hard, thinking about the body.

He pulls out #645. An unfamiliar face. A blond woman with a raised scar across her neck as if she cut her own throat.

"The original cadaver is gone."

Wally jumps, heart in his thoracic cavity, sweat on his temples. The fever is back, and worse.

It's Andrew Yu, holding their anatomy workbook to his chest. "I came here to prepare for next week. The lymphatic system. I really want to do well."

Wally pushes the body back into the drawer. "My good man, you will be excellent." He clears his throat. "Do you know why—did anyone say why they had to—"

"I don't know. Contamination of the medical material? I only overheard this from Brandon. They had to burn a body for safety reasons."

Wally feels another stab of pain in his groin, tries to cover it with a little bend at the waist, as if he is bowing. "That's odd." He doesn't want to push too hard. "Do you know why? That seems drastic."

Andrew Wu is staring at him strangely. Wally covers his crotch, afraid that maybe blood has soaked through his pants. "I couldn't say for sure. A virus." He picks at his forehead, thinking. "Dangerous. Contagious." He starts to walk away. "Oh, right—that weird new one. But you don't need to worry about it. We wore gloves. We barely handled her."

Wally stops him, touches his arm and is surprised by how warm he is. "Do you mean like—"

Andrew snaps his fingers. "I'm so dumb. Monkeypox. It was monkeypox." He sees the look on Wally's face. "You're fine, dude. It's only fatal through intimate contact. The worst you'll get is a rash on your forearms. Or, like, encephalitis." He pats Wally on the back. "I'm kidding!"

Wally nods. He feels woozy, his plan was to . . . what was his plan? A minute alone with Angie. The medical material. The contaminant.

Wally walks across the empty quad. It hurts to move too quickly. Maybe he should consider going home for the weekend. A two-hour train ride, he could say he's decided against medical school—(*You failed, you fucked up and now you're probably dying. Not to mention that you left semen behind in a cup. And then you go to the doctor and you, like, present yourself as this specimen? You committed a felony, a felony, you're going to jail where you will be raped and tortured, which you deserve, but that's if you survive.*) He starts to run, knowing that will make the bleeding worse, might cause something to rupture, but he needs to see it again, he has to *do* something.

Wally returns to his room. It hurts to move now. It's as if there is a seed stuck in the glans of his penis. Perhaps the infection will blossom out of the tip like a black rose.

His necktie hangs on the back of the bedroom door, the one he wore that night with Angie. He weighs an idea—a quick slip knot over the stainless-steel light, with the necktie tight around his esophagus, a kick of the chair, and just like that, no more shame. *(Do it, you stupid nothing person.)*

He won't do that—what if his parents thought he was into autoerotic asphyxiation?

He takes out his scalpel set with his initials carved on the front: *WAM*. He likes the way the instruments look in the leather pouch, untouched, unused, pure.

Wally's favorite book has always been *Gray's Anatomy: The Anatomical Basis of Clinical Practice.* As a kid, he studied the pages with the fascination other boys had for violent video games. He liked the exactness of the illustrations—the layers of skin peeled away to reveal muscle, muscle to reveal the circulatory system, circulatory system leading to bones and marrow.

He opens the book to page 459, the reproductive system. He looks closely at the diagram of the male genitalia. He takes out his shaving mirror and places it on a chair. If he can excise the dead skin on the scrotum, he might be able to root out the infection while also performing his very first own debriding.

He picks up the #3L scalpel. A part of him thinks, *Finally.*

He steadies his hand. He places the tip of the scalpel. He makes the cut.

BREATHING EXERCISE

BY **RAVEN LEILANI**

When she began to have trouble breathing, Myriam tried to wait it out. She monitored the daily pollen count, bought a neti pot, and tried not to think about the gallerists who no longer returned her calls. After an opening of her new work which had only three attendees—a pair of Danish tourists and a woman who wanted to know if the toilets were free—she went to a party in Poughkeepsie and received a crushing pep talk from a sculptor whose assistants were always under the age of twenty-three. *You're still young*, he said, and all night people offered similar condolences for her career. Later the host of the party corralled everyone into a room with an old tube TV. When he turned it on, she could hear the crackle of the cathode. He adjusted the antennas and said he was going to show them a documentary. It was about competitive tickling; as they watched, a hush settled over the room. A man looked into the camera and described being bound and tickled. *They told me it was about endurance*, he said. *I was thirteen*. It made Myriam uneasy, and she excused herself and took the earliest Metro-North into the city that she could find.

As soon as she got on the train, she put her head between

knees and tried to breathe. She called her mother, and they
a nice conversation until they came to the subject of her
rk. It had been eleven years since she'd left home, eight since
e'd graduated from a midtier art school and made her name
showing audiences how much abuse the human body could
withstand. *It isn't sustainable,* her mother said, and, technically,
she was right. As Myriam was getting off the train, the first
email came. *Hack bitch,* it began, before segueing into a surprising deconstruction of one of her more recent shows—soft
depictions of Black women in ornate Victorian dress: horsehair
crinoline, ivory boning, bantu knots. Subtler than her larger
body of work, meaning it involved significantly less self-harm.
Why not just kill yourself? the author wrote, after a long treatise
about the Round Earth conspiracy.

At home, she tried to open up her airways with peppermint
oil and steam. She took a Xanax and walked around in circles
with her arms above her head. A man was playing trumpet
across the street, and she opened the window and asked him to
stop. Not for the first time, her apartment felt as if it was too
small. It was 545 hyperutilized square feet, a one-bedroom in
Bed-Stuy that she could afford only because the closest subway
station was ten blocks away. She regretted going to the party,
but invitations were not coming the way they had when she was
twenty-five—when she fed yam and pig intestines through a
cotton gin and could still be someone's age-inappropriate girlfriend; when she rigged a voting machine to a hose and stood in
a glass tank as patrons cast their votes; when the confluence of
an unimpeachable pelvic floor and a strong debut made her into
a wanton, Brooklyn-dwelling monster—those were the days.
Days when her mother called and asked why she would do these
things to herself in public for white people.

Myriam didn't have a good answer, only that there
something pure about force, about a fervent belief in her
body, which could be technically boiled down to such clich
maxims as Mind over Matter and No Pain, No Gain. She four
a place in her mind that was dark and cool and still, and then she
opened a show at the Domino Sugar Factory and let herself be
repeatedly pushed down a flight of stairs. Now she was twenty-
nine, and her career was not going as planned. *Myriam Says Relax*, a show in which she sat for two hours with a lye relaxer in
her hair, had not been received well. After an hour, the sodium
hydroxide had begun to eat through her scalp, and she was hos-
pitalized. The reviews were embarrassing: articles on the vague
Hotepian undertones of the project, on the self-inflicted martyr-
dom for a problem as tired—as *nineties*—as Western European
beauty standards. And finally, the criticism which at first felt
shallow but now worried her as she moved beyond an age where
it was good enough just to shock and awe: that she was making
a spectacle of Black pain, feeding the machine she loathed.

She made attempts to remedy this, projects organized in secret with scrappy, progressive galleries unfazed or actively down
for the legal repercussions of not letting white people into her
shows, of charging them double, of making them wear signs
around their necks that said, *I am not welcome here*. She put on
shows like *George Washington's Teeth*, in which she collected the
teeth of white patrons and made bespoke silver grillz. But ul-
timately how she explained it to her mother was that she had
somehow broken into an industry in which *she* was not particularly welcome, and she was just doing what she could to
survive. She had made a Rube Goldberg machine—fifty domi-
noes, eighteen gumballs, seventy rubber bands, and one glass of
warm salt water poised above a synthetic hymen to terminate in

the utterance of the N-word. She branded herself with erasure poems she'd drawn from excerpts of *Huckleberry Finn.* White people came in giddy droves, excited to say the few words they were not allowed under the guise of discussing art.

A few days after the party, there was another message. She knew it was from the same person because of the email address, a generic dot org with no corresponding organization, but this time he signed his name. *Tragic Negress*, it began, *I read your interview with* _____ *and I had a few points*. She imagined he was normal, indistinct. To imagine him grotesque somehow felt less true, like a child's idea of evil, in which there is no dissonance between the heart and the face. It was just as likely that he was a competent and active community member, a new father, a guy on Lexapro with a dog waiting for him to come home. Of course, Hitler's dog must have loved him too. The only thing she knew was that he was local, as he spoke obsessively about an exhibit he'd seen recently at Hauser & Wirth, in Chelsea. *Dear Richard*, she wrote, *you think you hate me but you are actually obsessed with me and that is the thing you hate*, and even this made her feel out of breath.

She hoped she might feel better if she went to the gym, but after two minutes on the treadmill, she had to stop. It took her aback that her body, which she had punished thoroughly for years, was now incapable of accommodating such a small request. She started the treadmill again, but it was too much. She had the sensation that there was something hard and insoluble in her throat, like a diamond or some amalgamation of the microplastics in New York's water supply. Her trainer took her aside and asked if she was all right. He was a jarhead from Staten Island who didn't believe in excuses, and sometimes he pinched the fat that still remained around her stomach and made her keep going until she cried. But now he put his hand on her shoulder and told her to breathe, and she shrugged off his hand and said, *I can't.*

The next morning, she took the train to a clinic in Sunset Park and told her primary care physician that it felt as if she had wool in her lungs. While she described her symptoms, he kept glancing at his watch. In a way, this comforted her. If the situation were dire, she imagined, he would be a better audience. So she was relieved when he simply told her to go home and get some sleep. But a week later, she felt worse. As if every valuable organ in her chest were distended with dark city air. She logged into her health insurance portal—a poorly designed bit of JavaScript for patients insured through her artists union—and sent messages to her physician about the state of her health that did not receive a response. Richard kept in touch. As she expected, her response had not deterred him. It had encouraged him. *I'll find you*, he wrote. *It would be nothing to find your address. Maybe this is why your work has gotten so tepid? Maybe you feel a little too safe?*

She couldn't pretend that some of this didn't hurt her feelings. Comments about her cunt, about how her head might look on a stick—whatever. But the comments about her work, she carried them around with her all day. Although he was not alone. This particular critical response was familiar—that her level of self-exhibition corresponded inversely with her level of safety. *Who is this for?* her mother asked, and within the question was an accusation: that her work could not be for Black people, for Black women—creatures so powerless that to invite further subjugation was redundant, perverse. Myriam stammered when she tried to explain herself. She did not feel powerless. She felt searingly present in the world, and sometimes she wanted to be reduced.

When she didn't respond to his message, Richard sent a photo of a scimitar, then a Glock. She tried to report him. She put on her least threatening clothes and went to the precinct on Lafayette with a handful of printed emails, but as he hadn't actually done anything, there was nothing the authorities could do. After two days they sent an email to say that the ticket was closed, and she bought three cameras and mounted one in each room.

A few days later, she met with a pulmonologist. She sat in the waiting room for forty-five minutes after her appointment was supposed to start, and then a nurse ushered her inside and weighed her in a room with an overflowing garbage can. When the pulmonologist came, he did not make eye contact. He mis-pronounced her name and prescribed an antihistamine. The copay was two hundred dollars, the deductible a distant four-figure number that she could not hope to touch, the artists union's HMO a collection of inscrutable fine print that covered only routine checkups and visits to in-network gynecologists who said things like *Very pretty* about her transvaginal ultrasounds.

She took the pills and wrote a few emails to her mother that she didn't send. *I had a good childhood. You didn't do anything wrong*, one email began, before she filed it away in her drafts. When the pills didn't help, she found a nebulizer on eBay and hooked herself up to the machine twice a day each week. *This is what I'm going to do to you*, Richard wrote after sending a link to an upsetting pornography page. *Okay*, Myriam wrote back, lank from an hour on the nebulizer, the mask still strapped to her face and sputtering mist.

Of course, this only made him angrier. In her unfortunate tenure as a heterosexual woman she had learned that men, more than anything, did not like to be surprised. They did not like there to be any place inside you they could not touch. They were allowed to be certain of things, and they expected to be certain of you. Even her ex-husband, a performance artist whose oeuvre involved significant self-mutilation, had ideas about how she should conduct herself once they were married. When they were dating, he was happy to do joint projects in which they lived under surveillance in a room made entirely of Kanekalon hair. Happy to take turns spanking each other over clips of Bill Cosby's "pound cake" speech. But when they married, he felt differently. *Your body is a temple*, he said three days before he nailed his scrotum to the floor of the Guggenheim.

While she was out and about, Richard sent another message: *I can see you. I'm behind you.* She asked him what she was wearing and he said, *A blue dress*, which was right, and then, *Sandals*, which was wrong. She kept two knives in her purse. She didn't walk down ill-lit streets or ride in train cars that were insufficiently populated. If she had a husband, there would at least have been someone there to know if she didn't come home. When she got up in the morning and felt her body working against her lungs, she knew she was an easy mark. She looked around her apartment and took in the entirety of what it cost to breathe sparingly. To preserve energy, there were trade-offs, things that were left undone. The garbage, copious and cooking in the sun. The weapons fashioned from household items. The sink and shower, slippery with bacteria. Bed shirts and underwear, heavy with sweat from the exertion of breathing consciously. She took the cameras down, looked at the footage, and could not believe the person she saw. She made a copy of the footage and sent it to her manager, and in a few days her manager wrote, *Is there any more?*

And there were bills. The insurance company called once a week and then twice a day. She changed her voice mail to say that she was opening a show in Beijing and not answering her American phone. She dreamed it was true: low-lit, narcotic dreams in which she walked an adult panther through a Chinese tobacco factory and people flocked into the gallery and filled the air with Mandarin. In these dreams she could breathe again.

She used to live for the summers in New York. The stinky, shimmering avenues and everyone getting cooked underground. The body resisting a solid white arm of sun. Now it was hell. There were too many people and not enough air, and her chest burned no matter how carefully she drew breath. Now she drank barium as another specialist monitored a live X-ray of her throat. *Everything looks fine,* he said, and for two days all her meals tasted alkaline. For the next procedure, an endoscopy she spread over two credit cards, they lowered a camera into her esophagus and found nothing. She did not have an escort, and when she tried to hail a cab, three went by before one stopped.

No news did not feel like good news, and the longer there were no answers the more she was sure the answers were bad. It was not insignificant for her to believe so totally in a thing she could not see. Because she was a woman, she had been taught to distrust herself, and there was no certainty she held that had not been vetted for the cute, indelible madness of female error. To be able to insist fervently that something was wrong meant that all alternatives had been thoroughly explored. It meant defying the more natural inclination to defer and allow herself to be seen as crazy, and so she needed to be right. She had seen the news stories about richer, more powerful Black women. Dark, luminous women who always kept their faces partly out of view, who were emblems of what you could have when the long game was cautiously and brutally played. Even these women were sent home with aspirin as their brains were hemorrhaging.

She sent an email to her primary care physician and attached an article about respiratory illness and city smog. *I have done everything I'm supposed to do*, she wrote. *Please help.* It wasn't just that she couldn't breathe; it was that she still had to go about life. The errands, the electric bills, the sexually violent found poetry of loitering men. It was odd to be sick, to have the sensation that her lungs were full of blood, and still have to be wary of men. It was odd to feel as if she was dying and still have to field comments about her breasts. She went out to buy mucus thinners, and a man trailed her from Seventh Avenue to DeKalb. When she stopped to confront him, a group of men looked on and laughed. As she climbed the stairs to her apartment, another message came. *I'm going to pay you a visit soon*, Richard wrote, and outside, the man with the trumpet was still playing "Hot Cross Buns."

For two days, she didn't sleep. She cleaned the apartment, took out weeks' worth of recycling, and pulled hair from all the drains, and then she wrote her own obituary and addressed it to the biggest critic of her work, a prominent blogger who could not be pleased. She tried to make a case for some of the pieces he'd deemed irresponsible, but as she wrote, she wondered if he'd been right. Giving private dances to patrons for a nickel a pop had not been about anything other than being oversexed and twenty-six. Letting patrons choose between giving her a rose and holding an unloaded gun to her head had been, despite her cynicism, a severe miscalculation. The critic claimed to be among one of the faceless men who chose the .22, and in his review he wrote that there was nothing radical, nothing avant-garde about a Black woman's proximity to death.

She thought about this when she went for a full-body X-ray. She put on the lead apron, and a nurse warned her that the quarters would be tight. When she was inside, the radiologist noticed she hadn't had a bowel movement in a while. He joked that he could see an entire cherry tomato in her large intestine, and she pretended to laugh. The imaging took forty minutes, and she fell asleep. The technician shook her awake, and then the doctor took her into a room to tell her that nothing had been found. When she began to cry, he touched her shoulder and said, *Yes, it is a huge relief.*

For an hour, the city was entirely without sound. Everything was a labor—the stairs, the turnstile, the MetroCard machine which wouldn't take any coins. It was the most humid day of the year, and not even the city was indifferent to the heat. Across Brooklyn, wires were melting and lights were going out. There were fires and stroke victims and women wilting under parasols. She walked through the city and paid attention to everyone, and when she got home she began to reinstall the cameras.

One camera by the door, another in the bedroom. A bowl of apples with their bruises facing out, an open window, a book cracked along its spine. She put on the nicest dress she owned. Sheer blue chiffon studded with discreet zirconiums. Four years earlier, she'd worn it on the night of her debut. It had never been washed, and now it was two sizes too big. The insurance company called while she cinched the bust with safety pins. They left a voice mail with the information for a debt collection agency. She called her mother while she was doing her hair. *I don't have any more ideas*, she said when it went to the machine, and then she sent Richard her address. She wasn't unafraid.

As she knew it would, the city had opened to her the very moment she was leaving it, given her a sense of optimism that did not comport with the project ahead, and yet there was something else. The excitement that always preceded a new project, the composure, the freaky certainty about how the pieces fit together. A feeling that started in the chest and became a thing as inevitable as breath, an insatiable resolve to live beyond the body that she had tried again and again to turn into art—which she would try to do now, one more time.

MUZZLE

BY **CASSANDRA KHAW**

count my teeth. Over the top of my incisors, there's a crown of hard growth in the gum. *What the hell?* I think with a jump. What'd they say about rougarous again? That you can pass on the wolf if the burden is too much? That it bleeds into the ones you love? This *parasite*, this sickness in the spirit. No one's fault except for circumstance. Penned-up animals just don't do well in captivity, especially if you won't let them sleep.

I excuse myself from the table, bones thrumming, my skin too tight along a spine that feels suddenly compacted, scrunched up too short for far too long. It *aches*. All of me hurts with muscle burn and spurs of bone, pricking the underside of my flesh, crowding in the joints, and I want to scratch the meat from them and there are too many teeth, way too many, still blooming like it's the first springtime after a million years of cold. My lips ride up, my cheeks concave; a wet snap punctuates the moment my upper jaw elongates.

"Shit." I fling my hands over my face, elbowing past another guest and into the bathroom.

Bang, goes an indignant fist. *Bang,* again, and over and over. Someone curses me out but I don't listen, transfixed instead by the portraiture of my own face in the smudged glass. Graffiti—

Sharpied vulgarities, a phone number or two, nothing exciting except for their odor, a lingering stink of chemical and someone else's frustration, someone else's want congealed in the tiles, and *oh god*, it isn't lost upon me how wild it is that the smells read as loud as the riot act right now—surrounds the wrought-iron frame, distorted by the low light; my reflection pretends desperately to be human.

At least until my bones, all at once, become this roux of calcium, fat, and liquefied protein. Blood warms on the curve of my tongue, fills my mouth. I gulp down gelatin. As I stare into the mirror, my body reinvents its dimensions: it grows three feet vertically, bulks out at the shoulders. The muscles that mushroom around my scapulae make me hunch as bones widen, bend, bend, bend, break, *snap*. The pop of my vertebrae is a machine-gun noise. My lungs expand. And where the wolf breaks skin, I am bleeding in gouts, my body become glossolalia, alien as god; my red blood jeweling the white ceramic sink. There is so much of it, you can't see a break in the color. Somewhere, down in the dark of my belly, my wolf—not *him* although he started this, although he is the vector of infection, but my own wolf, the one that had slept encysted in my lizard brain up till this point of personal history—begins to low.

I shudder like a winded elk, legs slightly splayed, trembling. There's so much blood it's like afterbirth now, the torrent gone sticky and black. I'd never wanted to be a mother, aborted the thought when scientists prophesied the world burning. But here I am, moaning as gore pistons out of me. I look down. There's a sheen of yellow in the red where the fat, nearly boiling, washed through. And I am hungry, so fucking hungry, starved to my back teeth. I can barely think through the miasma of want and outside, outside—

"Is everything okay in there?"

I don't answer. I can't. If I open my muzzle, it won't close again, not until I've fit the owner of that voice into my mouth, until I have guzzled her down so far her hips bang on the hinges of my jaw, and she's kicking with those skinny legs until I can snap them off at the knee.

Bang.

"Hey, you okay in there?"

My stomach is cavernous. I could hold a village in there; I could eat her whole. I turn, still unsteady on these new legs, but that's okay. I'm still faster. The door, which I'd forgotten to lock, creaks open. Through the slit, I see bottle-blond hair, a pour of hesperidic light across the tiled bathroom floor. I could take her. I could gobble her down right now. I'm hungry as disaster and she smells *sweet* to my newly carnivorous palate.

"Hey? I said you okay in there?"

She smells like fucking up, like a life lesionous with the humble sins of coveting too much, commiting to too little: middle-aged suburban mediocrity is somehow mouthwateringly balsamic. Who the fuck knew? The light makes her pixie cut into a halo, sanctifies the pixie-ish face with its pinched and wary mouth. Her left eyebrow is serrated from when she'd worn piercings there, relics of a life spent squirming from her own nature. Funny how that works. No matter what you do, you come home to you, which, in her case, is a certain quintessential Karen-ness. I can hear it in how she whines my name. Complain until the world submits. Don't bend. Break instead into crocodile tears.

Her mouth is red as a heart on a butcher-block altar, and it comes softly ajar as her eyes meet mine, the stub of her tongue like a doorknob begging a hand to come and wrench its secrets apart.

Why the fuck does she get to grow older when better people can't? Why does she get to live?

My hunger alchemizes into justified cause right as her amygdala torques primacy from the rest of her brain, the conscious mind sequestered somewhere safe while instinct takes stock of the predator in its company, and I grin a salute as her eyes meet mine, the wreck of my face becoming double in the pinpoint dark of her pupils. Drool weeps from my shattered jaw, the fine details of my muzzle still being lathed into shape. My thoughts are an intemperate fusillade: she'd be one less stomach in a starving world, one less fulcrum of waste. The world would be better. The wolf exists to thin the flock. I could just eat her, could just swallow her face-first. I could, I could. *God.* I want to so badly. I should.

I press my furred cheek into her mien, a hideous satirizing of the relationship between pet and owner, the treble of her heartbeat transmitted through the contact. She is terrified. Poor woman, unfortunate lamb, dismal little bunny flushed from her hidey-hole. She isn't moving. She's practically slack, dangling from the meat hook of her spine. It is apparent to us both what her lizard brain has concluded: there really is nowhere to go. Better to play dead, to pray for the snap of a broken neck than the drawn-out decline of a pinned-down body, guts stretched to a nine-course hurt. A shiver chases down her spine, and her eyes squeeze shut. She is whispering: "No, no, no, no, this can't be real, this can't."

It would be so easy.

"*No.*"

And it is my voice, not hers, that grates out the word, a bark that fenestrates into human again halfway through. Whether it is the volume or the cogence of my anger, its incendiary rejection of the impulse to eat, to gorge, to tear, to open, to flatten into a word like *meat*, something in my shout causes the wolf to slough from me. The detritus floods the bathroom floor, a reeking inch-thick film of blistered fat and blackened protein.

"What the fuck?"

I wipe blood from my face.

"What the *fuck*?" she says again.

"I have no idea what you're talking about."

"You—" Her attention swings between points in the lowly lit bathroom.

Already, I can tell she is revising her memory of what happened, correcting herself, the supernatural components ejected in favor of more scientific excuses: a sleight of the light, cheap drugs, anything, anything but the predator breath wet upon her trembling cheek.

"Did the toilet explode? Fuck, did someone stuff the pipes with tampons? What is this shit? Is this shit?"

I shrug, preoccupied with staring at my hands, fingers still slick with afterbirth—after*death*? Macramés of still-wet muscle thread the webbing between each digit. I stare, aware that the world has become irreversibly *different,* and the body in which I woke up is not the same as the one I currently inhabit, that the telemetries of human science are just guesswork, a compass, no more real than the *lupa capitolina* canonized as the wet nurse of Rome. I remember every news article, every half-hour television special, alleging knowledge of how lycanthropy works; talk shows with esteemed scientists clarifying the process, assuring the public that it was revolutionary, yes, but safe, and performed only in controlled environments and only in times of national crisis. Reams of data, tables; excerpts from papers coauthored with legends. Every last one of them clinical in timbre, a choir of rigidly sanitized accounts, and not one fucking story about how something like this can happen, easy as waking up on the first day of being free.

"Did you do this?"

I don't realize she has hands on my shoulders until thirty seconds into her attempt at shaking some sense back into our night. Her face is so close to mine, it wouldn't take much to shear the skin from those high-cheeked bones. A pharyngeal tightness develops, and I press fingers to where the two halves of my jaw intersect. Underneath my touch: a stubbling of what I've come to recognize as teeth.

"Don't," I plant the heel of a palm on the tip of her breast-bone, and push hard, "touch me."

She lets go.

"I don't understand what is going on." The fight slinks from her posture. She weaves in place, almost punch-drunk, pupils blown so wide, there is no color to her eyes save for a perfect oil-slick black. I've seen boxers like this, catatonic but still on their feet, legs yet to receive notice that the battle is over, that this is done, and there is nowhere to go but down. "Are you one of them? Did you go to a war?"

Somewhere in memory, I hear my rougarou laugh: *It's the same war with different names.*

"I'm not."

"Please don't hurt me."

"I think you need to lay off the acid," I tell her, gentler than I thought myself able. She is older than me, and more brittle, fragile, ceramic-like, lacking in the kind of porousness that might allow her to survive this without repercussion. Then again, who am I to judge? I think I'm losing my mind in slow motion too. "You should get some water."

"Tell me what happened."

I run my tongue along its hall of teeth.

"I think it'd be the best for both of us if I didn't."

HER HEART MAY FAIL HER

BY YUMI DINEEN SHIROMA

Mina weaves garlic flowers into Lucy's hair. She starts from the scalp, a French braid, tucking in the stems. The buds poke out: little clouds of purple, virus-shaped, with purple spikes standing out. Lucy's hair is thick and black and it catches on Mina's bitten hands, skin chafed from the cold, nails chewed to a jagged edge.

"I thought I saw her out the window the other night," says Lucy, looking down at the street. A ginkgo tree grows through the sidewalk, dropping its pustules of foul-smelling fruit. Its leaves flutter gold in the afternoon light. Through them, Mina can glimpse the outlines of people passing by in denim and wool.

"You should have called me," Mina says. "I'll check on the wafers, or—"

"No," says Lucy, "that's the thing, it wasn't even her. She turned and I could see her face. It didn't look anything like her. Her head was buzzed on one side. She was walking a dog."

Mina gathers up the remaining strands of Lucy's hair, lifting them away from her neck, revealing the pale curve of her throat. The marks stand out there, white and slightly raised, the tight sheen of skin not yet healed.

"What time?" Mina asks.

"Maybe four p.m.? That's the other thing: I don't think it was dark enough."

"She must love this time of year," says Mina. "Dark all the time and cold as the grave."

Lucy shrugs, makes a sound, and Mina's hand slips, crushing the bud of one of the flowers. Pollen smears along her hand, accompanied by the faint scent of garlic.

"She always seemed happiest in the spring," says Lucy. "Not as many . . . episodes."

"Mm-hmm," Mina says.

Lucy fidgets in her chair, smoothing her skirt down over her thighs. "So I've been thinking . . . If we do it safely, like if I keep this on"——she fingers her crucifix——"and maybe you draw one of those circles, and we bring a big bag of garlic and wave it around . . . ?"

Lucy has recently expressed a desire to "get closure." Mina's protests only seem to strengthen her resolve. Mina doesn't argue anymore, just focuses on maintaining their space. Clearing out the garlic blooms at the farmers' market every Saturday morning, lining the windowsills. Twining the flowers every night around their necks and wrists. And there are the Bibles she stole from the old domed church on 47th and Springfield, gold flaking off its walls: one tucked beneath each of their pillows, one on the ratty living room coffee table, one on the bathroom window ledge. Another warped from the winter damp out on the fire escape, wedged between two of Lucy's plants. And the garlic, always the garlic, roasted with oil and herbs in the oven over an afternoon, mashed into potatoes and butternut soup.

"Uh-huh," Mina says. "We could try that."

"You don't think it's too . . . ?"

"I mean, I guess I'd just want us to have some kind of contingency plan in case—"

"No, no, of course, and I would definitely want to make sure—"

"—because we aren't really sure if she still—"

"—like, I can see why you'd worry—"

"—because if she still—"

"—but I don't really think she affects me like that anymore. I can see why you'd worry. But I've really been better. I'm feeling better. I haven't been having the dreams as much."

Mina doesn't know if it's enough, if any of it will ever be enough. Wave D— away from the porch with a crucifix and a head of garlic and she'll show up the next night with her face at Lucy's window, pale like the moon. The crumbled-up communion wafers summon roaches and mice, the garlic wilts on the windowsill, and she's never known where to find consecrated earth in Philadelphia anyway.

Maybe if none of it works they can get one of those gentrifier apartments in the old renovated church. No one believes in God anymore, Mina included; the city's supply of churches has begun to exceed the demand. A two-bedroom apartment goes for $2,400 a month, arched wood ceilings, a sliver of stained-glass Christ crucified above the fridge. D— would never find Lucy there, would burst into flames the minute she passed through the door.

"All done," Mina says.

Lucy turns, touching her hair. She looks like a May queen, a maenad, a reveler at a music festival in a forest somewhere. The scar on her neck catches the light.

Night, an indeterminate night. Mina startles awake. The trolley roars past on the street below. It's dark, as dark as it gets in the city. Faint glow of streetlamp, shadows thick in the park. The neighbors' dogs are barking on the other side of the duplex wall. Mina never sees them but she hears them every night, barking at someone or defending against something or just making their presence known.

As Mina stumbles to the bathroom, she catches a glimpse of Lucy through the window. She's standing out on the fire escape in boxers and an oversized tee. Crucifix glittering silvery in the hollow of her collarbones. She has that vacant look in her eyes, the sleepwalker's dreamy stance. She's staring out into the night, at something Mina can't see.

Her daily walks through the cemetery used to relax her. Mina prefers it at this time of year: the leaves half-turned, green warring with red. With the recent cold snap they'll be dead in a week, crunching underfoot.

Some of the graves are planters, fuzzy red brains and purple spikes and daisies poking up from the earth as though sprouted from the bodies of the dead. A row of tombs is carved into the hillside. One has had its door cracked open since Mina started walking here a year ago, though an oxidized copper chain still binds it closed. A plastic rose, its stem stuck through the chain, will never decay. Between the cemetery and the hospital, a shopping cart full of a homeless man's things sits abandoned in a sliver of woods.

Mina takes the winding path around. There are tombs with children's faces carved from stone, their features worn away by the slow attrition of time, by acid in the rain. A bronze tomb with a bronze angel shining triumphant on top, raising herself on one pointed foot. One like a Gothic church with spires, one with stained-glass windows glowing brilliant green in the sun, one with gargoyles, and one with battlements on which you can stand and watch the Center City lights wink across the river. An ordinary-looking one where if you peer inside you glimpse a blue glass skylight filtering the light, visible only to voyeurs and the dead.

Mina trails her fingers along the cold metal door. D— sleeps in one of these tombs, and when Mina figures out which one she is going to rip out D—'s throat.

Dinner. Chicken with forty cloves of garlic, celery, parsley, tarragon. A dash of vermouth in the sauce. Lucy plays with her food, shifting it back and forth on her plate, scraping flesh from bone with her butter knife. She is bare-faced today, and you wonder every time if this is because she can no longer see her own face in the glass. (Lucy used to keep a little pencil sketch of herself and D— in her wallet to show in lieu of a photograph. "She's just a little camera-shy," she'd say.)

It's drafty in the apartment today, aging radiators on full blast. Lucy is wearing a gauzy blouse and as she adjusts the neckline, you catch a glimpse of a rash on her skin: a burst of red between her collarbones, where a cross once hung.

You will have to shove a stake through her heart, but you don't own a stake or anything stake-like—unless there's some way to make one, to file down the handle of a wooden spoon—but come to think of it, you don't own a hammer either, and you don't have the upper-body strength. Lucy looks haler than she has in months, skin glowing, a touch of pink in her cheeks, and when she grins her incisors glint in the light.

PART III

OUT OF BODY, OUT OF TIME

Laurel Hausler

THE CHAIR OF TRANQUILITY

(FROM THE DIARY OF MRS. THOMAS PEELE, TRENTON, NEW JERSEY, 1853)

BY **JOYCE CAROL OATES**

So tenderly he wrapt me in warm-wetted sheets, the firmness of his grasp was not immediately evident.

A hood was placed over my head, of some light fabric, like muslin, through which I could see just light & not shapes, a suffusion of light such as one might "see" through closed eyes while facing the sun.

A thicker cloth was bound about my head & covered my mouth in a band. Not tightly—but with a hint, that tightness would ensue, if I took advantage of this courtesy, & cried out for childish attention, as I had been chastised.

This, like the warm-wetted sheets binding my arms against my sides, & securing my legs as I was seated in the Chair of Tranquility, was to pacify my more violent emotions, & my propensity for useless tears; that had led to such impatience, hurt, fury & despair in my husband, he saw no recourse but to bring me to the Asylum at Trenton where (it was believed) an illness such as mine might be cured.

An illness such as mine, in olden days, could not ever be cured. For it was believed to be "demonic"—possession by Satan. But there is a new era now, of moral therapy for female lunacy.

By moral therapy *is meant to an assault against illness, not* "demons." *A campaign waged by the guiding physician, to overcome the illness through the methods of common sense.*

The Chair of Tranquility is a very solid chair, of a size somewhat larger than the ordinary, & a height well above the height of most men.

The Chair of Tranquility is well-cushioned, the soft downy fabric seems to clutch at you, & surround you. Taking your breath away.

The Chair of Tranquility is designed for deep rest, "dozing."

It is true, I did harm to myself. Tearing at my hair & clawing at my face, & rending my garments.

It is true, I did harm to my "beauty." That my "beauty" was not mine to destroy but the possession of my husband was a lesson to be learned.

"Hysteria" is caused by a wandering womb, or broken-off parts of the womb circulating through the arteries, most virulent in the brain.

We were not impoverished like most of the patients at the Asylum. We were of comfortable parentage on both sides & lived in a most prestigious neighborhood south of Trenton. My husband was himself a physician, of general medicine, & had heard of the "revolutionary" ideas of the new director of the Asylum for Female Lunatics at Trenton, Dr. Silas Weir, in the cure of women's madness.

For we were of a (joint) wish, to have children. Heirs.

This vow, I had made in all but actual words, in marrying my husband at the altar of the First Presbyterian Church of Trenton.

Love, honor, & obey. In sickness as in health. Till death, part.

Yet, the crazed laughter bubbled up in me. There was released a frenzied kicking of my legs. If Mr. Peele should approach me in his nightgown on hands & knees like a panting beast. Kicked, kicked & kicked, biting my lower lip until it bled onto the white linen of the marital bed.

Arrangements were made. Arrangements between men. There are none other except arrangements between men.

My father too. Badly he wished a grandson. Grandchildren. Heirs.

There is little point to life, without heirs.

There is little point in accumulating wealth, except to leave to heirs.

God ordains. God commands, Increase & multiply!

My father, & Mr. Peele, & Dr. Weir. Arrangements were made, there was no need for my presence.

Private care, at private rates. In the State Asylum at Trenton, there would be a private wing, on the third floor of North Hall, for patients requiring special care under the auspices of Silas Weir.

None of us in private care would be required to brave the swarm of female lunatics in the dining hall, & none of us would be pressed into moral therapy *in the laundry, or the kitchen, or the latrines, or with* mop & pail *scrubbing the floors.*

We never saw. We never heard their shrieks. We never smelled their stench. We entered the facility, & exited the facility, by a special entrance reserved for private patients.

Our fates were decided by our husbands & fathers. Our fates were decided by handshakes.

Handshakes between the men behind the closed door. But you are free to imagine.

Your hand is too soft & the bones are sparrow bones. Crushed & broken in the man's handshake. You dare not risk.

Mrs. Peele!—you must lie still.

In his soft nasal voice instructing me. Through the muslin hood I could not see his face.

You must not resist, *it is a woman's duty to* submit. *You must meditate as a flower meditates. Each of the petals, in perfect stillness.*

The face of a clock whose hands have stopt. For in the Chair of Tranquility, time ceases to exist.

Do not think, do not recall. Do not summon back printed pages—

books. Your schoolbooks, these were in error. A girl-child does not need books. A girl-child of good family, of golden-haired beauty.

Rhyming verse, this is (sometimes) allowed. Verse carefully chosen for women, which will not excite or agitate them.

Do not allow (unrhyming) words to penetrate your consciousness. No more than tossing stones into a woodland pond. No more than tossing coals onto a pristine covering of snow. No more than shouting rudely in church.

Do not think, thinking is not natural in women. Do not think, thinking is harmful in women.

Thinking too freely led unhappy Eve to pick the fatal apple from the tree, to press upon Adam her husband, to incriminate him in her sin of disobedience.

It has been prescribed that for eight to ten weeks, depending upon your progress you will be seated very still in the Chair of Tranquility through the day. You will lie very still in the Bed of Tranquility through the night.

At all times, warm-wetted sheets will bind you. Your eyes will be closed, your mouth will be stilled. Your frenzied limbs cannot break free & will soon surrender. Your heart cannot race wild & crazed & will soon surrender.

If still the nervous womb becomes dislodged & sends its particles of disease to all part of the female body, most perniciously in the brain, a more drastic treatment will be added: the Waters of Tranquility.

Very gently, lowered into warm-lapping waves, while bound in the Chair of Tranquility. Five-foot copper tubs, kept at a temperature soothing to the skin. An attendant at all times, to prevent an accidental submergence.

Hydrotherapy, so-called, is a more risky measure than Tranquility, though it is an extension of Tranquility. It is not a punishment, though it may be necessary to quell the mutinous womb.

No, you will not drown! It is foolish, silly, childish, futile to fret over such a fate!—that will not happen, not under the watchful eye of Silas Aloysius Weir.

If you were a common lunatic, plucked out of anonymity, there might be reason to fret—but you are not common, your husband is paying a hefty fee (privately) to Dr. Weir. Thus, you are protected. As the common lunatics are not protected.

You will be protected by the spirit of Tranquility, as the male of the species is protected by the spirit of Activity.

The soul of the female, which is passivity & placidity; the soul of the male, which is activity & restive.

The soul of the female, best realized in rest; the soul of the male, best expressed in motion.

The flesh of the female, soft, yielding, ample, boneless; the flesh of the male, hard-muscled, strong-boned, & quick in reflex.

As it is unnatural for the male to exult in stillness, so it is unnatural for the female to express herself in motion.

In bed, abed, bedded, embedded; marching, hiking, riding (horses), & hunting.

In the Chair of Tranquility, you will consume eight meals a day. In calmness, in no hurry, you will chew your food following the Weir method, which necessitates chewing solid foods no less than 32 times until they are liquefied.

Never will you swallow any "solid" particles of food: you will only swallow liquid.

Rich broths & cream soups will be brought to you. You will consume butter, milk, specially prepared eggs, & rich breads & pastries. The hood will be removed, the cloth about your mouth will be removed, you will be fed by an attendant, you need not use your own hands.

As you are grievously underweight, & of a risk for childbirth, it is prescribed for you to gain 30-35 pounds.

You will become (again) an infant in the womb, to be nourished, to exult in absolute stillness as your (female) soul swells about you.

You will be given medications, prescribed particularly for you, & prepared by the hand of Dr. Weir, out of his own herbal medications.

In the treatment of hysteria it is recommended that calomel be ingested, several times a day. Calomel (mercury) will be in granule form, sprinkled on bread & covered with a thin coating of butter or honey.

In the treatment of female frigidity & barrenness, it is recommended that St. John's wort, black cohosh, castor oil, & milk thistle be administered in carefully regulated doses.

In the treatment of a spasmodic agitation of the limbs, to no purpose save agitation, a daily dosage of laudanum, to be increased if muscular agitation persists.

Never need you fear that the medications you receive will be bitter tasting. All of the medications you receive will have a tincture of sweetness.

You are privileged. You are blessed. Providence has brought you to Silas Aloysius Weir.

Repeat:

I will not read for a period of 6 to 8 weeks. I will not write for a period of 6 to 8 weeks. I will not imagine writing letters to my cousins, my friends, my mother, begging for me to be released from this horror of swaddling & suffocation.

I will not speak for a period of 6 to 8 weeks. I will not plead, scream, beg for mercy or release.

I will not agitate my brain for a period of 6 to 8 weeks.

I will not need to "relieve" myself—a nursemaid will see to it, that my bedpan is emptied whenever necessary & scoured clean.

Yes, I am very, very sorry that I clawed at my face. For my face was not mine to claw.

Yes, I am very, very sorry that I screamed & laughed & thrashed & kicked in spasms of madness in the sanctity of the marital bed.

In Tranquility I will drift to a place beyond words. In Tranquility I will exult.

In Tranquility I will gain 42 pounds of dense white flesh packed beneath my chin, swelling my belly, hanging from my thighs & from my bosom like great udders.

I will have a caregiver at all times. I will have a nursemaid to answer all my needs.

At all times repeat to yourself:

I am unique, I am in the care of Silas Aloysius Weir, a unique practitioner & pioneer of GynoPsychiatry.

When I am cured of my illness, I will be returned home to my husband. Only then will I be returned home to my husband to conceive our first son & heir.

In the interim, I have faith in Providence & in Silas Aloysius Weir, MD.

This, from a diary discovered among the personal possessions of Mrs. Thomas Peele, of 228 Lakeview Drive, Trenton, in April 1853, following her sudden death after her release from the Asylum at Trenton the previous week.

It did not seem to be known if the patient had died as a result of having gained forty-two pounds during her hospitalization, thus swelling her belly, torso, upper arms, and the flesh beneath her chin, which came to resemble a monstrous goiter, and placing a great strain on organs already weakened from weeks of inactivity; or whether, by some devious female method of overindulging in the daily dosage of laudanum prescribed for her by her physician, the unhappy woman had contrived to take her own life.

THE SEVENTH BRIDE, OR FEMALE CURIOSITY

BY **ELIZABETH HAND**

Livey played the seventh bride, her predecessors represented on the Royal Camden's stage by a series of macabre mannequins, three of them skeletal, the others papier-mâché, cloth, and wax figures depicting persons in varying stages of decay. Georgie Pye appeared opposite her nightly as Bluebeard. But not the towering, dark-skinned terrorizer of most versions of the play, shouting as his delicate helpmeet cowered before him, the gold key clutched in her trembling hand while his own raised the sword that would fall upon her smooth white neck.

"Foul woman! One thing only I asked of you, not to visit this room—and you have disobeyed me!"

And so on, the meek wife saved at the last moment when her sister (or brother, or mother; in one version a valiant passing troubadour) charges onstage and stabs the wicked murderer with a dagger.

Georgie Pye's Bluebeard didn't shout, or even tower. Scarcely taller than the actresses who had played the seventh bride (Livey was not the first), he wore high-heeled boots that added several inches to his slender frame. From the stalls he resembled a wiry sapling rather than a great oak, which made his success in the role even more mystifying. Slender, long-limbed, with handsome though delicate features and his own dark curls, rather than the fuliginous wigs favored by other actors in the role, Pye made an unlikely yet appealing murderer. His eyes heavily kohled, a touch of rouge on his cheeks, a gold bangle in one ear, he seemed more Blackbeard the pirate, an effect underscored by his (false) beard, which was small and pointed as a flint arrowhead. And not the deep indigo of most Bluebeard's, but an improbably bright peacock hue. Black trousers, a black tailcoat lined with peacock-blue satin, peacock-plumed hat borrowed from the actress who'd played Puss in Boots in the pantomime earlier that year. The oddity of his appearance was undoubtedly part of Georgie Pye's appeal, especially to female audience members. Bluebeard, usually a blusterer who from his first entrance intimidates his new bride, now seemed shy, gentle even. You could see why his previous wives fell in love with him, even imagine it might not be so bad to meet the thrust of the curved sword he wielded in the dungeon where their corpses hung.

Some people (mostly men) assumed that, offstage, he was an invert.

Not the case.

"You will take over for Jeanne tonight," the theater manager announced when Livey showed up for work. Her usual turn was as a dancing flower in *Harlequin's Honey Moon,* the playlet that preceded *Bluebeard, or Female Curiosity.*

Livey stared at him, alarmed but not surprised. "What about Doris?"

"Doris has taken unwell. She'll remain that way for some

time. I'll raise your wage, don't worry," he added. "Don't be alone with him, I can't afford to hire someone new and you're the only one the costume fits."

"I don't know the words!"

"Scream and sigh, Livey dear, that's all it is. Have your friend Roger walk you home after."

Doris had left because she was with child. Georgie Pye's baby. Everyone at the Camden Royal knew that Georgie wasn't a Molly but a bad shilling. Three actresses had left now in an interesting condition, and another two because Georgie's attentions had become over-avid, even violent. The house manager turned a blind eye—these things happened often enough. To be sure, at first Doris had willingly gone to Georgie's dressing room, little more than a closet with a mirror.

"He's married, Doris," Livey had warned her. "A wife and son in Blackheath."

"Two sons now." Doris wiggled her fingers, feigning alarm. "They bore him, he says he'll put me up in my own flat on Delancey Street."

Instead, Doris had left without a farewell to Livey or anyone else. Roger, the stagehand who moved the backdrops and scenery, operated the traveling curtains and also the trapdoor through which Bluebeard made his appearance, confided in Livey that Doris intended to see a specialist doctor.

"Oh, I hope not," Livey said, stricken. Another of Georgie's girls had died after such a visit.

"I'm sure she'll be sensible," Roger assured her. "She should have have been so before."

"Nothing to do with sense," snapped Livey. She loathed Georgie, with his tin charm and claques of charladies tossing him daisies and pinks from the gods.

Roger took her hand. "You have me, Livey. You don't need to fear him."

She'd climbed the ladder to the fly tower to join him before her debut performance. She and Roger intended to marry in the autumn, when he'd saved enough money and Livey got around to telling her sister and brother-in-law, whose flat she shared on Pratt Street.

"I hate him," she said, staring down at the set where the six mannequins hung from heavy manila rope. "I don't fear him."

What she did fear was the mannequins: ghastly figures, they terrified her even more than real corpses she'd seen. A naked man drowned in the Regents Canal, bloated like a spoiled sausage, tongue a curded yellow where it protruded from between his slack lips. Another man, very young and handsome, slumped on Pleasant Row; a sodomite, or unlucky enough to be mistaken for one.

And there had been corpses she knew when they were alive. Her mother had died when she was very young and she had no memory of that, but she'd seen a grandfather, her father, an uncle all laid out in parlors.

But no women. The sight of Bluebeard's wives dangling from the flies made Livey's hands itch with fear—she longed to remove her gloves so she could scratch them. The three skeletons were horrible because real: real bones, from a real woman, purchased at considerable expense from a resurrection man who plied his trade at Old St. Pancras. That was the first skeleton, its costume a shredded dress stiff with red paint. Real bones comprised the second skeleton too, though they came from different women.

"Not as costly," Georgie Pye had told Livey one day when he found her hurrying past the grisly shapes. She'd arrived late and hadn't yet changed into her flower costume. He'd accosted her, recognizing her fear as she darted around the expansive pool of stage blood—glycerine and carmine dye, speckled with dust and dead flies—in her anxiety to avoid the mannequins, and Georgie himself. "But it was difficult to match all the different bones—some were from a very large woman. But this one—"

His long fingers grasped a leg bone of the second skeleton, marbled brown and black. "See, this is from a much smaller person, probably a girl like yourself. She must've died a long time ago, that's why her bones are so discolored. They didn't bother bleaching them, like this one—"

He'd taken Livey's hand and pulled her after him, gently but irresistibly. "See how white she is? They bleached these bones then reassembled them. This one I think is from a horse," he went on, frowning as he ran his free hand along a skeletal arm, flicking at the blue ribbons twined around it. "But the rib cage is definitely a person's."

"I have to go," Livey gasped. She pulled free, and heard Georgie's amused voice as she fled to her dressing area.

"Timor mortis," he called. She didn't understand the first word but knew that mortis meant death. Rigor mortis—someone had used the term after her father died. They'd had to break his arms to dress him in his burial suit.

The other figures were worse. Wax faces, one had glass eyes that lolled in their sockets, lidless, with pupils blue-gray as eel skin, cheeks gouged so that clots of wax, daubed with cochineal, drooped to its jaw. The next mannequin wore a bridal gown, white lace spattered with red, the bodice torn so the audience had a glimpse of ice-white flesh, porcelain not wax, but from the stalls it looked like real skin. The skin had been flensed from her neck in ribbons. Ragged pink satin, again alarmingly realistic, spiraling away from the bones of her neck—a white ladder leading to a skull with jaws wired open in a scream.

The sixth and last bride terrified Livey more than the others combined. It resembled a real woman who had recently been alive, its face that of a large doll, perhaps a shop mannequin's, pink cheeks and eyes closed as if in sleep. A wig of dark curls perched atop the doll's life-sized head, topped by a black bonnet, and it wore a plain slate-blue dress very like Livey's own best dress, padded beneath with old sheets to suggest layers of undergarments. The Camden Royal Theatre, despite its name, had a very limited costume budget.

Livey couldn't describe what it was about this figure that gave her nightmares. She'd tried once, with Roger.

"Is it because the dress is like yours?" he asked, bemused. "We could buy you another one."

"It's not that," she'd said, though in part it was. "I think it's because it still has skin on it. It hasn't rotted yet. It makes me think that he's just killed her."

"He doesn't kill *you*—I mean, Jeanne," Roger corrected himself quickly, "your part. He gets killed instead. It's all very happy at the end."

"I suppose. But please come fetch me as soon as I change afterward." She'd only been performing as Jeanne for a week, another girl having taken over the flower in *Harlequin's Honey Moon,* and already Georgie Pye had furtively bumped against her onstage, rubbing against her leg.

"I'll be there. Of course." He blew a kiss at her and headed backstage.

But he wasn't there when Livey finally left the dressing room. The other girls had gone home long ago, along with the other players, the audience, the two boys who worked under Roger, raising and lowering the battens and the flying rig used by the Conjuror in *Harlequin*.

Livey waited impatiently, cracking the door to peer out. She knew Roger wouldn't have forgotten. The manager might have waylaid him, or there might have been a problem with the flying rig, which had nearly dropped Mr. Spale, who at twenty stone made an imposing soaring Conjuror but an unwieldy one.

She headed toward the manager's office. The quickest way took her backstage, which meant she could look for Roger.

"Roger?" she called out, peering through the shadows. The chandeliers in the house had been extinguished after the audience left, but a single gaslight still guttered on the dungeon set. The Camden Royal was famous for the depth of its stage, rivaled only by that of the Royal Marylebone; ideal for transformation scenes and flying rigs (as well as flying rugs; the Camden Royal presented a wonderful *Ali Baba* one Christmastime), less so for unaccompanied young women having to traverse its mucky boards late at night. "Roger, are you there?"

"*I'm* here."

Someone wrapped his arms around her, pressed his hand lightly over her mouth, and pulled her behind the painted flat, to the cyclorama. Georgie Pye, now in his street clothes, a garish blue-and-green check jacket and matching trousers. He'd dressed too quickly and carelessly, with no tie and his collar askew. Before she could protest or question him, he pushed her against the back wall of the theater, one hand still on her mouth, the other fumbling at his trousers. She tried to kick him, hindered by her skirts, which he now tugged at. When she attempted to scream, he flattened his hand so his palm covered not just her mouth but also her nostrils, so she couldn't breathe. She could feel his hand groping at the place between her thighs; how could he even find it amid all that cloth?

Because he's done it before, she thought. To Doris and Amelia and Lydia and Clara and Bridget . . .

His mouth opened, he moved his hand—he was trying to kiss her. Livey spat at him and he laughed. In a rage, she pushed at him, felt his weight shift, off-balance. With all her strength she shoved him to one side, slipping from his hands as he spun and struck the brick wall.

Not the wall: the foot-long iron spike protruding from between two of the bricks. Usually it held a long coil of manila rope that weighed as much as Livey did, but the rope had been removed. Georgie Pye's head smacked against its point with enough force that it pierced his skull. Livey watched as the spike emerged from one eye, the metal filigreed with bits of pinkish mince and a translucent jelly that darkened as blood seeped from around the spike. Georgie's other eye rolled, as though he was exasperated that she'd forgotten her line (again). His mouth gaped and she saw blood filming his teeth, a red line drawn between the corner of his mouth and his lower jaw so that he resembled a marionette she had once seen outside Covent Garden, as tall as a child. The marionette had jumped up and down, chanting, "I saw yers, I saw yers," in a thin frantic tone while Livey clapped her hands over her ears.

Georgie Pye didn't jump, didn't make a peep, he didn't move at all. He was dead.

"Timor mortis," whispered Livey.

"Livey! Are you—"

She took a deep breath as Roger ran up alongside her. "My god," he said. He'd gone white as a sheet of canvas.

"He accosted me." She spoke the words as though reading from a timetable.

"But you . . . He's dead."

"I didn't kill him. He fell against that—" She pointed at Georgie, his head impaled upon the spike, the rest of him beginning to sag from the body's weight.

Roger stared at the corpse, then at Livey. "We need to get the police."

"Why? They'll arrest me. Probably you too."

"But you said you didn't kill him."

"I didn't. But they won't believe me." She thought of poor Lydia, splayed upon the floor, a doctor tugging a homunculus from between her legs as Lydia breathed through a cloth soaked with ether. And Bridget, sent to a laundry back in Ulster.

"Then what—"

Livey set a finger to her lips, turned, and walked around the backdrop for the dungeon. She stood and regarded the half dozen women hanging there: not dead, they were the fortunate ones. She stepped over to the one that had so frightened her, in its limp black dress and sad bonnet. She removed her gloves and began to unbutton the dress, wishing she had a button hook. There was one in the dressing area, but no time.

"Come here, Roger," she called in a low voice.

She didn't need to explain to him—one of the many things she loved about Roger. The two of them undressed the mannequin, Livey careful about where the dress and bonnet fell. She tossed aside the bundles of sheets and soiled blankets, wrinkling her nose at the old smells of perspiration and sour milk they'd absorbed in an earlier life. She let Roger remove the porcelain head, eyeless and mouthless, its smooth cheeks smeared with rouge, a crushed spider stuck to one temple. Livey shuddered, pointing to where he should set it with the padding.

Next they removed Georgie Pye from the wall. Livey held his head firmly between her hands, eyes squeezed shut and teeth gritted as she pulled it toward her, pretending she was sliding an oversized cooked apple from a skewer. The head did not come smoothly from the spike—it must have caught on the broken eggshell of Georgie's skull. She yanked again, tears streaming from her eyes as Roger supported the body, hugging it to him like she'd seen men hug their drunken friends. At last something tore loose inside and the head flopped down, a bit sideways but still mostly intact. Livey didn't look at the back of the skull, the front was bad enough. Pretend it's strawberry jam, she thought, which almost made her gag, but then she thought of his hands going up her skirts. I'm glad, she thought instead.

They undressed him behind the backdrop, in the near dark. No time to worry about someone finding them there, no time to talk. She breathed through her nose, a superstitious fear of inhaling some miasma, though she could only smell herself and Roger's tobacco breath, the faint acrid scent from the gas chandelier high above the stalls. She rolled Georgie's outer clothes in a bundle, gazed at his wool long johns. They reeked of fresh urine.

She recoiled in distaste, as Roger quickly removed them. For a moment she stared at the wormy thing at Georgie's groin, the hairy plums to either side. All for that? She grimaced and got back to her feet.

Dressing the body took a bit longer, mostly because of the buttons. They jammed his feet into the boots worn by the sixth bride—supple leather, fortunately, they didn't bother to lace them all the way up.

"What about his face?" asked Roger, the first time either of them had spoken.

Without replying, Livey hiked her skirts and raced to the dressing area. She returned with a pot of face paint and powder from Harlequin's dressing table. She smoothed the white paste over Georgie Pye's face, dusted it thickly with powder; applied rouge to his cheeks and lips. Pressed a wad of cotton into his mouth to absorb the blood, of which there was very little. Brains didn't bleed, she supposed.

She tugged the curly black wig onto Georgie's head. There was no hiding the hole in his eye, or the flap of flesh like raw bacon that hung beneath it. But really, that only added to the intended effect.

"It looks very realistic," said Livey.

"It does," agreed Roger,

Another quarter hour and the sixth bride had been hoisted onto its hook. Livey and Roger stepped back to regard their work.

"Can you tell?" she asked.

"No. No one will notice. Not till it starts to smell."

"When will that be?"

He shrugged and looked around the vast space, the trailing drapery and Harlequin's glitter curtain, the vast tidy web of ropes and rigging, blocks and tackle, huge painted canvases and flats, some as tall as a house and decorated like a palace, or dungeon or moonlit canal. "Well, it's cold, so that will help. A few days, at least. Maybe longer if it snows." He reached for her hand. "I'm sorry I wasn't there. Robbie got sick, I had to clean up after him and strike the set alone."

"Is he alright?"

"I think so. Catarrh."

"We can say that Georgie caught it from him and won't be able to perform. You can write a note and leave it in the office."

Roger frowned. "What about us?"

"I don't know yet."

They returned backstage and finished cleaning up. Roger looped the thick coil of manila rope back onto the spike, patting it. Livey returned the cosmetics she'd borrowed and retraced her steps, looking for any sign of struggle. Other than a few spots of blood on the floor, there was only a chunk of black hair on the spike, which she wrapped in a handkerchief. Anything else would be taken for part of the set, she thought approvingly.

Roger left a note for the manager, imitating Georgie Pye's handwriting, saying that he was feeling unwell. They might want to consider canceling tomorrow night's performance of *Bluebeard* so he could recover. Then he and Livey left the theater together, as they often did, Livey with the bundle of old sheets hidden beneath her shawl. They walked alongside the canal path, also their usual route, pausing several times to drop one of the pieces of fabric into the noisome black water.

"Here, puss," Livey called softly when she spied a stray cat sitting on the wall beside the path. The cat blinked, observing her with wary yellow eyes as Livey set the bit of scalp bristling with black hairs onto the brick. Livey continued walking, and when she looked back, she saw the cat swiftly leap upon the tidbit and carry it off.

Late the following afternoon, Livey arrived at the theater. The manager met her at the door.

"You're off tonight. Georgie's taken ill."

"Oh dear. Is it serious?"

"Probably the itch," the manager said with a grimace. "I

think we'll start rehearsing *Ali Baba* again next month. I'm a family man, I don't like that sort of behavior. I'm sorry about your wages. But your lad Roger says the two of you are off to be married on Saturday. I gather he's found work up in Bedford-shire. I gave him a shilling, he's a good man."

"Yes, he is!" exclaimed Livey, pinking. "And thank you, perhaps we'll come see *Ali Baba*."

Livey and Roger did marry, though not so quickly as Saturday. They moved to Leigh-on-Sea, not Bedfordshire, where he found work as a bargeman and Livey gave elocution lessons. After ten months, they moved again, to a small farmstead near Stroud Green. Georgie himself was discovered, though not for several weeks—there had indeed been a cold snap, and the players were so absorbed in breaking in the actor who took over Georgie's part that no one noticed the stench until one of the *Harlequin* singers complained.

"Wasn't that the play you were in?" Livey's sister asked when she visited the following year. "*Bluebeard?*"

Livey nodded, shuddering. "Yes," she said, and nestled the baby closer to her breast. "But it was far too gruesome for the likes of me."

NEMESIS

BY **VALERIE MARTIN**

When Maurice returned from college that summer, he was accompanied by a school friend, Eric Jeffrey, whom he had invited to stay with us for the long vacation.

My youngest daughter, Cici, came out to welcome her brother. She is like a young animal, high-spirited, destructive, and fond of her own way. Her attention is erratic, ever flickering from one object to another, but when Eric Jeffrey dismounted from his horse and stood casually brushing the front of his riding coat with the backs of his fingers, Cici fell silent and absolutely still.

He appeared to be made of solid gold. His thick curling hair was spun gold, his complexion was gold beaten thin as paper, and his eyes had the greenish gold of verdigris patina on copper, lustrous yet opaque, like a lion's eyes. There was something leonine in his build, wide shoulders, narrow hips, a powerful and muscular physique, elegant even in his rumpled coat and doeskin breeches. He took Cici in with a glance and smiled broadly. I was relieved to discover that his teeth weren't gold but white and even. "You must be Cici," he said.

Cici, flustered, lowered her eyes, stepping back like a child.

"You didn't tell me your sister is shy," Eric said to Maurice, who, having handed off his horse to the groom, now joined his friend. To the breathless Cici, he added, "Your brother says you are as wild as an ocelot."

Cici sent her brother a sharp, reproving look, but Maurice only laughed and said, "This is my friend Eric. I've been telling him about you all the way from Virginia."

So Eric Jeffrey came among us, with his easy ways and confident address. Maurice clearly thought him a superior being. I wasn't inclined to disagree, but I detected beneath the genial good manners a detachment that puzzled me. It was as if he watched himself charming us. When I mentioned this to my husband, who had taken to the young man at once, he pointed out that our family society was so small and intimate that our guest must necessarily feel himself an outsider.

At dinner, Eric explained that he was an avid hunter, and that Maurice's effusive description of the plentiful sport available in our vicinity had persuaded him to pass his school holiday far from his home in Boston, where his father "has a bank." He personally found everything about banking repugnant. He had abandoned accounting for medical studies. "I'm fascinated by everything to do with the human body," he concluded.

I saw my husband's eyebrows lift and his mouth compress at this remark, which was inappropriate in the presence of young ladies, but I thought it a revealing confession. Cici, who at fifteen would never be sillier, put down her fork and said, "I couldn't agree more. Everything about the human body is fascinating. Just this afternoon I was thinking how much I enjoy having hands." And she raised her pretty hands, waggling the fingers before her eyes.

Eric cast her the mild, uncomprehending look we were to

see often in the weeks that followed, and my husband, now visibly displeased, said, "Cici, do shut up." Then he turned to Maurice. "What rifles will you be using tomorrow?" thereby changing the subject from the marvels of the human body to the more acceptable topic of animal slaughter.

That night Cici followed me to my dressing room, her feet fairly dancing on the smooth oak boards of the hall. Inside, she closed the door carefully and said in her breathless voice, "Oh Mamère, isn't he divine?"

"He's very attractive," I said. "And much too old for you."

"I don't think so," she replied.

"Don't let your father see you mooning around after him. And don't embarrass Maurice."

"I don't moon," said my daughter.

"You sat there with your mouth ajar. And what was that foolishness about your hands?"

"It wasn't foolish. What he said was true, and I had really just thought this afternoon, when I was watching Bugle try to hold a bone between his paws, that it is just such a wonderful gift to have hands."

I sat down at my dressing table and began unfastening my hair. "It's not so wonderful if the hands are always idle."

"It wasn't foolish," she repeated. "Did you see how he looked at me? He thought it was a most interesting thing for a young lady to say."

So I understood that Cici was going to make a fool of herself and wouldn't see what was right in front of her eyes, which was that Eric Jeffrey had no real interest in anyone but himself.

I was never beautiful, though my children are. At my best, I was plain. As a child, I contracted smallpox, which left a line of pitted scars across my jaw and chin. Sadly, this remnant of childhood is now the least of my deformities. Five years ago I suffered a brain fever that left me partially paralyzed on my right side. My mouth drags down and the muscles around my right eye don't respond, which gives me a ghastly affect. My body, after bearing three children, is stout and flaccid, and I don't bother with the wretched stays and laces that young women are expected and willing to tolerate. I dress in loose gowns of my own manufacture, capacious and many-pocketed, made of fabrics appropriate to the season. My good husband approves of my industry and invention, as his fondest wish is for my comfort and ease. Bless him; he still looks on me with steady affection.

But beauty loves only beauty, and I knew that in spite of his elaborate courtesy, Eric Jeffrey was offended by the sight of me.

At dinner, that first night, his eyes carefully coasted past me until I felt pity for him. He clearly wanted and expected to charm every one of us, but he couldn't bring himself to look steadily at my face. This incapacity allowed me to observe him without the distraction of conversation. I said very little, though I had many thoughts. As Cici nattered on about the provenance of a hair ornament Eric admired, I noticed that his eyes drifted from her coiffure to the windowpane just past her right ear. For a moment I thought he was distracted by something moving outside, something he was evidently pleased to see, for his expression softened as a mother's might when her dearest babe toddles into view. It was a few moments before I realized that what engaged him so agreeably was his own reflection. This unconscious display of personal vanity so surprised me that I expelled a little huff of amusement. Eric heard this, and as he turned abruptly toward me, our eye-beams crossed at last. In that exchange, I believe, hostilities were declared.

"I don't trust that young man," I said to my husband when we retired for the night.

"He seems an amiable fellow," replied this credulous soul.

"Mark my words," I said.

He grinned. It was a joke between us. Charles is often cheated by devious business cronies whose unscrupulousness is apparent to me long before he recognizes that he has been too trusting. I dread what might become of our daughters should they be left solely in their father's care. Even Maurice would need protection, as he shares his father's too-ready reliance on the good intentions of his fellow men.

My husband laid his hand on my shoulder and bent to kiss my brow. "Iris," he said, "don't be so suspicious."

"Mark my words," I said again.

A few days after his arrival, the post brought a letter for Eric from his father, or so I presumed—the sender was Alton Jeffrey, and the postmark was Boston. I laid the envelope inside the folded napkin at the breakfast table so that I might see his expression when he found it.

Maurice is an early riser, as am I. Since his childhood we have enjoyed our café au lait in the early morning light while the birds chitter outside and the air is at its coolest. Now that he's away much of the year, I miss those companionable hours. Often he told me of his reading, which changed as he did, from romances and fables to texts on botany and biology, or occasionally ancient history.

My husband was next up, followed by Henriette, Cici, and

our guest, in that order. Eric came in, still dazed from sleep, and went directly to the coffee urn—he has taken to our coffee with chicory as quickly as he has to my daughters—where he filled his cup with milk and coffee, stirred in a spoon of sugar, and turned upon us his irresistible smile. "Good morning, all," he said.

Cici tore off a piece from the baguette and set it on his side plate. Henriette took up the jam pot and passed it across the table so that it would be near to his hand. Eric pulled out his chair and took his seat, lowering the cup and saucer to the cloth. When he reached for his napkin, his fingers found the unexpected brittleness of the paper. I watched him closely, focusing his sleepy gaze on his own name written in a strong masculine script across the creamy vellum—it was expensive stationery. A momentary flash of something that wasn't pleasure passed his lips, his nostrils flared, and his eyes went cold. Conscious that he had the attention of everyone at the table (save my husband, who was slathering his bread with butter), he smiled and, tapping the letter against the edge of his plate, said, "My father. At last."

That day, the young people were much occupied in preparations for a dance at my cousin Adele's. In the afternoon, I coaxed them to walk to the cutting garden and gather flowers, some for the girls' hair ornaments and others for Adele, who loves roses but has no luck growing them. Cici was in a crisis about her gown, which required some last-minute alteration, and Maurice was distracted by an unusual butterfly he wished to capture for his collection; he always has his collecting bottle with him, though he had no net. So when we reached the pool at the edge of the garden, only Eric and Henriette were with me. It's a lovely spot, an oblong of smooth, dark water, hemmed in by a half circle of flat stone on one side and a bank of wild forget-me-nots and alyssum spread in a colorful carpet on the other. To Eric's question about its history, Henriette replied, "It's called Treasure Pool, but I don't know why."

"Is there treasure in it?" Eric asked.

"There might be," I told him, though actually I knew there wasn't. The original owner of this property was Alphonse Trésor, hence the name. "The story is that some bank robbers threw a bag of gold there for safekeeping, but couldn't retrieve it because the pond is too deep."

Eric cast me a glittery look. An affected smile disguised his interest.

"I've never heard that story," Henriette commented.

"It was a long time ago," I said.

Eric took a few steps out on the stones and gazed down into the still, dark water. He tilted his head to one side, brushing his hair back with his hand. *He's looking at his reflection,* I thought.

"Maurice likes to bathe here," Henriette informed our guest. "But it's spring fed and the water is too cold for me."

Maurice appeared on the path, holding aloft his collecting bottle in which a captive flapped its last. "I caught it in my hands," he declared.

Later, as we were returning, laden with blooms, Eric hung back with Henriette, teasing and dallying with her. She was a fountain of giggles and sighs. I stopped to adjust my bonnet. Glancing back, I saw that he had passed his arm around her waist.

The festivities at Adele's house went on until nearly dawn. I didn't enjoy myself, as I spent the evening watching Eric Jeffrey's attempts to seduce both of my daughters and Adele's pretty niece Lisette into the bargain. Adele took me aside to ask about him. "He's a charming young man," she said. "What do you know about his family?"

"Very little," I admitted. "The father's in banking."

"That sounds promising," she said.

"He could be a clerk, for all I know."

"But he attends college with Maurice. That's not something a clerk could afford."

"Perhaps he's a scholarship boy."

We watched Lisette's lithe figure whirl by in the arms of this mysterious youth. "It might be a good idea to find out," Adele said.

I couldn't have agreed more. Eric was secretive about his family. He'd had no communication from them beyond that one letter, which seemed to have disturbed him. He took it away to read in his room and didn't come out for some time. I assumed he was writing a reply, but when I asked if he had letters to post, he said no.

Everyone slept late the next morning. When we were all gathered, Maurice put forward a plan to take the open carriage to the old fort and have a picnic lunch there among the ruins. Henriette and Cici went off to the kitchen to pack a basket and Maurice went out to the barn to alert the groom to their intentions. This left me sitting over coffee with Eric, whom I assumed would make some excuse and slip away. To my surprise, he refilled his cup at the urn and returned to his seat opposite me.

"It's a fine day for a picnic," I said.

He laughed at this, pulling his collar open with two fingers as if throwing off grievous restraints. "Yes," he agreed, "blessedly overcast."

I attempted to engage him with a series of questions. His manner was dutiful, courteous, with an earnestness I recognized as disingenuous. I pretended concern for my son's progress at college, though I knew Maurice was solidly at the top of his class. I inquired more deeply into Eric's father's view of his studies, and received the banking-versus-medicine comparison. He was clearly so appalled to find himself in the near vicinity of a body as unappealing as mine that the effort to disguise his discomfort forced from him the occasional honest answer. "Banking is a soulless enterprise, Mrs. LeClerc," he said. "Everything is reduced to transactions and investments. It kills the spirit. Don't you agree?"

"Oh yes," I said. "Medicine offers far more in the way of both mental and moral challenges."

He considered this. "Just between you and me, medicine doesn't interest me that much either."

"So you're not *particularly* fascinated by the human body?"

He gave me a blank look, trying to connect my question to his casual remark. Then it dawned on him that I was referring to his dinner repartee. For some reason this pleased him and his expression softened. "Well," he said, "I think the young ladies like that idea."

I rested my chin in my palm, stretching my free hand to tap his sleeve in the manner of a flirtatious confidante. "Don't worry, your secret is safe with me."

At the touch of my fingers, he recoiled, drawing his arm away. "I really must change for this expedition," he said, pushing back his chair.

* * *

The picnic party rode off in good spirits, though Cici cast me an anxious look as she tripped across the drive to the carriage. Eric had taken the seat next to Henriette. I smiled and waved until they turned off at the road. I had made up my mind to investigate Eric's room and read the letter from his father. I knew that once my husband left for his office, I would be at liberty to carry out this plan.

I found the room in disorder, clothes scattered across the bed, the armoire doors left ajar, his riding boots caked with mud and tossed into a corner. Everything about the dressing stand was neat, though he'd left the pitcher outside the basin. The desk was scattered with books, none of them medical texts, one a boy's novel about the French aristocracy, another a treatise on horse breeding. The letter wasn't there, nor was it in the desk drawer. I looked about, at his shaving kit, a jumble of cravats on the dresser, his silk dressing gown, the open trunk which had arrived from the college two days after its owner. This trunk was full, its contents spilling over the sides. I knelt before it, running my hands under a few items; there were notebooks, hats, and at the bottom, more clothing. My eye fell on a loose leather pocket sewn to the inside of the lid from which a pen case protruded. Quickly my fingers found the stiff envelope neatly folded in half. I withdrew the page, stood up, and stepped into the light near the window. It wasn't long, but it told me everything I needed to know. I read it several times, memorizing important phrases.

My Dear Nephew,

In time, your father's anger will subside, but currently he is distraught and has asked me to write to you and advise you that under no circumstances are you to return to his house. You will find no welcome there. He maintains that to harbor you would make him an accomplice to your crime. You have been Permanently and Irrevocably dismissed from the college and the unfortunate young woman has brought charges against you, though there is some hope that your father will arrange a settlement with her mother, who is a widow, and that the matter will not go to court. For the present, you'd best stay where you are.

"He is a scoundrel!" I announced to my husband, who looked up from his newspaper with eyes as flat and chilly as an owl's. "He is hiding out here in disgrace! He has ruined one young woman and now he seeks to add one or both of our daughters to his list of infamy."

To my dismay, my husband showed more alarm at my having invaded the privacy of our son's guest than at the revelation that this infamous youth had been cast out by his own family for his abuse of an innocent girl. "We can't ask him to leave without revealing that you've been investigating his room," he reasoned, at which point I thought my poor brain would explode.

"Why in heaven's name should we care what he thinks?" I replied.

"It's not what he thinks that concerns me, but what Maurice will think, and frankly my love, what *I* think. How could you do such a thing? It goes against every rule of hospitality. If, as you say, some settlement is underway and his uncle advises him to stay among us, he may yet recover his reputation and be the wiser for his close call. Any young man may make a mistake, especially one as well-formed and agreeable as Eric. His friendship with Maurice may be the saving of him."

I couldn't bother even to respond to such sophistry. "Very well," I said, "I will say nothing. But forewarned is forearmed, mark my words," and I left the poor, foolish man to his paper.

The young people returned in time for supper. They appeared in good humor, though I thought Henriette looked a bit downcast. She retired first, saying she was exhausted from the long drive, which all agreed had been a bumpy, miserable business. If Eric had bothered to look at me, he would have noted at once the change in my demeanor. I watched him with a baleful eye. But he was busy tantalizing Cici with some chatter about the dance and her overcrowded card. She hardly ate for giggling and blushing.

At the close of the meal, Charles invited the young men to join him in sampling a fine cognac he'd just received in a shipment from Paris, a proposal agreed to with alacrity. So that was his strategy, I thought. Keep the interloper ever in his sight. As my husband rose from the table, he gave me a look of mild inquiry and I returned a firm nod. He's not a fool, that man, but he's too trusting.

My morning conversation with Maurice was brief but informative. I asked how he was enjoying his friend's visit, and he replied that Eric was fine company and that all young ladies were strongly drawn to him, which meant that Maurice received more than usual attention from that quarter simply by standing near his friend. Eric was excessively fond of dancing and liberal in his choice of partner; he danced with all the prettiest girls.

"How amusing," I said.

My son studied me for a moment over his coffee cup. "I know you don't like him."

I was startled by this frankness. "I don't know him."

Before he could say another word, we heard footsteps in the hall and there he was, leaning in the doorframe, drowsy and smiling, bidding us good morning.

"You're up early," said Maurice.

Eric nodded, taking us in with that expansive good humor that proceeded from his confidence that we were exalted by his presence. "It's this country air," he said.

The country air was already steaming, and after breakfast, at Eric's urging, the young men went down to the pool for a bath. Cici repaired to the piano and Henriette, to my surprise, joined me in my sewing room with a roll of lace and a plain summer dress. "Aunt Adele gave me this," she said, displaying the frothy trim edged with a thin pale-blue ribbon. "I think it will improve this frock, don't you?"

We discussed the best stitch for attaching the lace, picked a thread of the same hue as the dress, and set to work companionably. *All is well,* I told myself. *My daughters are safely occupied in profitable pursuits and that overheated young man is cooling down in a chilly pool.*

But we had not worked long when Henriette said. "I'm worried about Cici."

I continued pulling my thread, but my attention was entirely upon my daughter. "What is it that concerns you?"

"She's so . . ." She paused, laying a strip of lace in her lap. "She's so infatuated with Eric."

"And you fear he's leading her on."

"Yes."

"And that he is insincere."

"It's worse than that."

"How could it be worse?"

"He's persuaded her to run away with him."

At this point, I too laid my needlework in my lap. "Has she told you this?"

"Not exactly. She's hinted at it."

"I see." My brain was so abruptly ignited with rage that I struggled for control.

Henriette regarded me, tears welling in her eyes. "Oh please, Mamère, don't tell her I told you. Promise me you won't tell her."

"Dearest," I said, taking her hand in my own, "be assured. Cici will never know you've spoken to me on this subject."

She dabbed her eyes with the lace. "Thank you, Mamère."

"Do you know when this elopement is planned?"

"No. I don't think it's settled. I told her to have Eric speak to Father, but she says he won't because he's certain Father will say she's too young and they should wait."

"And Eric doesn't want to wait," I said.

"That's right."

"You've saved your sister from a mistake that might well have ruined her life. But now you must put it out of your mind. Your duty is done, and well done."

In a visible flush of color, relief flooded through my poor daughter. "What will you do?"

"I'm not sure," I replied. "I'll think of something."

I had a few dire thoughts—turn the villain out or call the police—but I was giving my daughter such sound advice that I understood the need to temper my own impulse to revenge. I put my sewing aside and went out to consult with our cook.

When I came down for lunch, I found the young people lounging in the drawing room with tall glasses of lemonade. Eric was stretched out listlessly on a chaise, his collar open, his sleeves rolled back, and his eyes closed.

"He's worn himself out diving to find that gold you told him about," Maurice said. "He told me he thinks he saw it."

"I don't know what I saw," the treasure hunter said testily.

Cici, sitting near him, her back straight and her hands folded, caressed him with her eyes in a way that made my stomach turn. "It's dangerous to dive so deep," she said. She raised her eyes to her sister, who joined the group, perching on the piano bench. "Maurice said he stayed under for nearly two minutes!"

He might drown, I thought. And a fantasy in which I could facilitate this outcome began unfurling like a bright banner in my mind.

At breakfast, Maurice and I discussed an invitation he'd received to a boating party on Lake Borgne. He thought it would suit Eric as it would be cooler on the water. Cici and Henriette drifted in, then my husband. The conversation lagged, the coffee urn was visited and revisited, but Eric did not appear. "He was feeling poorly last night," Maurice said. "Perhaps I should look in on him."

"Oh, do," said Cici.

Maurice went out and returned quickly to tell us that Eric had passed a sleepless night and was feeling so unwell that he thought he'd best rest in his room.

Cici's head drooped on her long neck. "I hope he isn't seriously ill," she said, craning past me toward his room.

Maurice turned to me. "He looks pretty rocky."

"I'll go and see him," I said.

I found him collapsed upon the chaise, half dressed, having tried but failed to make himself presentable. "You must let me help you," I said. He was so weak, he made no protest. I laid my palm across his forehead. He was burning with fever, his face was flushed, his skin dry to the touch. I helped him to the bed and poured water from the pitcher into the basin. As I removed his shirt, he was barely able to raise his arms. The shutters were half closed and the room was dim, but when he fell back upon the pillow, his eyes caught a stray beam of light and I saw that the whites were shot with blood. "Once you're comfortable, I'll send for the doctor," I told him.

"Send for him now," he demanded. "I'm very ill. My head aches, my throat hurts. Something is wrong with my tongue."

He lay still while I pressed a damp cloth to his forehead, patting his face and neck. "Let me see your tongue, please," I said. Listlessly, he opened his lips and thrust forth his tongue.

There were two dark spots on one side; another, nearer the throat, had progressed to an open sore.

My heart lifted. The furies had delivered him into my hands. *You are all mine now,* I thought. "Cook will bring you some orgeat water," I said. "Be sure to drink it all."

I went out and sought my husband, who was waiting for his horse to be brought up as he had business in the town.

"Our guest is feeling unwell," I said. "He's a little feverish. Would you stop in and ask Dr. Landry to come by on his rounds?"

"I will," he answered. When he was gone, I went to the kitchen and told Cook to bring Eric some soft eggs, bread, and a pitcher of orgeat water. Then I went upstairs to sort out linens for the laundress who comes on Wednesdays.

At lunch, Cook told me Eric had eaten nothing, complained of headache and nausea, and wished to see the doctor as soon as possible.

"Well," I said, "he's on his rounds, but he'll be along. Though it may not be until morning if my husband doesn't find him in town."

"He's very insistent," said Cook.

"Is he?" We smiled at each other.

After lunch, Maurice briefly visited his friend. Eric encouraged him not to delay joining the fishing party. "I'm good for nothing," he said.

When my son had set off with his poles and hooks and lead sinkers, I brewed a pot of strong coffee and carried it in to our patient. He lay flat on his back across the counterpane, groaning pitifully. When he saw me, his greeting was, "Where have you been? I've been waiting too long. Where is the doctor?"

I set down the tray and approached him. "I thought you might need some rest," I said. His face was damp, his forehead and upper lip dotted with a prickly rash. "Are you feeling any better."

"Worse," he croaked. "I can hardly move. My joints ache. I'm burning up. It's unbearable."

I pressed my palm to his forehead; his fever was very high. "Cook told me you haven't eaten."

"My mouth is too sore."

"Will you drink a little coffee? It might help."

"Where is the doctor? Why is it taking so long for him to come?"

"We're in the country here," I said calmly. "The doctor ranges far afield. But I've sent for him and he'll come soon, I'm sure. Will you drink some orgeat water?"

"Yes, that seems to help a little."

I pulled the pillows up behind him and he propped himself upon them. He was able to drink a glass of water, and when the coffee was cool, a cup of that. I bathed his forehead, chest, and arms with vinegar, which soothed him. "Where is Maurice?" he asked.

"He's gone on the fishing party."

"Yes, I remember now."

"Try to rest," I said. "I'm sure the doctor will be along soon."

"All I can do is rest," he replied bitterly. "I'm too weak to move."

Dr. Landry arrived in the late afternoon, having spent a long day on horseback. I gave him sandwiches and coffee before bringing him to our guest. I stayed only long enough to witness Eric's evident relief at the appearance of a medical professional. As I left, I heard him inform the doctor that he had never been so ill in his life, and he knew our infernal climate had bested him.

It didn't take our doctor long to determine the nature of Eric's illness. When he offered his diagnosis, I nodded. "I thought as much," I said. "Are there many cases around?"

"There's a small outbreak in Natchitoches, but it's under control."

"I believe he and Maurice stopped over there on their way down."

"You know what this means, Iris," he said.

"Quarantine."

"You're immune, I believe."

"I had it when I was a child," I said. "Then my father caught it from me. My case was mild, but his was very serious. I remember how terrifying he looked, especially when the pustules began to weep. And then the scabs."

"Did he recover?" the doctor asked.

"Yes. But his looks were ruined."

"That may be the case here. It's a pity. He's a handsome young man."

"And a vain one," I said.

"Well, the treatment isn't complicated. It's mostly a matter of keeping him comfortable. I'll stop in to follow his progress. He may have a few days of vomiting; just give him nothing but water. When the fever breaks, he should regain some strength and be able to eat, though you may have to mash his food. Once the blisters form, just keep him clean and as dry as possible. If he develops a cough, send for me. Respiratory engagement is the most dangerous complication."

"I understand," I said.

"We've got a day or two. He won't be contagious until the rash spreads. I'll make the arrangements. Are your children at home?"

"I'll send my daughters to my sister in New Orleans today," I said.

"The sooner the better. And Maurice?"

"Fishing on Lake Borgne. He can stay with Adele until it's over."

"Your husband?"

"He's in town now. He should return this evening."

"I'm going back to town now," he said. "I can carry a message to his office if you like."

"Yes. If you won't mind waiting, I'll go and write it at once."

I went to my desk and wrote quickly, urging my husband not to come home.

Dr. Landry took the envelope and slipped it into his coat pocket.

"I've asked him not to enter the quarantine," I said.

"I think that's best. I'll come again on Friday. We should have a clearer idea of our patient's situation by then."

"Do you think he'll recover?"

"It's too early to tell. He's a strong young man. He should

survive. But his temperature is unusually high for the pox, and I don't like the blood in his eyes. It may be a virulent strain, in which case he might succumb."

I escorted Dr. Landry to the door, where we stood for a few moments exchanging family news. As he was leaving, he paused on the step to make one last recommendation: "I notice there's a cheval glass in the young man's room. It might be a good idea to have it removed."

In the weeks that followed, it was my dismal fate to gaze deeply into the soul of Eric Jeffrey. I found no shred of nobility there, no courage, no patience, no self-control at all. That he had come among us with ignoble intentions, I did not doubt, so it shouldn't have surprised me to find, beneath his handsome, confident facade, a cowardly beast. Once the fever broke and the pox, which was, as Dr. Landry feared, a virulent strain, bloomed over his face, his torso, his arms, legs, and extremities, his suffering was exacerbated by strange fantasies and obsessions, chief of which was that I was trying to kill him. He was weak and could barely walk, yet he was determined to break out of the quarantine. No counsel by Dr. Landry could persuade him of the folly of this; no appeal to the safety of others, or the public good, carried any weight with him. We were forced to batten the shutters and lock him in his room. He clung to the doctor's arm, whispering accusations against me—that I was not to be trusted, that I hated him, that I was poisoning him. He begged for food and water from the town, and swore he would not eat or drink anything prepared by my hands.

"He calls you his nemesis," the doctor told me after a difficult visit. "He's making himself worse with this madness. He believes you've not contacted his family."

"I've written to his father," I said. "He gave me the address. He saw the letter."

"He says you didn't mail it."

Eric didn't pursue these fantasies in my presence. He seemed to believe he had enlisted Dr. Landry's confidence against me. When I entered his room, he was often lying on the chaise, his eyes closed, his hands pressed against his temples—he suffered greatly from headache. He would only answer my questions in monosyllables. He refused all food, muttering that his stomach could keep nothing down, yet I knew the truth. I instructed Cook to prepare a bowl of boiled eggs and I took this, with a bottle of champagne, to his room, so that I could shell the eggs and uncork the wine before his eyes. He was persuaded that even a witch of my powers couldn't poison an egg in a shell or corrupt an unopened bottle of wine, and he agreed to eat and drink a little.

When I told Dr. Landry of this diet, he laughed. "That's wonderful," he said. "You're ingenious."

I reminded him that the wife of the equally suspicious Caesar Augustus murdered him by injecting poison into figs still hanging in their garden tree.

The doctor knit his brow. "Are they certain it was his wife?"

Daily, I went out pulling a little cart to meet my husband at the entrance to our drive. We stood a few feet apart and spoke briefly while he loaded my wagon with various supplies and carefully worded notes of sympathy for Eric from my daughters, which I didn't bother to read to the invalid. These messages evidenced a cautious restraint. There were no undo expressions of affection or hopes for the future beyond their friend's speedy recovery. They knew, we all did, that if their handsome darling survived the brutal course of the disease, he might not be be so pleasing to look upon.

The rash progressed speedily, spreading and forming blisters, which filled with an opaque fluid that made them appear soft, though they were hard to the touch, like peas in a pod. These I treated with cool compresses, to little effect. He complained that the back pain and headache were beyond endurance, and he was convinced that he was going blind. The doctor dosed him with laudanum, which quieted him.

By the second week the pustules covered every part of his body, packed so tightly that in some places, especially on his hands, the soles of his feet, and his face, the outer surface of the skin appeared to be lifting off in a pellucid sheet. His skull was covered in sores and, to his horror, his golden hair began to fall out in handfuls. His mouth was a white, swollen slash, his tongue protruded thickly between his lips, his green-gold eyes glared fiercely from beneath red swollen lids encrusted with white pustules.

I had not, as the doctor suggested, removed the cheval glass from his room. I'd simply turned the oval so that the wooden back faced the bed. One morning, when I found him still asleep, I stood for a moment, studying the wreck of his body, and particularly, the profusion of pustules on his face, some still hard, some weeping, some bloody, a few scabbing over. His breath made a thin whinny between his blistered lips, which were swollen to twice their normal size. The doctor agreed with me that this virus was particularly furious; it seemed bent on destroying tissue to the bone, and, should he survive, which was by no means certain, his face would be much disfigured. I stepped away and turned the cheval glass so that the mirrored side faced the bed.

A few minutes later, as I was rinsing bandages in a basin near the open window, I heard him waking behind me. He moved, rustling the sheet; there was a low groan. He was silent a moment. Then he cried out, "No!" in mortal agony and horror.

I smiled to myself.

"Let me die," he moaned. "Let me die."

But I wasn't going to let him die.

By the third week the pustules were all burst and suppurating. As Dr. Landry feared, Eric began to cough. It was a dry, rasping, racking cough that doubled him over in the bed. We wrapped his sores in gauze, which soaked through rapidly, and had to be changed every few hours. I worked tirelessly, with little rest, trying to keep him clean and fed, but he persisted in his hatred of me, and I received not a word of gratitude. Dr. Landry expressed anxiety for my health.

No word arrived from Eric's family, which vexed all concerned. My husband sent a second message; he feared it would be too late.

Gradually, the sores crusted over with scabs and our patient began to mend. The cough lessened; he could eat soft food. We left the bandages off a few hours a day, drying out the wounds. Eventually his body was covered with thick black scabs, wrapping him from head to foot in a crust like a shell that cracked and bled when he moved. Now it was only a matter of healing and Dr. Landry declared the quarantine no longer necessary. My family could come home.

As the scabs began falling off, we received a message from Eric's father, who complained that we had not informed him of his son's illness in a timely fashion. The first letter had evidently been lost in the post. He would set out at once to retrieve his son.

By the time his father arrived, Eric was well enough to dress himself and leave his room. The scabs had come off in patches, the thickest ones clinging to deep wounds. Though he removed the bandages when he was alone, he kept his face covered in company. He wrapped his head in gauze, leaving slits for his eyes, nose, and mouth. Then he made a ghoulish presence in the drawing room, where he sat in silence, nursing a glass of brandy.

All his charm had vanished; he was sullen and moody. Cici and Henriette avoided him, and even Maurice, who was always kind and considerate when they were together, admitted that it would be a relief to have him return to his family.

Though I knew his son had disgraced himself and his family, when John Jeffrey arrived, he carried on as if we were uncivilized brutes who had destroyed the great hope of his life. He stayed only a few days, making preparations for their return, shipping Eric's trunk, selling his horse, arranging a carriage to New Orleans from whence they would take a steamer back to Boston.

The day they left, the sun was out and the air had a note of crispness to it. Summer was at last easing its torrid grip. I went to Eric's room to tell him the carriage had arrived. When I knocked, there was no answer. Cautiously, I opened the door.

He was sitting on the chaise, fully dressed, with his elbows on his knees and his head resting between his hands. A straw Panama hat lay on the seat next to him. He lifted his head, but his eyes didn't meet mine. His expression was hectic and defensive, the haunted stare of a lunatic. He gazed into the middle air, presenting his face for my inspection.

The face that he would wear until he died.

A circlet of raised red flesh following the lines of the veins surrounded his left eye as if it had been painted on with an artist's brush. On his right cheek, a purple wedge of deep pockmarks spread from the bridge of his nose to the corner of his mouth and back to his ear. A thick white scar pushed out his lower lip, dividing it at the center, and folding it down so that the pink inner flesh was exposed. Another raised red scar pinched his left nostril, ending in a ugly knot on his upper lip. Most of his golden hair had fallen out, though some patches remained, trimmed close over his ears and well back from his forehead. Where the scalp showed through was all crinkled pink flesh that looked like it had been burned.

"Here is your handiwork," he said archly. "Are you satisfied?"

"How can you say that?" I responded. "I nursed you as if you were my own child."

He made no response, but refocused his gaze, so that his cold eyes drilled into me. As I stood there, I became acutely conscious of my own appearance, of my ruined face, my wispy gray hair combed back in a tight knot at the nape of my neck, my dead eye and lopsided mouth, my aged, heavy body, wrapped in the equivalent of a sack. Exhaustion weighed on me as well; it had been a struggle to keep this brute alive.

"My God, you are ugly," he said.

I took a step away from him. *Of course,* I thought. *Of course.* He wasn't brought down so low that he couldn't find contempt for me. I smiled with the side of my mouth that can smile. "The carriage is here," I said.

He took up the hat, and set it on his head with a rakish tilt to the front. "Tell them I'm coming."

I relayed this message to his father, who was fretting about the horses on the carriage. Then I went to the kitchen and sat shelling peas with Cook until we heard the carriage wheels crunching the gravel on the drive. "How is the young man?" she asked.

"He's lost his mind," I said. "He thinks I gave him the pox."

"What? After all you did for him?"

At length my husband joined us and announced that the Jeffreys had begun the long trip back to Boston.

My daughters were naturally crestfallen by the cruel transformation and departure of their once-handsome and interesting suitor. Maurice expressed his sadness and regret that a friend he had found so agreeable should undergo such grievous suffering while a guest in our home. Yet as time passed and we heard nothing more of Eric Jeffrey, other interests claimed them, and my children recovered the vivacity and high spirits to which youth and beauty are entitled.

SYDNEY

BY **SHEILA KOHLER**

I

As a writer, I feel obliged to portray reality as I have perceived it. This has, of course, serious risks. I fear upsetting others, revealing information that may be used to destroy a reputation, and in this case the reputation of a learned man, a doctor, who was my husband. Yet in the end, it is only on the page that I can hold onto what I have lost.

II

I was almost thirty when I married. At that point no one, including myself, really expected or perhaps even wanted me to marry. It was not that I was particularly plain or stupid, but my parents had very little money, and I had very little education, having been compelled to leave school at seventeen. We lived in a remote area on a game farm on the border between Zimbabwe and South Africa. The Limpopo River runs through the bottom of the property, and the sound of it and the cries of cicadas became part of my early dreams. It is a beautiful place, the sun shining almost constantly with only brief, hard spells of rain, often accompanied by the loud clap of thunder and spectacular lightning, which sometimes sets a tree or even a house on fire.

From our veranda you can see the blue hills in the distance. There is a big dam where we swam. No one dares to swim in the river because of crocodiles. Lemon trees surround the house, the ripe lemons just falling to the ground for anyone to pick up freely.

As the schools in the area were themselves at a considerable distance, I had initially been sent as a boarder to Johannesburg; however, when Mother died, shortly after I matriculated, Father brought me home to take care of the house for him and his elderly mother. I did not go on to university, as many of my classmates did, or even look for a position of employment.

My father ran the game farm. A tall, thin, and silent man, he spent most of his days out on the land with his rifle slung over his shoulder, watching out for poachers or freeing animals caught in traps, or fixing fences. Sometimes he had to cull the deer or shoot a leopard, if it was killing off too much of the game. The owner of the farm, whom we rarely saw, gave us a small house with a corrugated-iron roof which was very hot in the summer and cold in winter as there was no heating except for a fireplace in the kitchen and a few small radiators in the bedrooms. Fortunately, the winters are short.

Though we had some local help, I was kept busy with the many household chores. I rose early to tend to the two ridge-back dogs, the horses, the chickens in the henhouse, the pigs, the vegetable and flower gardens. I learned to ride and curry horses, to slaughter and pluck chickens, to bake bread, to make jam, and to put up pickled cucumbers and onions. In the evenings my grandmother and I embroidered tablecloths or sheets that were rarely used.

"We'll put them away for your trousseau," Ouma would say with a little laugh—she was the only one who maintained the illusion of a possible wedding—slipping the cloth into the bottom drawer of the English chest with her gnarled and trembling hands. It was a hard and monotonous life, but I felt useful and appreciated.

III

My future husband came to the farm quite by chance. His car, a white Jaguar, had broken down on the road to Harare where he was to attend a medical conference. Spotting our house from the road, he walked a considerable distance up the dust path in the noonday sun without a hat, arriving at our door with sweat running down his thin cheeks, his fine blue shirt plastered to his chest. This was in November, one of our hottest months, in the late eighties.

Through the screen door to the kitchen he asked me if he could possibly use our telephone to call the nearest garage for help. He must have been in his early fifties, I thought, though already white-haired, with his small, uneven, slightly yellow teeth. Even in distress there was something distinguished about him.

After he had made his call, I gave this doctor, which he told me he was, looking as if he was about to expire, a glass of homemade lemonade and some of my *koeksisters*. He thanked me profusely but said he felt dizzy, probably from too much sun. He said he had driven a long way and was very tired. So, I ushered him into my small bedroom, closed the shutters, and helped him onto my bed. I bent down to take off his good English shoes now caked with dust, and noticed, as he put his thick, tortoiseshell-rimmed glasses on the bedside table, that he had no ring on his ring finger. I gave him a cool flannel for his forehead, and left him to rest, shutting the door. Then we waited for the mechanic from the garage to arrive.

Though it was evening by the time he came, the doctor must still have been fast asleep, because he did not come out to meet him. I was out in the garden pulling up carrots for dinner. My father, who had just arrived home, told the mechanic that he had come to the wrong house. Had he not been told of the doctor's arrival? Nor did my grandmother, who must have seen the doctor walking up to the house, bother to correct my father. My grandmother, who had once been a schoolteacher, was a resourceful woman, and in her mind a proper woman's role remained as wife and mother. I remember her once asking me as I came in with a basket of eggs from the henhouse, straw caught in my ponytail, "What did women's lib do for you? Can you tell me?"

By the time the mechanic finally returned the next day, in response to my call, the doctor was restored. I had served up delicious, crispy lamb with roast potatoes, just as my grandmother had taught me to make, along with my own mint jelly. The next day, the doctor left for the conference.

But he returned, quite unexpectedly, a few days later. It was then that he asked me to marry him. He did not kiss me or even hold my hand or bring me so much as a bunch of flowers, he simply stood in the middle of our veranda with its polished red floor and looked out at the blue hills in the distance. "I would like to marry you," he said softly, as though he were talking to God or perhaps to the sinking sun, the orange sky, and the lemon trees, which surrounded us so beautifully.

I was not sure what to say. I wanted to ask him above all why he wanted to marry me. Was there something mysterious that attracted him to me? I had seen him watch me when I mounted one of our more frisky mares and held her firmly between my knees, and I had caught him staring at my face and my body as I worked in the garden, pushing a heavy wheelbarrow filled with stones for a new path. Was it my light-blue eyes, my light-brown hair, my long legs, my broad hips? I wondered. Or was it the good cooking? Whatever it might have been, he seemed strangely sure of his choice, which made an impression on me. He was a man, I could see, of a certain arrogance or anyway of great assurance, probably used to telling his patients what was wrong with them. Perhaps he was the oldest in a wealthy family, I surmised, or certainly someone who had grown up with the knowledge of art and song as well as medical matters, someone familiar with the classics, used to ordering others around, to getting his way. He obviously did not think any explanation was required.

I was not in love with him; I hardly knew him, after all. He looked at least twenty years older than me—my father's age. But he was not unattractive: tall and slim, with an aquiline nose and close-set brown eyes and a pleasing mouth. He told me he lived in a large house in Johannesburg where he employed a couple who had come from Germany along with his parents: an elderly housekeeper and her husband who kept up the garden and lived in a cottage on the property. There were many books in the house and even a pool in the garden. I would have an easy life, he promised. I told him I had no money and no professional qualifications, but he said that had no importance.

Laughingly, he called me his savior, something I was to think of later and continue to recall with sadness even now. The wedding was small, just the family, and a few old school friends who still lived in Zim. I wore a short beige dress with a crown of flowers from the garden. I kissed my grandmother and my father goodbye, shed a tear, and promised to visit soon.

"Don't come back without a bun in the oven," my grandmother said, laughing at me. Then we drove off in the car that had brought him to me. Somehow it seemed fitting.

IV

We spent our first night at Meikles, a grand hotel in Harare. We had a splendid dinner with champagne and foie gras followed by filet mignon in the dining room, and then retired to our room. I went into the bathroom to put on the transparent white nightdress I had chosen for my wedding night. I brushed my hair until it shone and put a daub of cream on my cheeks. I looked at myself in the mirror and decided that though I was not beautiful, I was pleasing enough: tall and slender and with my thick brown hair with its russet lights on my shoulders. I might even be considered appealing. I could only hope my husband would guide me on this first night of lovemaking, something new for me. But that is not what happened.

When I emerged from the bathroom, the doctor was already tucked into one of the twin beds in the room. He did not even look at me, he simply said we would have to get to know one another before he turned out his light and went to sleep.

V

The doctor's house in Johannesburg was grand and not gloomy. It was a white Cape Dutch with gables and a thatched roof, built in the nineteenth century. It lay at the end of a long alley of old oak trees. Bougainvillea climbed up the walls and its flowers of bright purple grew in profusion.

The housekeeper, Ingrid, a stout, severe woman, and her husband, Johann, were waiting on the steps of the house to welcome us. Ingrid, who dressed in black and spoke heavily accented English, smiled with sly servility at my husband. She offered to show me around the house. I followed her upstairs into the room where I was to reside: a big pleasant bedroom with a four-poster bed, a large armoire, a dressing table with a frilled skirt, a small desk under the window, a standing mirror in a corner, and a private bathroom with a large bath.

"You will have everything you need here," she said, looking my crumpled traveling clothes up and down, "and the doctor will be sleeping next door."

Then she showed me the dining room with its beamed ceiling, long shiny mahogany table, Chippendale chairs, and French windows which opened onto the garden. Down a few carpeted steps was the cool and shadowy sitting room. She took me into the doctor's office, a large room accessible by an entrance at the back of the house. The walls were lined with books from many countries and in different languages, stretching from the floor all the way up to the thatched open ceiling.

"You have to dust all of this!" I said with sympathy to the housekeeper.

"Not quite—I don't go up there," she said, and added, lowering her voice and looking at me from the sides of her eyes, "and I wouldn't if I were you either," waving to a sort of balcony which ran all the way around the room, accessible by a curving wooden staircase.

Ingrid explained that my husband saw his private patients in his office in the early mornings before breakfast or the late afternoons and occasionally after dinner. In between, the doctor left to visit certain patients in their own homes or in his hospital office. "A busy man," she said, smiling proprietarily.

The garden was large with many old oak trees and well-tended flower beds. In the back there was a long pool shaded by a jacaranda tree.

When I asked to see the kitchens and the pantry, she showed me, making it quite clear that she did not expect me to interfere in any way with her running of the house. She would continue to do all the shopping, the cooking, and the cleaning of the rooms. She would make, as I was to discover, the heavy German meals which my husband was apparently accustomed to: sauerkraut and wurst—big white sausages; schinken and kase—thick slices of ham and cheese; schnitzel—breaded cutlets, apple strudel. We were served in the long dining room by the husband, Johann, a quiet man who also cleaned the silver and worked in the garden.

When I offered to take on even the smallest of tasks—the making of a cake or the ordering of the wine—Ingrid demurred, telling me I could pick the flowers and arrange them in the vases if I had nothing better to do with my time.

VI

At first I would wake in a panic, forgetting where I was, imagining I needed to rise and attend to the farm animals, my grandmother's breakfast which I had always brought to her bed on a tray. Then I would realize that in my new life, nothing—absolutely nothing—was required of me. I took my time dressing without looking at the clock. I found the plentiful buffet breakfast on the dining room table. I drifted aimlessly around the house, swam backstroke in the heat of the day in the long pool, going up and down endlessly, my gaze on the feathery leaves of the jacaranda, recalling the wide dam of my youth.

At first I enjoyed the complete freedom of my days, something I had never known. I wandered through the flowers in the garden in the bright highveld light, beneath a white sky, delighting in the silence and stillness of the sun. But after a while, I missed my father and even more my grandmother, who for all her antiquated ideas was a lively companion with a wry sense of humor. The endless empty days weighed heavily on me. What purpose did my life serve?

When I suggested to my husband that I would now have time to go to the university, to further my limited education, and perhaps make some new friends, he objected, "But you have all the books you need right here. And am I not companion enough?" He suggested books that I might read by the German authors in his collection. He had white statues of Goethe and Schiller, his idols, on a high shelf. He gave me *The Sufferings of Young Werther, The Metamorphosis of Plants, Faust,* and *Wilhelm Meister,* along with some Hesse as well as Schiller's poetry. He recommended books by the nineteenth-century Russians: Tolstoy, Dostoevsky, and Gogol; the Italians: Landolfi, Ginzberg, and Dante; and the French, as well as my old favorites, the English writers I had read with much pleasure in my boarding school.

Occasionally, I met an old school friend in town for lunch.

One of them, Pippa, a plump girl who had been almost as bad as I was at math, asked me, after a few glasses of wine at the Oasis, a restaurant in Johannesburg, if I was happy.

"Happy?" I replied. "Of course—who would not be? Such a beautiful house and garden, servants, a generous, kind husband. Why do you ask?"

"You know how people gossip," she said, staring at me.

"Gossip? About what?"

She thought for a moment and then said, "There was the first wife disappearing so suddenly."

I took a sip of wine. I was not sure what to say. It was the first time I had heard of a previous wife. I waited for her to explain.

But she just shook her head and said, "Probably nonsense, such an excellent doctor."

My husband, indeed, was always perfectly polite, considerate, and generous. He gave me a liberal allowance which I found difficult to spend. I had not been in the habit of buying myself clothes. For many years I had worn a school uniform, and then on the game farm work clothes: blue jeans and overalls, an apron. "Buy yourself some decent clothes," he urged, looking me up and down critically. "You are now the wife of a doctor."

At dinner he asked me about my day, what I had done, commenting at some length on the books I was reading, the authors' lives and times, but told me little about his own. I respected his silence on the lives of his patients but I would have liked to know more about his past. Why had he never mentioned the first wife, for example, I wondered but did not dare ask. I gathered he had been a brilliant student, had matriculated very young, and was already a doctor by the time he was twenty one. He had done some graduate studies in Munich at the Max Planck Institute and had once considered, he told me, becoming a research scientist. I gathered he had read just about everything.

When I asked him why he had become a doctor, he told me that as a young child he had suffered from an irregular heartbeat. Sometimes it went too fast or too slowly, but what mattered was that it didn't work efficiently as a pump. He had feared at moments his heart might stop beating altogether. He had always felt it was essential to know about his body, in order to control it. Above all, he was interested in the essence of life: what produced the first spark, what kept us alive. He was gifted at mathematics and chemistry, and fascinated by the role electricity played in keeping our bodies functioning.

"I aced organic chemistry, which others found difficult," he said with a smile.

I asked him if he had found the dissection of a dead body disturbing.

"Not at all. Well—perhaps a little. There was the unpleasant smell of formaldehyde, but how else can we learn how a human being is put together? We were lucky to have so many opportunities to study the various organs firsthand: heart, lungs, kidneys, even the brain." He explained that in the nineteenth century they would have to go to graveyards to dig up corpses to study.

"Now we can leave our bodies, our brains, to science to be used productively, which I certainly intend to do." He peered at me as though he expected me to make a similar commitment.

None of this made much sense to me. I had never been interested in science and had wept when asked to cut up a rabbit in science class. I continued to wonder what purpose I served in the doctor's life. After months of marriage, I was still a virgin. All my skill lay in organizing a home, cooking, gardening, tending to animals, even mending—which were all frowned upon here, the sock or the shirt snatched from my hands immediately by the housekeeper. Occasionally there was a dinner party for my husband's colleagues, and I would arrange the flowers for the table, go to the hairdresser, and put on a suitable dark dress, but even so, I knew no one, and no one seemed very interested in getting to know me.

Only on Sundays were the servants off, resting quietly in their cottage on the property. In the afternoons, my husband would go to visit his mother who lived at some distance from us. At first I was invited, but she spoke very little English and did not show much interest in me, so eventually I stayed home.

I enjoyed having the whole house to myself and preparing a simple supper of scrambled eggs and baked beans, or baking a cake for my husband when he returned.

VII

One Sunday afternoon, after my husband had called to say his mother was not well and he would stay with her for supper, I found the reason why he had married me—a woman of a certain age, healthy, respectable, sufficiently decorative, undemanding, and poor—and why he had never bothered to have any but the most distant relations with me. He had found other sources of satisfaction, a satisfaction so perfect that he needed no other, a source that he had perhaps even provided for himself right under his own roof, and which I found upstairs behind the books on the balcony that Sunday afternoon by chance.

I had been looking for something more amusing to read. Probably because Ingrid had told me not to go up on the balcony of his library, that is just where I headed. Leaning against a wall of books to adjust the strap of my sandal, I nearly fell over when a hidden door behind the books suddenly swung open, letting me into a shadowy room in the eaves.

I peered into the room with its sloping thatched ceiling with wooden beams and a small window. I was able to make out a bed against the wall and a round wooden table in the corner with an object on it. It appeared at first, the curtain drawn on the sunlight, as if someone was lying on the bed under the sloping wall. A woman, I thought, was reclining, head on one hand, trying to peer out through the gap in the curtains, her thick black locks undulating down her beautiful bare back. All I perceived was the hair, the back, the firm buttocks, the backs of shapely legs, and the bottoms of the crossed feet. For a moment I believed I had come across a perfectly formed naked woman, one of my husband's patients, perhaps someone quite mad, who he must have shut up there for some reason, someone who was longing to escape. Perhaps I was thinking of the wife in Charlotte Brontë's *Jane Eyre*.

"Oh, excuse me!" I said, and was about to retreat, almost closing the door, my hands trembling, but something about the complete immobility of the figure made me instead tiptoe slowly into the hidden space, draw open the curtain, and touch the shoulder of the figure.

Then I discovered this was not a woman or a man, nor even an animal or a vegetable, not anything human but rather an artificial doll, a sort of mannequin, composed of rubbery material which had the appearance of pale skin with a glow that seemed to come from within. When I turned her over, I saw at once a lovely face with large, dark eyes which seemed to stare soulfully up at me, a slightly drooping nose, and full lips, well-formed breasts, generous hips, and under the light hair, her labia. The only thing that seemed out of place was a thin electric cord which emerged at the back of the head, and led to a small computer on the table.

After a few fumbles I managed to turn the machine on. There was a menu where I understood I could enter commands by speaking, or if I preferred, typing them directly into "Sydney," which was apparently her name. There were different options: masculine mode; female mode; and something called hybrid. Curious to see more, I immediately chose the masculine one and watched fascinated as the breasts slowly seemed to melt, the shoulders swelled, the hips narrowed, and the thighs thickened and lengthened. The labia dropped down, became crenellated, while between them the clitoris swelled up until it became a nicely formed penis. Even the long dark hair seemed shorter and somewhat lighter, and the face too, of course, changed, the skin becoming somewhat darker—café au lait, with a faint hint of a mustache on the upper lip and a dusting of hair on the cheeks. An Adam's apple protruded from what was now his neck, moving up and down. His eyes, though, remained as dark and expressive as before, still filled with loneliness and longing. They seemed to say, *I'm so glad you have found me here. Now help me!*

What was I to do? I looked back at the screen and saw that the menu now offered other choices. There were various new possibilities under the masculine mode, one of which was an erection which could be followed, if desired, by intercourse. I looked at Sydney, who seemed to smile an invitation at me, his lips slightly parted, his eyes filled with tenderness and desire. I thought I could almost hear in the quiet of the afternoon a brief lonely sigh—though it may have been my own. It had been so long since anyone had held me close. No one had done that since my dear mother died.

After a moment of hesitation, I chose the intercourse command. Sydney then slowly stood up to his full height. He must have had some sort of rudimentary skeleton, perhaps made of whale bone, with a spine to hold him up and give him a firm pelvis and a cranium. Standing, he was taller than I, but his expression was always the same, the eyes unblinking, filled with understanding and empathy and delight in my presence, or so it seemed to me. His lips opened slightly, inviting me. He even had a little shiny freckle or mole like a sequin on his left cheek, which pleased me.

He advanced slowly, almost shyly, shuffling with small, even steps on the balls of his feet. He took me firmly in his strong arms. With his chest thrust against me, I could even feel a beating heart and, lower down, his swollen sex, thrusting against me. I hastily slipped my panties down, my cotton skirt up, and let the smooth, firm penis enter my flesh, gently thrusting back and forth, while he ran his hands pleasurably over my buttocks.

All the while I had to keep my gaze on the small window, which looked out onto the driveway with its alley of oaks. Darkness falls fast in Johannesburg. I was now looking into the leafy night to see if my husband was coming up the driveway, arriving home. It was just as I felt I was diving deep into a warm pool of joy, and giving a low cry of pleasure, that I saw the lights of the white Jaguar piercing the dark. Then, as they say in the books, I knew no more. This first and, I am afraid to say, only orgasm was so extreme it brought about a complete loss of consciousness.

VIII

When I awoke I was lying in my own bed in my own room. Only the small bedside lamp was lit, and I could barely make out the two dark forms, one behind the other, emerging in the dim light, hovering above me. Ingrid and my husband, I realized, were bending over me. I had the distinct impression that they were laughing at me, their yellowish teeth glistening. Or they had been laughing at me, and now they simply smiled.

How had they found me? What had happened to Sydney? How long had I been unconscious? These were my first waking thoughts. "What happened?" I asked them, my heart hammering wildly: going fast and then slowing down.

"I believe you must have been looking for a *book* on the balcony," my husband said, with only a hint of irony, still smiling at me.

"Perhaps not a good idea," Ingrid said softly, straightening up the bedcovers and looking at me severely.

"You seem to have fainted," my husband said.

I could only stare up at him. What, I wanted to ask, had happened to Sydney?

"You must rest now," my husband said. "Ingrid will bring you some soup."

"I'm not hungry at all," I responded. The room was spinning around me, and I was filled with nausea.

"Ah, but you must eat. It is necessary, my dear," my husband said.

"Indeed," Ingrid said severely.

IX

For several days I was confined to my room, limp, helpless, utterly bereft, hardly able to stagger to the bathroom. Nights I lay awake, or if I slept it was a shallow, restless sleep, and in the early mornings I awoke, overcome with nausea, bile rising into my mouth, so that I had to rush into the bathroom to reach the toilet in time, sweat pouring from me. I retched so continuously and became so disgustingly incontinent that I was obliged to lie on the cool tiles in the bathroom, to be near the toilet, in order to relieve myself again and again, a yellow liquid pouring from all my orifices. There was a terrible taste in my mouth, and my gums became black. It was as though my body was in a basic revolt, attempting to rid itself by any means of what was within me. I was becoming weaker and weaker, despite Ingrid's valiant efforts to feed me. She brought me a sort of thick gray gruel which she spooned into my mouth, but it only added to my nausea. My stomach rebelled and refused to accept food. Indeed, I ate almost nothing, the sight or even mention of food making me sick. My head ached and when I tried to lift it I was filled with an extreme dizziness, with a humming and buzzing in my ears. My eyes misted over, I could barely see.

Writing this now, the horror comes back to me so clearly. It was as if the whole pleasant room and the beautiful garden which lay beyond had been transformed into a place of death. All the sounds from the garden—the calls of the doves, the cries of the crows, the twitter of the starlings, the soft breezes stirring up the leaves of the old oak trees—were stilled. Day after day, the white sun continued to shine endlessly, heartlessly, it seemed to me, the sky an almost transparent blue, and in my mind again and again Sydney came to me, tall, bronzed, beautiful, his arms longingly outstretched toward me.

How long had I been with him? How long had my pleasure lasted? How long had I been unconscious? What had happened to Sydney now? Why was I so ill? I longed to make my way down the stairs and up into the little room behind the books, but I could hardly move from the bathroom floor where I spent much of the day sprawled helplessly, filled with a loneliness I had never felt in my life.

I had always been surrounded by people: first in my home, with my loving mother and father, then at boarding school, where we slept in long dormitories and ate at long tables of ten or twelve chattering girls. Then as a young woman, I had spent my days with my father and grandmother and all the farm animals: the horses, the dogs, the chickens, even the pigs. Now there was no one. There was nothing but fear that I was dying, that life was ebbing from me.

My husband, it is true, visited me each morning and every evening, but somehow these brief visits only added to my panic. He would come in with some cheerful comment about the weather: the sun, or the pleasant breeze, or the blue sky. He would bring a thermometer in a glass of Dettol to my bedside, shake it with a skillful flip of his narrow wrist and thrust it under my tongue, glance at his watch and feel my pulse, and take the thermometer out after three minutes, looking at it with a small, satisfied smile. He placed cool compresses on my feverish brow, plumped up my pillows, and even inquired as to how I felt. "A little better this morning?" he would say, his voice rising with optimism. He had a mellifluous voice, but somehow his constantly cheerful statements, which obviously ignored my extreme distress, only added to it.

One morning, feeling particularly weak and sick, I asked if it would not be possible for me to see a doctor. He looked surprised by the demand, and smiled. "But we have a doctor in the house, my dear, do we not? Do we feel we need anyone else?" he asked as though I were a small child or an idiot.

I was not sure what to say except that I felt increasingly ill, that I feared dying. I could eat nothing, spent my days retching, a ghastly yellow liquid pouring from me.

"We will take care of you," he said gently, and added, "You are very important to us. Particularly now . . . Besides," he went on with his habitual assurance, half turning from me, going toward the door, "a doctor is hardly necessary. Your symptoms are obvious ones, are they not?"

"What do you mean?" I asked.

"Fainting? Nausea? Have you had your period?"

I stared at him, bile rising in my mouth. "But how could I be pregnant?"

He sighed. "I think you know the answer as well as I do, though it might be wise for your sake to keep it under wraps."

"And even if I *am* pregnant, why would I be so suddenly and so dreadfully sick?"

He smiled and said softly, "Intercourse between the different species may once have been possible; the fly and the flower perhaps produced the butterfly, the tuna fish and the cow may have brought forth the dolphin, bats might have come from the coupling of an owl and a mouse. Perhaps the animate and the inanimate are a particularly fecund combination. There are more things, my dear, in heaven and earth than are dreamed of in our philosophy." Then he turned his back on me and left the room.

I thought of how my father had explained to me once that in nature, different species cannot mate, that the donkey and the horse can produce only a sterile mule. By what means could a mannequin and a human create a child? Was it not against nature? Was the doctor's sperm somehow transmitted through the mannequin? Was I the surrogate bearer of the doctor and Sydney's child? What was my role here?

Whatever it was, it filled me with panic, aware that I had perhaps walked unwittingly into a trap. Had all of this been planned from the start? What could I do? I thought of writing to my father or even my grandmother, or telephoning them, but what could I say? Could I tell them I was pregnant and have them congratulate me? I thought of my grandmother laughingly saying, "Don't come back without a bun in the oven." What if I came back with a doll? A dummy? A mannequin? Some half-artificial creature in the oven?

X

That night, lying with the curtains drawn open, the moonlight flooding my room, I grew determined to make my way down the steps and back up onto the balcony, even if I had to do it on my hands and knees. I needed to see Sydney, to reassure myself of the mannequin's existence, of my own rational mind. I reminded myself of my active, hard life on the game farm, my ability to swim and ride and dig in the earth.

I dragged myself from my bed. In the light of the moon, I caught a glimpse of myself in the standing mirror in the corner of the room. In my pale nightdress, spotted with yellow stains, my hair in wild knots around my dead-white face, I looked like a specter of myself. *Courage!* I told myself, as my mother had once told me, her hands on my shoulders, standing on the platform before I took the train at seven years old, when I was first sent off alone on a voyage which took a night and two days to reach my boarding school.

Now I dragged myself slowly down the stairs in the dark. I found my way, my arms stretched before me, going into my husband's office. There I turned on the small lamp on his desk and climbed up to the balcony and pressed against the books as I had done before, but nothing happened. I tried again and again, my heart beating wildly, the nausea coming over me in waves. Had I, in my need and loneliness, invented Sydney? Was there no room under the eaves? Yet it seemed to me I could hear faintly in the distance cries of distress.

"Oh Sydney," I called out, "I'm here," before retreating down the stairs, tears running down my cheeks and nausea rising in my throat, my stomach clenching.

I made it back to my bed, only to lie there in the depths of despair.

XI

Then I thought of my old school friend Pippa and her question that day at lunch. I decided to telephone her, to get her to come to the house, if that was possible. I would have to let my husband know.

To my surprise, when I made the suggestion the next morning during his visit to me, he seemed pleased. "Good idea," he said, and encouraged me to rise and make the call and even offered to drive me to a restaurant where we might meet. "It would do you good to get up and out, move around a little. Show yourself in town. You can't lie here forever. I'll send you Ingrid to help."

I managed to bathe and dress with Ingrid's help. She filled a bath with warm water, washed every part of my thin body, and helped me dry myself. She pulled a clean dress over my head, slipped on pantyhose and shoes on my feet; she brushed out my tangled hair, even outlined my lips with gloss. With my husband's help, I staggered down the stairs. He settled me beside him in his car and drove us fast into town. He dropped me off at the restaurant where I was to meet Pippa, a pleasant place with an outside courtyard, palm trees. My husband promised to come and pick me up shortly. I walked slowly into the courtyard, holding onto the backs of chairs as I went. The air felt good on my face; I took in great gulps, and my courage revived at the sight of Pippa sitting at a far table by the palm trees, her plump pink face turned toward me, watching me advance.

She got up and came to me, took my arm. "What on earth is the matter?" she said as I dropped down into the chair opposite her.

"With *me?*" I said.

"You look as white as a ghost."

I pushed the menu away and grasped her hand. "You came for lunch with me, but I can't possibly eat."

"Has something happened?" she asked.

"I've been ill—I am still ill. But I had to see you." I held fast to her hand.

"What can I do for you? Shall I take you home?"

"I wanted to ask you about my husband's first wife. You said there was gossip."

"I gathered your husband has never spoken of her to you?"

I nodded my head. "Not a word. Who was she? Where did she come from?"

"Italy, I believe. She didn't speak much English. I met her only once briefly at a cocktail party. She was young, very pretty. I remember she was wearing those long, dangling pearl earrings which she kept shaking back and forth as she laughed."

"What happened to her?"

"People said the doctor was using her in some sort of experiment . . ."

"An experiment?"

"Some said it was a dangerous cure for his wife's infertility."

"And did the cure work?" I asked.

"She became ill, fatally ill . . ."

"How awful! Poor girl," I said, imagining it all too well.

"Why don't you just let me take you home. You would be safe with me. I'll look after you. I can't bear to see you looking like this."

I shook my head. There was nowhere safe for me to go now. If the doctor was working on a problem of infertility, this time he had succeeded. I could already feel something moving inside me: a foot, a hand, a head? The living thing, whatever form of life it had taken, even if my body had initially rejected it, was now firmly planted within me.

Besides, looking around the restaurant, I now saw my husband walking into the courtyard. "He's here," I said.

XII

As the days went by, I grew slowly stronger. My husband was surprisingly affectionate, thoughtful, giving in to my slightest whims. He joked with me in a new playful way, bringing me little presents: bonbons, brooches, ribbons for my hair. He encouraged me to walk with him in the garden in the cool of the evenings, talking to me all the while. He knew the names of the birds and the trees, the Latin names for the flowers. He told me the word *delphinium* came from *dolphin*. He pointed out the constellation of stars that lit up the southern sky so brightly. I even took up my swimming again, floating on my back, my stomach swelling above me.

My nausea decreased, and I began regaining the weight I had lost. Indeed, I developed an almost insatiable appetite. No matter what I ate at the dinner table, despite Ingrid's heavy German fare, I remained ravenously hungry. Nights, I rose and slipped down the stairs to forage in the kitchen for something to eat. I opened up the refrigerator and stole whatever I could find. I gobbled up Ingrid's wurst, swallowed down her schnitzels, ate large slices of the apple strudel, bolted bricks of black bread smothered in thick cheese. I stuffed the food into my mouth hastily, like a starving wild animal. I gulped down large glasses of beer or knocked back snifters of schnapps. Only with enough food within me could I get back to sleep.

As I said, my husband had always been generous with my allowance, which he now increased, and which I spent more lavishly. "Your taste has improved, my dear," he said, seeing me in my bright, loose dresses. I cut my hair short, and streaked it with blond highlights, had my nails painted bright pink; I outlined my lips with gloss; I had massages and facials in a spa in Rosebank.

"You look positively radiant, my dear," my husband said. It was true. When I looked in the mirror, I could see my skin shining with an inner light that reminded me of Sydney's. It looked almost transparent, my cheeks round, buttery, and slightly freckled.

Our dinner parties were now well-attended. The notables in both the literary and medical worlds sought our invitations. I received compliments from the dinner guests, though I often excused myself before the end, professing fatigue.

I was an asset from my husband's point of view in several ways, I could see. His success as a doctor in the town was more assured. His investment in a decorative wife, now obviously pregnant, was paying off. Even Pippa, when she visited, told me I was looking well. "You both look well—you look almost alike," she said, peering at my blond highlights and my husband's white hair.

And all the while I felt the offspring growing and stirring restlessly within me: hands, feet, and, so it seemed, heads, greedy mouths—at any rate, a gluttonous creature, never satisfied. I had heard the expression "eating for two"; I felt I was feeding a small army.

As the days went by, I thought increasingly fearfully of the birth and what this might bring forth, and what would happen to me.

XIII

At dinner one evening, as I drank a second glass of beer, my husband reached across with an affectionate gesture to wipe the foam from my upper lip with his napkin. I asked him who would assist me at the birth and if the hospital in town had been notified.

"I don't think that will be necessary," he said.

I just looked at him, trying to divine his intentions. What did he intend to do with this offspring, whether it was Sydney's or his? What did he intend to do with me once my purpose was fulfilled, once I had carried the baby to term? Would I then become extraneous, an unnecessary witness?

It was then that I made my own plan.

I had assisted with the birth of several animals on the game farm. Birth, like death, I told myself, was a natural process. In the best of cases, it happened without too much pain. Plenty of women had done this unaided, I knew, simply going off alone into the bush and coming back with a child at their breast. I remembered a foal being born to one of our mares and how the little animal had staggered to his feet and how the mother had licked him lovingly all over. I thought of how my mother had told me that childbirth is indeed painful, but that nature does its work well, and the pain is soon forgotten, once the child is there. I determined to do this alone without my husband, and to take our baby to Sydney. It would be my gift.

At first all went as planned. I was lucky that the labor began in the dead of night, well after midnight, when I was alone in my dark room, and the house quiet. I did not even turn on the lamp by my bed or cry out at the moments of greatest pain.

I had always read that this is a long, drawn-out process, particularly for a first child, sometimes lasting for days, the contractions gentle at first and spaced out, and only coming close toward the end. In my case, the labor was short and particularly brutal, as if the infant was in a great rush to enter life. From the start, the pains came fast and furiously.

Yet I cannot call it a *natural* process: there was such haste, such a mad searching, a sort of competition for air, space, and life. I remember thinking at the worst moments, *I don't care what this is—a cow, a dolphin, a bat—just let it be over.* The creature ripped through my body, the contractions coming like the crash of a wave, one following fast on the next. I thought of what my mother had said about childbirth and could not imagine I would ever forget such pain. Indeed, I remember those dark hours so precisely, each contraction clear in my mind.

What I cannot tell you is what I saw when the creature came forth. My eyes were dim in the half light of dawn and I swiftly turned my gaze away in horror, simply wiping away the blood and quickly cutting the umbilical cord, eager to free myself of this encumbrance. I camouflaged it as best I could in the blanket, covering it up with what I had prepared for this purpose, aware from the movement that it was alive.

Weak as I was, I staggered down the stairs with my heavy burden. That I can still recall clearly, the weight in my arms. Surely the infant weighed more than ten pounds. I had one purpose in mind: to get to Sydney.

It was day by then, dawn lighting up the sky. Through the open windows the sound of birdsong filled the air; the sweet scents of the garden came to me. I went through my husband's office and, panting and sweating, slowly mounted the steps to the balcony, my knees like water, my thighs trembling with weakness under the weight. This time the door behind the books was already open. I stood there exhausted, leaning against the books, hardly able to hold the creature in my arms, listening.

I could hear my husband's voice, a voice so soft, so tender, saying with love in tones I had never heard, "It won't be long now, darling. I promise you this time you will have your baby. You will have your companion for the rest of your days. You will no longer be alone, you have my word."

Even at such a moment, and weak and burdened as I was, I could not help thinking with sadness that my husband had never spoken to me in such a way; he had surely never loved anyone as much as this being which he had himself created.

Then, to my surprise, and I have to admit with a certain annoyance, I heard Sydney's voice for the first and last time. "Master," she said, "I believe you. I know how brilliant you are and how hard you have worked."

I hesitated a moment before entering the room, but weakened as I was, I no longer had a choice. My head spinning, my knees giving way, I could only stagger into the small room in the eaves where I had found so much pleasure.

The curtain was open and the bright highveld light filled the room. Sydney, as though she knew I was coming, was waiting there in feminine mode, sitting up in the bed, her lovely dark hair loose around her bare shoulders, a white sheet drawn up over her body. In the shadows in the corner, sitting on the stool before the lit computer, my husband was waiting for me.

"Here you are," I said, dropping the child beside Sydney as she sat up on the bed, her gaze fixed on me.

She looked down at the child but reacted immediately as I had done, averting her gaze in horror, reaching her arms out to me. "Oh! No!" she said.

I collapsed beside her. Sydney held me close. I stroked her soft hair, and I kissed her on the lips. There were tears in her eyes, on her cheeks. "I'm so sorry," I said.

My husband stood up and came closer, staring down at the child with revulsion. He looked at me and said, "This is what you have produced?" I nodded my head sadly. He gave a great wail of grief. "I've failed once again," he said wildly. "All my efforts, knowledge, and skill have brought nothing but suffering in the end!" He lifted a hand as if to strike me, but instead sank down on his knees.

My husband was in such inexpressible despair that despite his desperate deeds, I could feel nothing but pity for him at that moment. I realized that this man, who had always seemed so composed, so detached, so cold, was capable of extreme emotion. This endeavor, the creation of a new life for Sydney, was dearer than his own. He held his head in his hands, his close-set eyes filled with tears. He shouted at me, "I feared something like this! This is enough! It's the end!" He rose to his feet, turned from me and Sydney and the baby, and headed over to the computer, turning it off with one harsh click of the keys.

Sydney's whole body crumpled into a heap on the bed, head on her knees, turning pale. The mannequin seemed to almost be praying for mercy.

The doctor pulled savagely at the cord at the back of Sydney's bowed head. Then he lifted the head by the hair, tilting it back so brutally that the bones in the spine seemed to crack. A spark of electricity ran through all of Sydney's body, lighting up the waxen figure from head to toe.

"No! No!" I said, trying to reach out my arms to protect Sydney, the baby, to stop my husband—but it was too late. I could only watch in horror as the lips which I had just kissed with such longing began to twist and melt, the cheeks to blacken and sink in, and the whiteness of the bones underneath became exposed by flickering flames. Sydney's whole body was lit up, struck by lightning like a tree or a house in a violent storm in the fields of my native Zimbabwe.

"Get out of here! Get away from me! Get out of my house!" my husband shouted, thrusting me out of the room, closing the door on me, but not before I caught a glimpse of the child—

here I cannot be completely sure of what I saw, but it seemed to me it was a little boy, the huge head falling back, the gash of the mouth open in a silent cry, the skin shining with small scales like sequins, as Sydney cradled him in her burning arms.

I stood outside the door, the smoke pouring out onto the balcony. I stumbled down the stairs and out the back door which led into the garden. Then I turned to see the very house itself lit up with flames. The conflagration was accompanied by a terrible explosion which I could only imagine was Sydney itself, the wildly beating heart of Sydney bursting into flames. I staggered to the cottage in the garden to beg Ingrid and Johann for help, but it was too late by then. The thatch and the wood, the books, the fine furniture, the Persian carpets, the flowers in the vases, all the refinement of the grand house, and with it my husband with all his erudition, his knowledge of the human body, the human mind, and the human heart, art and song, were already destroyed, carried away by the flames, transformed into ashes. By the time the fire department arrived, all was gone, and with it my husband, Sydney, the strange sequin-covered baby boy, and all our dreams.

XIV

I lay bleeding for several nights and days on the sofa in the cottage. Eventually, the couple called a local doctor, who examined me and said I would recover but would never bear a child again. Soon, with careful nursing, I was strong enough to rise. Ingrid gave me a change of clothes, a black dress, and a cardigan—it was August by then, the air cool in Johannesburg in the early morning.

I called my father and told him I would like to come home. My grandmother had recently died, and he was on his own, he said, and only too happy to have me back. The couple loaned me enough money for my trip, which I promised to repay. I said goodbye to them, and embraced them warmly. I had come to appreciate the couple over the months I had spent in the house, for their loyalty, tact, and hard work. I never found out how much they knew of my husband's time spent with Sydney, or if they even knew of Sydney's existence at all, though I suspect they did know and kept the doctor's secret better than I have.

Then I took the bus to the train station, carrying only a small bag, leaving with less than I had arrived. On my arrival at the station in Harare, my father was clearly glad to see me, though he gazed at me with wonder. "You seem a completely different person. Marriage has changed you," he said.

I just smiled, but I thought, *Ah! that was Sydney.*

With the money I eventually inherited from my husband's estate, I was able to pension off the housekeeper and her husband and buy the land around our house. I had the old edifice knocked down and a more suitable place for us built with a large office that I lined with books. I even had a balcony constructed with a secret door that opened behind the books on a small room in the eaves. I hired some local help to manage the place, bought a computer for the first time in my life, and, sitting at the window with the view of the blue hills, began to write up this account, with the sound of the river running and the cries of the cicadas now part of my imaginings. This, as I said at the start, though it reveals my husband's secret, has enabled me to keep Sydney alive on the page and in my heart, and—who knows?—once I have made some inquiries into the matter, and perhaps with the help of my readers, an avatar of Sydney may soon appear in the room behind the books.

ABOUT THE CONTRIBUTORS

Nina Subin

MEGAN ABBOTT is the Edgar Award–winning author of ten crime novels, including *You Will Know Me*, *Give Me Your Hand*, the *New York Times* best seller *The Turnout*, and, most recently, *Beware the Woman*. She also writes for television, including *Dare Me*, the series she adapted from her own novel, now streaming on Netflix.

Luis Mora

MARGARET ATWOOD is the author of more than fifty books of fiction, poetry, and critical essays. Her 1985 classic, *The Handmaid's Tale*, was followed in 2019 by a sequel, *The Testaments*, which was a global number one best seller and won the Booker Prize. In 2020 she published *Dearly*, her first collection of poetry in a decade, followed in 2022 with *Burning Questions*, a selection of essays from 2004–2021. She lives in Toronto, Canada.

Max S. Gerber

AIMEE BENDER is the author of six books of fiction, including the best seller *The Particular Sadness of Lemon Cake* and the *New York Times* Notable Book *The Color Master*. Her work has been translated into sixteen languages, and she teaches creative writing at the University of Southern California.

Melissa Hibbert

TANANARIVE DUE is an award-winning author who teaches Black Horror and Afrofuturism at UCLA. She is an executive producer on Shudder's groundbreaking documentary *Horror Noire: A History of Black Horror*. She and her husband/collaborator Steven Barnes wrote "A Small Town" for Jordan Peele's *The Twilight Zone*, and the graphic novel *The Keeper*, illustrated by Marco Finnegan. Due's short story collection *The Wishing Pool and Other Stories* was published by Akashic Books in 2023.

Judith Clute

ELIZABETH HAND is the author of twenty award-winning novels and five collections of short fiction. She is a longtime contributor of book reviews and essays to the *Washington Post*, among many other places. *A Haunting on the Hill*, a follow-on to Shirley Jackson's classic *The Haunting of Hill House*, was published in 2023. Hand teaches at the Stonecoast MFA program in creative writing, and divides her time between the coast of Maine and North London.

Laurel Hausler

LAUREL HAUSLER is a mixed-media artist from the Washington, DC, area who paints the dark prom of life. Her ghostly work is shown and collected internationally. Her artwork is included in the anthology *Cutting Edge: New Stories of Mystery and Crime by Women Writers*, edited by Joyce Carol Oates.

Cassandra Khaw

CASSANDRA KHAW is an award-winning game writer. Their recent novella *Nothing but Blackened Teeth* was a British Fantasy, World Fantasy, Shirley Jackson, and Bram Stoker Award finalist. Their debut collection *Breakable Things* is now out.

Beowulf Sheehan

SHEILA KOHLER is the author of eleven novels, three collections of short stories, and the memoir *Once We Were Sisters*. Her work has been translated and published widely abroad. She has taught creative writing at Columbia University and Princeton. Her novel *Cracks* has been filmed with Jordan Scott as director, Ridley Scott as executive producer, and starring Eva Green, and is being reissued by Open Road in 2023.

Dan Fernandez

AIMEE LABRIE's short stories have appeared in the *Minnesota Review, Iron Horse Literary Review, StoryQuarterly, Cimarron Review, Pleiades, Beloit Fiction Journal, Permafrost Magazine*, and other venues. In 2007, her short story collection *Wonderful Girl* was awarded the Katherine Anne Porter Prize in Short Fiction. Her short stories have been nominated three times for the Pushcart Prize. She works as the senior program coordinator and an instructor for the Writers House at Rutgers University.

Raven Leilani

RAVEN LEILANI is a National Book Foundation "5 under 35" honoree, and the recipient of the 2020 *Kirkus* Prize, the VCU Cabell First Novelist Award, NBCC's John Leonard Prize, the Dylan Thomas Prize, the Clark Fiction Prize, and the Center for Fiction's First Novel Prize. She teaches at NYU, and *Luster* is her first novel.

Adam Lim

LISA LIM is a comic storyteller born and raised in Queens, New York. Her work has been featured in *Guernica*, *PANK*, the *Rumpus*, *PEN America*, and *Mutha Magazine*. Find more of her storytelling at lisalimcomics.com

Tess Steinkolk

JOANNA MARGARET holds a PhD in history from the University of St. Andrews, an MFA in creative writing from NYU, and a BA in French and history from Columbia University. She has taught history at the University of St. Andrews and the University of Dundee. She is the author of the novel *The Bequest*. She lives and writes in New York City.

Michael Lionstar

VALERIE MARTIN is the author of eleven novels, including *Mary Reilly*, which won the Kafka Prize; *Property*, winner of the Women's Prize; and, most recently, *I Give It to You*; as well as four collections of short fiction, and a biography of St. Francis of Assisi. She has been awarded a grant from the National Endowment for the Arts and a Guggenheim Fellowship. She resides in Madison, Connecticut.

Carissa Gallo

JOYCE CAROL OATES is the author of a number of works of fiction, poetry, and nonfiction. She is the editor of *New Jersey Noir*, *Prison Noir*, and *Cutting Edge: New Stories of Mystery and Crime by Women Writers*; and a recipient of the National Book Award, PEN America's Lifetime Achievement Award, the National Humanities Medal, and a World Fantasy Award for Short Fiction. She lives in Princeton, New Jersey.

JS Wu

YUMI DINEEN SHIROMA is a PhD student in English at Rutgers University, studying postcolonial and queer theories and literatures. Her poetry has appeared in *BOMB*, *Hyperallergic*, *Peach Mag*, and *Nat. Brut*. She lives in Philadelphia with Signora Neroni the cat.

LISA TUTTLE began writing professionally in the 1970s. Although she also writes novels and nonfiction, her preference is for the weird short story. Her most recent collection is *The Dead Hours of Night*. Born and raised in Texas, she has lived in Scotland for many years.